Sleight of Hand

A Blackbridge Security Novel
Marie James

Blackbridge Security

Hostile Territory
Shot in the Dark
Contingency Plan
Truth Be Told
Calculated Risk
Heroic Measures
Sleight of Hand
Controlled Burn
Cease Fire

Copyright

Synopsis

Gaige Ward, acquisitions expert for Blackbridge Security, obtains things for the team.

As far as your mind can take you is how far he can go.

If it exists, he can get his hands on it.

If he can't, he'll find someone who can.

He never fails.

As with all things when growing in popularity, Blackbridge is also taking on scrutiny.

His boss, in an attempt to counter being called misogynistic and discriminatory against women, needs a female with the ability to handle the same tasks his guys can.

Leighton Redmond fits the bill perfectly.

Only, according to her, she isn't for sale, for employment or otherwise.

Gaige loves a challenge but has NEVER had to fight so hard to procure something for his boss.

Maybe next time he'll think twice before having a one-night stand the day before a very important business meeting...

Chapter 1

Gaige

"Business is good?" Sherman asks as I lift my glass of whiskey to my lips.

"Business is always good." I give him a sly grin as I look around the packed bar.

I wouldn't call us friends, but we're both two like-minded men who run into each other in this hotel bar often.

We're busy, as are the women we meet here, and that's exactly why we choose this place. We aren't looking for love or a long-term connection. We want fun, a single night of great sex, no connection or need for excuses once the sun comes up. Hell, most of the time we're back in our own beds long before that happens. The women we meet here expect nothing less.

The bar, the closest one to the airport with a five-star rating, hosts mostly business professionals just as busy as we are. If they're interested in letting their hair down for a few hours, that's as far as they want things to go. It's the perfect situation, and the fact that they're going to be on the next flight out of town makes it all the more ideal. It's less likely for them to get clingy or expect more.

"I love convention weeks," Sherman says, his eyes wandering around the room. The selection varied tonight.

Most people privileged to our conversation would think we were complete assholes, men who think they could bag any woman in the place, but experience is what makes us cocky. We strike out. Of course we do. Occasionally, we approach a woman who happens to be here just to unwind, wanting to sip a glass of wine in peace before heading up to bed alone, but it's a rare occurrence. More often than not, we don't approach those women. They send off an unapproachable vibe, and working for it really isn't my thing, unless I'm up for a challenge. After a long day's work of acquiring things for Blackbridge Security, I tend to lean more toward a sure thing.

"What happened with that new girl at work?" I ask, remembering that Sherman was complaining about someone last week.

He mutters something about the new woman being the bane of his existence when I notice a woman down the bar. Waves of dark brown hair along her bare back and a sinful red dress. She showed up tonight to be noticed, and I'm not the first tonight to set eyes on her.

Several men in the bar are looking her way, building their courage to approach her. I get the bartender's attention. Being a regular and a very good tipper has a fresh glass of white wine in front of her within seconds. The bartender dips his head in my direction. She smiles at me, her teeth sinking into the flesh of her daring red lips right before the wine glass meets her lips. She doesn't break eye contact as she sips, her tongue dashing away a rogue drop as she lowers the glass.

"See you later, man," I tell Sherman as I clap him on the back.

"Lucky fuck," he mutters at my back, but I'm already walking toward the goddess in red.

My approach could be smoother, but because of the convention Sherman mentioned, the bar is overly crowded tonight. I have to turn sideways more than once to get through the throng of people. I manage to make my way to her without spilling my drink, and I like how she keeps her eyes on me the entire time. It increases the chance of getting what I'm after tonight. Many women will play coy, keeping me in their periphery, darting their eyes away as if they're shy. This woman locks her eyes on me, shifting them up my body as I walk closer. I don't hide the sweep of my own, starting at her crossed legs and working my way up her exposed thighs to the swell of her breasts in that sinful dress.

The second I reach her, I lean against the bar and place my hand on the exposed skin of her back. She's warm to the touch, and much to my liking, she doesn't flinch away.

"Hi." I trace her spine with the tip of one finger.

"Hey." Smoky, sultry, full of promises. She takes another sip of her wine. "Thanks for the drink."

"John," I tell her, not offering her my hand because I'm already touching her. We're a few steps past formalities already, and I like where this is heading.

"Ginger," she returns, the tip of her red fingernail tracing the rim of her wine glass.

She's full of shit with her name, just like I am with mine. We both know it, and it doesn't matter. This woman knows the game, and she came here to play. If I believed in love, I'd be halfway there already. She's utter perfection.

I tip my drink up, draining the remaining whiskey. She mimics the action, placing her empty wine glass next to my tumbler, offering me her hand as she stands, and releasing it the second she's on her feet.

She's confident, not needing the touch to maintain her confidence. I press my palm to her lower back as I guide her from the bar, taking her lead as she moves toward the elevators. If she didn't have a room here, I'd get one. Being a frequent patron means I get a great discount, but if she's got a room, that's great, too.

The elevator ride is silent. Neither of us needs small talk to ease any discomfort because neither of us is feeling any. We don't feel the need to placate the other. We know what this is. We know what we're doing, but it isn't business-like either.

The sexual tension swirling around is so thick it's damn near suffocating, and I know she's not immune to it either as I watch her pulse flutter in her throat. She jolts, her body hitching the slightest little jerk when the elevator dings on her floor.

Her stride to her door has her regaining her confidence, her hips the perfect sway of seduction in tall heels, her calves strong and sexy. My fingers itch to grip her ass and guide her movements, but letting her take control has its own appeal as well.

"Night cap?" she offers as we step inside her room.

"Sure," I say as I focus on her.

The room is pretty basic, so I don't bother looking around. I've been in plenty of them before. There's only one attraction inside these four walls that I'm focused on.

Ginger heads to the mini bar, pulling out a small bottle of Jameson, but I press my front to her back before she can twist the metal top off.

"Not really thirsty," I whisper, my lips against the column of her neck.

"Me either," she says, angling her head so I can have better access.

"Did you go to the bar tonight looking to get fucked?"

"Yes," she pants as my hand drifts down her body, first skating over the swell of her breast, then traveling down her stomach before flirting with the hem of her dress.

"Does this red dress always work for you?"

"Always. Mmm."

My fingers tease up her thigh as I move her dress higher up.

"You're gonna be a lot of fun. I can already tell." I nip at her neck, and she shudders. "Tell me what you need."

My fingers trace circles on her thigh. I'm inches from touching her center. Her hips roll, wanting more, but I can't give it to her just yet. One-night stands are tricky. We both have needs and desires. Those things are easier to satisfy usually for a man, but for a woman it's trickier. Many things are either left unfulfilled or they're learned after long-term exploration. We don't have the luxury of lengthy bouts of play, and I'll be damned if I leave a woman unsatisfied, so a quick conversation is a must.

"Ginger," I prompt. "What do you need?"

She whimpers when I pull my hand free. Clearly it's too much of a distraction for her, but I press my palm flat to her stomach and urge her against my straining erection against her back.

"A confident lover."

"That's a good start. What else?"

"Umm..."

I smile against her temple. Her head seems to be just as clouded as mine.

"Do you need pain?"

She shakes her head. "No, but a little aggression never hurts."

"So you like it rough?"

"And hard," she pants, her hips rolling against me. "Bossy."

"What else?" My fingers work open the single snap holding her dress up at the nape of her neck, my hands replacing the fabric at her perfect tits as it falls away. Utter damn perfection. The warmth of them makes me groan, and I turn her around to face me, lowering my mouth to her flesh.

"I think that's it. I like that. Mmm. That, too." She moans when my teeth sink into the furled tip of her nipple.

"Unzip me."

Her fingers work open the button and zipper on my slacks, and although I didn't tell her to, she slinks her hand behind the fabric of my boxer briefs, her hand making contact with my shaft. I hiss in pleasure, standing still for a long moment as she explores the length of me.

When I stand to my full height, she seems reluctant to let me go. Her eyes stay on her working hand when I take a step back, her jaw slack.

"Ginger?" Her teeth dig into her lower lip. "Ginger?"

"Huh?" Her eyes snap up to mine.

"Get naked."

Her eyes stay locked on me as I begin to unbutton my shirt, the head of my cock peeking out of the top band of my underwear. She works her dress over her hips, leaving her lacy black panties on as a tease. I like the sight of them on her milky skin. I'm going to like the marks they leave behind when I twist and stretch them against her skin as well.

"How wet are you?"

Her wide eyes finally find mine, even though she seems reluctant to pull her eyes from my throbbing cock now that I've tossed my slacks away.

"Soaked," she says, no timidness in her tone. She has the same confidence she had downstairs at the bar.

"Show me."

I expect her to slide her panties to the side, maybe dip her fingers against her little pink slit, but no, that's what one of those coy women would do. Ginger is far from coy. Ginger shocks the shit out of me—the man who thought he has seen everything—by walking across the room, then climbing on the bed and getting on all fours. She spreads her legs, then she pulls her panties to the side. While looking over her shoulder, the little minx then spreads herself for me and fuck if she wasn't lying. I have the perfect view, visual proof that she's slick and ready, no preparation needed for my cock.

My cock leaks at the sight, my mouth watering for a taste for the first time in a very long time. Eating pussy isn't my thing. It never really has been. Oral—giving not receiving—isn't something I do very often, and that's a safety thing, not a selfish thing. STDs and STIs are serious shit and living the life I live isn't something I want to risk.

But Ginger is looking like someone I could snack on. I mean, I'm not going to risk it because seriously, no one is worth the risk, but that's one delectable looking pussy.

"Play with it," I tell her. She wanted bossy, and fuck if I don't need to see it myself. "No, baby, two fingers, not just one. You need more than just one. It's a greedy little thing, isn't it? There you go."

I bite my bottom lip, hand stroking my cock, begging it for patience as I enjoy the show.

"John," she moans, two fingers dipping in as deep as her position will allow.

"That's it, Ginger. Can you get three in there?" I grab my slacks and pull a rubber from my wallet. "You've touched my cock. You know you're going to have to open up a little more for me than that."

She moans again, her fingers shifting, her pussy working tirelessly to accommodate one more.

"That's it," I praise as I crawl up the bed, knee-walking until I'm inches away from her.

Unable to resist, I bend down and bite her ass, my finger playing with the ones she has inside of her.

"Can you take one more?" I press one finger in between hers slowly, groaning when she pushes back against my hand. She does like a little pain with her pleasure, I realize when I stuff her full. "Move up. Forearms on the wall above the headboard."

I know from experience the painting above the wall is anchored so it won't move, and Ginger doesn't even hesitate to obey. On her knees, she presses her arms to the picture.

"Legs wide. Sit back."

I guide her with one hand, but keep the touch light, my fingers toying with the lace still clinging to her hip. My cock slides between her damp thighs, finding purchase right where our fingers were moments ago. We both groan in pleasure, her head rolling forward and smacking the painting.

She chuckles, but I can't have her hurting herself, so I grip a handful of her hair and angle her head back, resting it on my shoulder. She mentioned liking a little aggression, and this is part of that. I anticipate her telling me to stop if she grows uncomfortable, but her low groan tells me that she likes what I'm doing.

"Work my cock," I growl.

She bounces, her trim thighs just muscular enough to carry her the length of me. Up and down, back and forth. It's my turn to lose focus, my head rolling on my shoulders, chin resting on her shoulder as I watch her tits bounce. Fuck, she feels good, almost too good. The perfect amount of heat and pressure, the grip of her enough to make me lose my damn mind. I knew it was going to be amazing just from the glint in her eyes at the bar, but fuck, I never imagined this.

The scent of her skin combined with the damn arousal surrounding both of us is more intoxicating than the whiskey I drank earlier.

I'm drunk on the combination of it. My mind is muddled, overstimulated with everything, unable to focus on any one thing.

"That's it, faster."

My grip on her tightens, fingers twisting the fabric of her thong until I lose circulation in the tips. I move my hips, counterthrusting, meeting her halfway, the slapping of our bodies echoing through the room, the symphony of our fucking the perfect soundtrack for the night.

"My clit," she wheezes. "Pinch it."

Not play with it. Pinch.

Fuck. Pure. Fucking. Perfection.

She said she wanted bossy, but it seems this woman has a little of that in her as well.

I untangle my fingers from her panties, unwilling to release the grip I have on her hair and reach between her thighs. She's slick and swollen, a low mewl escaping her lips when I do her bidding. She must've been waiting until the very last second because the instant I clamp my fingers over her clit, she detonates, her core clamping down on my cock in rhythmic pulses. Her body locks up, muscles hardening, and I have to grip her throat to hold her to me. I fuck her through it, relishing in the sound she makes even when her body seems incapable of doing anything other than fluttering down the length of me.

"God damn," I gasp. "Fuck."

She takes a huge intake of breath as if coming back to life, jolting in my arms.

"Arms out," I hiss, and somehow she manages, her forearms reaching out before she ends up face-planting into the painting on the wall.

I release her neck and the grip I have on her hair and grip both of her hips.

"Damn it. Never in my life," I complain, but really, it's not a complaint. I don't think I've ever felt a woman orgasm so strongly in my life.

I slam into her over and over and over. I may have to apologize when it's done, but I fuck her hard and fast, my hips slamming against her, my arms locked in place, the only thing keeping her from slamming into the headboard.

"John!" she screams, but it's not a complaint.

If there's anyone in the rooms on either side of this one, we may have a problem, but we can worry about that later. I don't give a shit about anything else right now but chasing my own orgasm, but then this naughty bitch moans again, that same damn sound she made before.

"Really?" I hiss with a laugh, my hips slowing.

"S-s-sorry," she groans. "Just one more."

"I can't stop," I tell her. "You have to do it."

My hips speed up again, my balls tight and ready.

"Please," she gasps. "I'm right there."

"Me too."

"Johnnn!"

I grind my teeth, my body unable to drive over the edge while she's begging.

"You have to do it yourself," I tell her, grabbing a handful of her hair and pulling. I spin us around, throwing her to her back.

Chapter 2

Leighton

I squeal in surprise when he practically bends me in half. My knees are in the crooks of his elbows, and I barely have time to take a breath before he slams back inside of me.

"Get your fingers on your pussy," he hisses.

"Oh shit," I whimper "So fucking hot."

Who the hell is this man, and how in the world did I get so lucky to find him in a hotel bar in St. Louis of all places?

My fingers work, the tips of them brushing the base of his cock each time he finds the end of me. He pulls back a few inches, eyelids growing heavy as he watches my red-tipped fingers working my pink flesh, his thickness disappearing inside of me. It's filthy and erotic, and something I never thought I'd experience from a one-night stand. Most people are too shy for this level of intimacy. It's actually refreshing, giving and taking, knowing we'll never have to see each other again.

"Your other hand," he grunts, indicating the hand I have gripping the sheets. "On my back."

I lift it, placing it low on his back, near his ass.

"Higher."

I oblige as he lowers his face and sucks one of my nipples into his mouth. His groan makes my fingers flex against his skin, and I think that's exactly what he wants. The man wants me to mark him. He asked what I wanted, and I was so turned on, I never opened my mouth to get his list of needs. If this is what he craves, I can give it to him in spades. I'd love to see my mark on him when he slides that pristine white shirt back up. I'd love to see him walk out of this room all put together, knowing my scratches mar his perfect skin.

When he bites down on the tip of my nipple, he brings me to the cusp of no return for the second time tonight, and I do the exact same thing he did earlier. I pinch my clit, only this time, I take him with me. He doesn't come silently like some men. He doesn't release a low grunt or whimper. The man fucking roars, a feral growl from his lips like a wild beast, making gooseflesh pebble my skin. It prolongs my orgasm, making it more powerful than the first one, and that's saying a lot because that one was an out-of-body experience like nothing I've ever had before in my life.

If I thought my orgasm earlier was miraculous, it has nothing on ours happening together. Nothing exists but the combined throbs, the sweat dotting our skin, the pulse of our bodies, and the thundering hearts in our chests.

"You're crushing me," I say with a wheeze after reality crashes back down.

The hand on my clit is locked between us, and I'm beginning to lose feeling in my legs.

He doesn't laugh or apologize, and honestly, I didn't expect him to.

I'm too lost in the euphoria to worry about a man I just met in a bar and fucked.

I'm breathless, boneless, yet cognizant enough to pray he has enough energy for another round before he leaves. I have a lot of shit going on in my life, and I'll be busy for a while. No sense in letting a good thing go to waste. There's no telling when I'll get the chance for good sex again.

There's a lazy smile on my face when he rolls out of bed and heads right to the bathroom. He has literally no tan lines, no delineation from his back to his ass, and as smooth as he was in the bar, that shouldn't surprise me. His body is utter perfection, from his smile to his impeccably shaped almost beard. Hell, even his balls are manscaped flawlessly.

I roll my head on the pillow, looking up at the ceiling. If only all aspects of my life could be as perfect as the man I ended up with tonight. I'm usually pretty selective, can usually spot a really good time from a mile away, but John went above and beyond. The man oozed confidence from the other side of the bar. Walking up and putting his hand on me before even opening his mouth was bold. He said two words before I stood, telling him he was welcome to join me in this room, but it wouldn't have even taken that. The look, the swagger, the way he carried himself on the walk over was enough. He told me I was his for the night before he even reached me, and my body said *yes, sir*, my pussy growing wet before my brain had a chance to disagree.

Before he even leaves the bathroom, I've already decided I want more. I have two more days in St. Louis, longer if I get the job I came to interview for, and there's nothing worse than the cat-and-mouse game. Why waste time at the hotel bar when I already know what I can get from this man?

I smile at him when the bathroom door opens. His cock hangs between his legs, still thick even at rest, and I lick my lips. I scrape my teeth over my bottom lip, lifting my eyes to meet his. He has a hand towel in his fist, but before I can open my mouth to call him a gentleman, he tosses it at me, hitting me in the face with it. I'm a little shocked, but I pull it away, laughing.

"Wow," I say, lowering the thing with a chuckle because he has to be joking, right?

I can't tell because he has his back to me. It's a point against him, seriously, but he has a long way to go—because the sex was just that good—before he ends up in the red.

He bends, picking up his slacks from the floor, struggling to turn them right side out. Seems he was in as much of a hurry to get out of them as I was to see him naked. He shoves his legs into them before grabbing his socks and tugging those on. Next are his shoes. His shirt is over his broad shoulders.

I guess he has no interest in round two, and I can't fault the guy. This was never meant to be a romantic interlude. His fingers work down the row of buttons on his shirt, his back to me the entire time, and all the charm and swagger he had down at the bar seem to have evaporated along with the sexual chemistry we had. At least for him. I'm still riding the sexual high. Hell, I haven't even bothered to right myself after he rolled off of me. My body is still trying to calm down after two very spectacular orgasms, and I refuse to feel any sort of shame for what I've done despite the way he's acting.

"Do you have plans tomorrow? I'm in town—"

"Can't," he says, reaching into the front pocket of his slacks.

I think he's doing it to situate his pockets but then his fingers come out, the very two he used to pinch my clit earlier and send me over the edge. Fuck my life if he doesn't have a goddamned wedding band between them. The bedside lamp glints off the gold as if I need the extra slap in the face.

"I have to get home before the wife and kids wake up. I have carpool duty tomorrow. Thanks for a great lay."

I'm frozen, much like I was when that orgasm hit me. I can't move. My body is locked in place as he walks out of my hotel room. Only it's not from pleasure. It's not from experiencing the greatest feeling I've ever felt in my entire life.

How I've gone from the highest high to the lowest low in a matter of an hour, I'll never know.

As if my life can't get any worse. As if I didn't just discover that my dad has been cheating on my mother for the last fifteen years with a woman from the office. As if my entire personal and professional life isn't in jeopardy. Now I've put myself in the position of being the other woman. Granted, this sin is on John's shoulders, not mine, but it doesn't make me feel any less like a whore.

I'm all about sexual freedom, but it's pieces of shit like him that make it impossible for women—or men if the tables were turned—to enjoy no-strings sex because there's always someone in the group who fucks it all up by being a horrible human being. There are women who would sleep with married men with their eyes wide open to that fact. Bamboozling women who aren't interested is the lowest of low.

I feel sick to my stomach as I rush to the bathroom to shower him off of me. There isn't enough soap in this entire damn hotel to make me feel better, and despite having a serious meeting tomorrow, I know I'll show up looking haggard. It'll be impossible to get any rest tonight.

It's just another way to prove I'm thirty years old and I don't have my life together.

Chapter 3

Gaige

"What the fuck just happened?" I mutter as we all watch Jude disappear down the hall with Parker Maxwell.

I know my jaw is hanging open, but I just can't seem to get my shit together this morning.

"Is that Hayden's best friend?" Finnegan Jenkins asks, his Irish accent thick this morning.

"Yep," Wren answers from near the coffee pot. "But that's been building for a while."

Of course Wren knows what the hell is going on. As Blackbridge's IT specialist, he's always in everyone's business whether we want him there or not. It wouldn't surprise me if he knew exactly where I went after Quinten and Hayden's wedding last night, or who I spent the night with. Hell, I don't even know the woman's real name, but I wouldn't put it past him to not only know that information but have a full workup of her entire history including pictures of her from grade school.

I narrow my eyes at him, but he seems more focused on fixing a cup of coffee than anything else.

"Weren't you guys just giving him shit for being a virgin?" I look to Brooks for confirmation.

The man nods, a frown on his face when I expect to see the quick grin he's known for. Something is going on with him, but it's not really my place to grill him about his personal shit, so I don't.

"She's a real looker," Finn adds. "Did you see the way he kissed her? That wasn't a virgin kiss."

"Nope," Wren confirms, and leave it to the not-so-closeted-kink-master to know that piece of information.

"What are we discussing?" Kit asks as he walks up, placing a rifle case to the side of the sofa before walking toward the coffee pot.

"Jude just disappeared into his exam room with Parker Maxwell," Finn helpfully supplies as he makes a god-awful noise moving bits and pieces of who knows what around inside a metal box. The man is always tinkering with something, but I guess as the resident mechanic and safe cracker, it's sort of his job.

I didn't drink enough to have the headache that seems to be hell-bent on splitting my head wide open this morning, but here I am suffering anyway.

"That sexy friend of Hayden's? Man, the way she looked in her bridesmaid's dress last night made me want—"

"She's off the market, man." Wren slaps him on the back. "Jude's locking it down right now."

"In his office?" Kit asks with disbelief, his eyes darting down the hall in that direction. "Impossible. The man is a vir—"

"Apparently, not any longer," Finn says with a quick laugh.

"Women are fucking trouble," Kit says.

"Sex is the trouble," Finn argues.

"Great sex is the trouble," Brooks clarifies, and it isn't lost on me that he didn't speak up like he normally does when Kit mentioned *women* being the problem.

"I can drink to that." I hold up my third cup of coffee for the day in commiseration before taking a long swig, draining the cup.

I stand to prepare the fourth one, knowing it's going to take a lot more caffeine to make it through this damn day. I felt like a complete ass for the first time after pulling the wedding ring bullshit last night, and I have no idea why. I don't have to use it often, but I saw the look in that woman's eye. She was all hearts and flowers, and I get it. The sex was earth-shattering for her. Hell, it was for me, too.

I had the inclination to walk out of that bathroom, clean her up myself and put my mouth exactly where my cock had been. That was the first warning sign.

The second had been to agree to whatever her offer had been when she opened those perfectly plump lips of hers. It didn't matter what my plans were for today. I was seconds away from canceling them and spending the day with her. So long as it ended with me inside of her again, I wanted to be a part of it.

It couldn't happen. I wouldn't let it.

That would be too much like a relationship.

I don't do relationships.

I've never done them.

I don't want any part of them.

I've never had any inclination to want to spend any length of time with the same woman.

I didn't have a fucked-up childhood.

I had two great parents growing up. They loved each other. I grew up surrounded by love. I wasn't deprived or abused. I just don't want to be tied down. I don't want to answer to anyone. I don't want to have to call and check in. I don't want to have to run my plans by anyone else.

I want freedom to do what I want when I want to do it.

Plain and simple.

I want to sleep alone.

I want to fuck who I want and when.

I want variety.

There's no hidden pain, no suffering, no inner trauma.

There's nothing to be fixed, nothing broken in me.

But I'll be damned if that fucking woman last night didn't make me stutter.

It only happened for a second. Just one slow blink, one misstep, but I fixed that shit quickly, and telling by the way her jaw was hanging open when I walked out of there, I fixed it well.

Bachelorhood restored.

Now all I have to do is stay away from that particular bar for a couple of days, and all is right in my world. It'll be perfectly fine. There are other bars, not ones as great as that one, but next week, things will be back to normal.

"Are you just going to stand there blocking the damn machine?"

I look over at Brooks. The man is scowling like I've personally offended him.

"You seem grouchy this morning," I mutter, inching away so he can make another cup of coffee. We both seem to have the need to mainline the stuff today. "How's your ass?"

He shoots me the bird before placing his coffee mug under the machine and dropping a single-serve cup into it. Recently, our covert-ops guy ended up with a dog bite on his ass. He refused to explain how or why it happened, vowing that it occurred on personal time, but I get the feeling it has something to do with the very foul mood he's been having lately.

"My ass is fine."

Wren snorts. "Did you try that—"

"I swear to God—"

Wren holds one hand up near his ear in surrender as he grins, lifting his coffee mug to his lips. The man is full of our secrets, but to his credit, he doesn't seem to share them with others until the news comes out.

Brooks makes his coffee, grumbling to himself before walking away. I'm next at the coffee pot, ignoring the burn of his eye on the side of my head as I make mine.

"Deacon is coming in this morning."

"Anna just had the baby last night."

"He has a meeting he couldn't reschedule," Wren explains. "He'll only be in for a little while."

"Okay," I say, finished with making my coffee and heading back to the sofa.

I can feel his eyes on me the entire time, and I opt to not engage any further. Yep, the man definitely knows something.

"Wild night?" Wren asks the second I get settled on the couch.

I'm not looking at him, and I don't lift my eyes, praying he's talking to someone else.

Before he gets the chance to put me in the spotlight, a door closes down the hall. Finn looks up from his box of junk, a wide smile spreading across his face, green eyes shining. When he starts to slow clap, we all join in. Giving each other a hard time is a rite of passage around here. Jude and Parker walk toward us, and there's no denying what those two have been up to. Parker's cheeks are flushed, and not just from embarrassment. Her hair is a mess, and Jude looks like one satisfied man—a man in love with empty balls.

"Yuck it up, fuckers," Jude mutters, but the smile on his face says it all. He bends low, talking to his woman before making his way over to the coffee pot.

Wren speaks to them for a second before heading to his office, and then it's Brooks's turn to approach them. Parker had some shit go down recently with a psychotic stalker who ended up being a misinformed half-brother. I knew BBS was working with her, but I had no damn clue that Jude had any involvement with her past the time he spent one evening watching over her apartment.

"Everyone!" Deacon Black, our boss, grabs our attention. "I'd like you to meet Leighton Redmond."

Leighton Redmond, my ass. She looks no less sexy standing in the middle of the Blackbridge Security Office in black heels, a white blouse, and a black pencil skirt than she did in that damn sexy red dress she was wearing last night at the bar.

I stand from the sofa, drawing her eyes as she scans the room, a small, professional smile on her beautiful face.

"I'm trying to convince her to—"

"You!" she snaps when her eyes land on me.

Deacon follows the point of her red-tipped fingernail, his eyes widening when he doesn't see it pointed at Brooks, the man who would normally pull such a reaction from a woman.

"You two have met?" Deacon asks.

"Briefly," I respond, doing my best to hide all emotions because honestly, I don't know how to react. I want to smile, but at the same damn time I want to yell at her for infiltrating my safe place. "Leighton? Or should I call you Ginger?"

She narrows her eyes at me, hatred filling every feature on her beautiful face, but then the walls go up, and the mask comes down, and I wouldn't believe it if I wasn't witnessing it myself. She just shoved it all away as if it never existed.

She turns to Deacon, a placating smile on her lips. "Sorry to waste your time, Mr. Black, but this just isn't going to work out."

Without wasting another glance in my direction, she spins on her heel and walks out of the room, leaving everyone staring after her with jaws hanging open. I watch too—the sway of her hips, that perfect ass of hers as tight as it was last night. I'm entranced, and it's not the first time since I laid eyes on her.

"What the fuck did you do?"

I snap my eyes back to Deacon, scoffing to save face when he notices me staring in the direction of her ass. "Nothing she didn't do first."

We barely spoke to each other last night. She stood up. She offered. I accepted. I didn't proposition her. We were on mutual ground. It was consensual. I was an asshole, but hell. Was she looking for a commitment in a hotel bar? Love matches could possibly happen in a hometown bar where happy hour lasts from open to close with Tuesday two for ones, but not a five-star establishment meant for business moguls needing to get their rocks off before an important meeting.

"You'll fix it," Deacon growls.

"You'll have better luck turning water into wine. That's never going to happen, boss. There will be more clients."

"She isn't a client, Gaige. She's the headhunter we need to help start the newest branch of BBS."

My face falls. "Really?"

"Yes, really. Like I said, fix it."

Fuck.

Deacon leaves the room, heading toward his office as he mutters about idiots and why he feels like he's running a damn daycare rather than a business with grown-ass men. He grumbles louder about leaving the damn hospital, leaving his newborn baby and his wife for this meeting only for it to be fucked up, and it makes me feel like complete shit.

"Let's go," I hear Jude urge Parker who is looking around the room with a wide grin on her face.

"This place is like a soap opera," she whispers as they walk past me.

I stand there frozen, wondering where I need to go first. Wren is going to have the information I need, but I also feel the urge to apologize to Deacon. I've stirred up a shitstorm. I'm normally the one working hand-in-hand with Quinten to calm shit down, to get the man the things he needs, not cause more trouble.

I head to Deacon first, knowing Wren is already going to be working on what I need because he's a nosy fucker and he's aware of what just went down even though he's shut away in his office.

I knock on Deacon's door, but he already knows it's me, so I shove the damn thing open and step inside. He's going to give me shit, but then he's going to settle down. I've never been on the receiving end of his ire before, and it makes me feel like a complete asshole.

"I can't tell you who to fuck, Gaige, but I need you to move your hunting grounds a little further away from the office."

"I was all the way across town, by the airport," I answer.

His jaw clenches, and I know I can't say a damn thing right now. Action is the only thing that will make this better.

"I'll get her back," I vow, and it's the first time I've opened my mouth to him with something that may be a lie.

Sometimes I say things and I'm not sure, but there's not a fucking chance this woman will ever agree to come back up here, not after the shit I pulled last night. But I know I have to try.

When I leave the office, I pull that damn gold band back out of my pocket and slide it right back on my finger, and I know it has more to do with me and less to do with her. She tempts me too damn much, but I don't have time to unpack that shit right now. I made a promise to a man I respect, and I have to try my hardest to keep it.

Chapter 4

Leighton

My world has never felt smaller than it does right now. Of all the damn men in the world. I thought it was bad walking into my father's office on Friday and finding him in a lip lock with our chief financial officer, Margaret. Apparently, them being in love for the last fifteen years was supposed to make it okay, was supposed to erase the thirty-five-year marriage he had with my mother. Their marriage is a complete joke. It has been for as long as I can remember, but that's why they make divorces, right? You don't love someone, leave them. Don't cheat on them behind their back for a decade and a half.

Men suck. All of them. Every last one.

And yes, I know that's why the disclosure of John's little golden band last night hit me harder than maybe it would've two weeks ago, but shit, men are just useless when it comes to commitment. The grass is always greener and all that, I guess. They're never happy or satisfied. Why get married in the first damn place? If love is such a fucking joke, then don't make vows, don't tie a woman down then go looking for someone else. Let that woman find someone willing to be faithful. Unless men like that don't exist at all, which is the direction I'm leaning toward more and more these days.

But then again, some people find love, I realize when I see my sister's name flash on my phone. I quickly pay the cab driver and step out of the car before answering.

"Men suck," I mutter instead of hello.

"Still not over Dad and Margaret?"

"I can't believe you knew and didn't tell me," I mutter as I enter the hotel lobby.

The place is bustling with people, and I have to keep to one side of the lobby to avoid getting my toes run over by rolling suitcases from people not paying attention to where they're going.

"It wasn't my place, but honestly, you've always had rose-colored glasses where Dad is concerned. You wouldn't have believed it."

"I don't," I argue. "I know Mom and he aren't happy, but—"

"But what?" she challenges. "You think he's just living in misery? The man deserves a little happiness."

"He could've left her."

"If he leaves, he loses everything."

Chelsea is right. Mom is the one with the control in the relationship. It's Dad's name on the building, but she's the one who brought the money into the relationship. Legally, she owns everything.

"I told him I couldn't work for a dishonest man. I think I broke his heart."

The elevator dings its arrival, but before I can step on it, a man pushes me out of the way to take the last available spot. I stand, glaring at him, but he's too busy on his phone to even notice me giving him the evil eye.

"Men suck," I say loudly, but even that declaration goes without response.

"Not all men," Chelsea says with a soft sigh.

"Well, you got the last good one, that's for sure. How is your boy toy?"

"He's fine and quit calling him a boy toy."

"Still makes you a cougar," I say, reaching over and pressing the button to call another elevator. I tug open the top button of my blouse. The damn thing is suffocating me, or it could be the damn heat traveling all over my body from the anger I still feel from seeing John at the Blackbridge office.

"I believe the definition of a cougar has the woman at over thirty-five and the man has to be eight years younger. Gabe is only four years younger than me."

"Seems you've done some research. That's what old women do."

She scoffs. "I'm only eleven months older than you. Don't forget it."

Silence fills the line as the elevator opens. Several other people get in the car, and I refuse to speak with others around. Chelsea knows this about me, so she waits. Once inside the hotel room, I pop my AirPods in so I can move around the room and still converse with her.

"Have you decided what you're going to do?"

"I told you what I'm going to do."

"And I thought you'd take a few days and calm down."

"I can't work for a man who would cheat on his wife."

"Even knowing what a hateful woman she is? You lived with her for eighteen years. You know she's terrible."

"He should've divorced her."

"It's not that simple, and you know it."

"I know I'd rather live poor than do what he did."

"I don't think it's that simple."

"It may not be, but this is my life."

"You've always planned to take over Redmond Enterprises. You've planned everything around it."

"I didn't say it was going to be easy."

"So that's why you're in St. Louis."

"I'm coming home." Tears sting my eyes, and I do my best not to cry. I've cried enough the last couple of days. It's hard realizing that your future is changing, that you put too much hope in things and people that had the power to destroy your plans. It's heartbreaking. My throat threatens to close, and I stop in the middle of the room, looking up to the low ceiling, willing myself to be strong, but the tears refuse to stay back, falling in rivulets down my cheeks.

Saying home doesn't even have the same feel to it any longer now that I have no real place to land. New York City has always been home; Redmond Enterprises always my future but Dad managed to destroy that. More than a hundred times I've wished I could've just remained blissfully ignorant to the whole affair, blind to what was going on.

I pull my suitcase from the closet before heading into the bathroom to pack the toiletries. The job with Blackbridge was going to be the one thing I was hoping to have on my resume, the one thing I could do on my own to help start a new foundation for my future. One night of bad decisions managed to set that on fire, but I refuse to go home with my tail tucked between my legs. I'm resilient. I'll go back to my apartment, regroup, and think of the next couple of steps.

"Are you still there?"

I clear my throat, praying she won't be able to hear the emotions clogging my throat. I'll have time to sob later after I end the call. "I'm here, just getting my stuff together."

"I think you should call Mom."

I stare at the phone like Chelsea can see me, the tears now steady rivers down my face. "You've got to be kidding me."

Anger is good. Anger is a sure way to dry the tears.

"I'm not. I think you'll be surprised. I bet Mom already knows. I bet she doesn't even care."

"I am not going to be the one to tell the woman her husband has been having an affair for fifteen years, Chels. It's not my place."

"Maybe not."

"It's not. Dad said he loved her. That's ten times worse. It's not just loneliness or sex." I shudder at the thought. No child should have to even have notions of parents and sex in their heads. "Love. I've never even heard that word and them in the same sentence."

"Maybe it'll blow over."

"Blow over? Are you listening to yourself? There's nothing to blow over. It's been going on for years. It'll continue. Dad and Margaret seem quite content to just go on living this alternate life right under Mom's nose, and you know what, let them, but I'm not going to be a part of it. I told him I quit. I won't be going back."

"Then Mom's going to know. What are you going to tell her when she finds out?"

"How is she going to find out? It's not like she's going to come to the office or check the financials."

I shove my toiletry bag into my suitcase with so much force it moves one of the heels I was wearing last night out. I bend to pick it up from the floor just as a knock hits the door.

"Not now!" I say.

"If not now, then when?" Chelsea asks. "She's going to be upset even more if—"

"Not you. Housekeeping is knocking."

"Oh. But seriously with Mom, you know how she gets. If you don't—"

More knocking.

"Come back later!"

"Insistent, aren't they?"

I huff, turning to drop the shoe back into the suitcase.

"I'll deal with Mom when the time comes. She has no control over my life."

I spin around to give housekeeping hell when I hear the electronic whir of a keycard in the door.

"Leighton?"

"Chelsea, I have to go."

"What's—"

I press the button on my phone to end the call because housekeeping isn't standing in my damn room. It's the man who was in here less than twelve hours ago.

Chapter 5

Gaige

The sultry woman from last night is gone, and so is the scent of sex from her room. The bed however is still rumpled, the red dress discarded in the exact spot on the floor when she shoved it down her hips. My eyes dart to it. Instead of running to it in shame, she stiffens her spine, nose raising a little higher in the air, and good for her.

Honestly, she looks a little bored with me standing in front of her. She doesn't look agitated or irate for me using a key I have no business using, but then I really look at her, noticing the redness around her eyes, the small imperfection in her makeup.

She's upset, has been crying.

On instinct, I reach for her, and for a fraction of a second, I think she's going to let me comfort her, but then her eyes dart down to my hand—the one with that fucking ring on it, and it's like I've slapped her in the face a second time with it.

She takes a step back, more disgust on her face than she had last night at the sight of it. Leighton looks like she has swallowed glass and I'm trying to hand her a cup of battery acid to wash it down. I needed the barrier, the protection for myself.

Post-nut clarity is a very real thing. I can get all wrapped up in a woman, my head going all sorts of crazy places while I'm in the moment. Last night inside of her, feeling what I felt when she came on my cock the way she did, I would've given this woman every damn penny in my bank account. I would've robbed for her, murdered for her. I would've given trade secrets for her. I would've promised her the world. I've gotten close to feeling those things before, and maybe even touched on one or two of those, but never had I scored all of them at the same time. The only difference is, last night after I came, it didn't fade quick enough. Once I orgasm, that shit is supposed to just dwindle away to nothing. It's supposed to be gone by the time I toss the condom in the trash.

It wasn't.

It wasn't gone when I walked out of the bathroom.

It sure as fuck wasn't gone when I walked back into the room and saw her fucking panties still pulled to the side, her creamy fucking pussy just begging to be filled again.

And that's why I had to do what I did. I can blame the look in her eye, the way she looked clingy all damn day, but I'm the one with a problem here, not her. I wanted to shower with her. Get her clean, then get her dirty again. Fuck, I want to do it now. Was her blouse unbuttoned this much when she came to the office?

"Stop it," she hisses.

I realize my eyes have been roving over the length of her for who knows how long. I'm slow to lift them to her face because fuck, she's tantalizing as hell. My tongue skates over my bottom lip, unbidden and desperate.

I clear my throat, wondering if she isn't some type of succubus on a serious level because I feel wholly entranced right now, and I never feel this way. It's to the point that I'm growing angry about it, almost unable to control myself, another thing to be irritated with.

"I'm here to take you back to BBS."

"I'm not going back to Blackbridge," she says, moving for the first time since she ended her call with whomever Chelsea is.

She rummages around in her suitcase before sliding past me to grab the sexy red dress from the floor, and despite knowing what it's going to do to me, I watch her ass in that fucking pencil skirt as she bends down to pick it up. Without care for the thing, she tosses it on top of the other items.

"It's imperative that you come again."

She freezes as if the words carry the innuendo I didn't intend.

I watch her throat work on a swallow.

"I'm going back to New York." She zips up her suitcase as if to prove her point.

"I'm a professional," I say, stepping out of the way as she drags the case from the bed to the floor. "You're a professional. We shouldn't let a night of consensual sex get in the way of doing our respective jobs."

"And John, what exactly is your job with Blackbridge Security?"

She stands in front of me, all prim and proper, with her hands clasped in front of her like she didn't come on my cock twice last night.

Fuck, I hate that I didn't tell her my real name. It would've been a real pleasure to hear her calling it out when we hit that high together.

"I'm an acquisitions expert. You're a headhunter."

"I'm an executive recruiter," she corrects, and it seems like a little of a sore spot for her. "And I'm not something for you to acquire."

"I already got you, babe." As if that wasn't the worst thing to fucking say right now, my fucking ego gets the best of me, and I top that shit off with a damn wink.

Her mouth hangs open, her pink tongue just sitting right there, and instead of apologizing, I picture her on her damn knees catching my cum. I'm in desperate need of therapy. Seriously, why did my head go in that direction? Deacon needs her, and I'm thinking of painting her damn face with jizz.

"Leighton, I didn't—"

She stomps on my damn foot with her heel, the spike of the daytime sensible thing no match for the expensive leather before grabbing the handle of her suitcase and rolling right past me.

"Fuck!" I roar, falling to the side and crashing to the bed.

I'm going to need fucking stitches. I just fucking know it. As if the goddamn pain isn't bad enough, I can smell the both of us on the damn bed. Jesus, what a heady scent. I'm not a psycho. I don't roll around on the damn thing. I do cringe when I sit up and check my foot. The heel of her shoe didn't actually go through my shoe, so I don't bother taking mine off, but I do end up having to walk through the BBS office with a limp I refuse to explain.

"I was wondering when you were going to get here," Wren says with his eyes still on his computer screen.

He either clocked me from the parking garage or he's been watching since the hotel. Either wouldn't surprise me.

"Where is she?" I snap.

"At the airport."

"You couldn't give me a fucking warning this morning?"

"Wasn't enough time."

"Enough time? All I needed was to duck into my fucking office. Deacon could've met with her, and everything would be fine."

"Where's the fun in that?" He spins around to face me, a sly smirk on his face.

"Do you like fucking with other people's lives?"

"More than you'll ever know."

"This isn't going to end up like everyone else, Wren. I'm not some sad sap, waiting for the girl of my dreams to come along."

"Not everyone is going to fall in love with a girl, Gaige, and it's pretty narrow minded of you to think in such a *straight* line." He looks to the side like he's some fucking Morpheus incarnate, able to predict the future like he's lived it before or something.

"Where's the fucking file?" I hiss.

He grabs a file, holding it in his grip before handing it over completely. "Get that foot looked at. High heel injuries are dangerous if not treated properly."

Chapter 6

Leighton

Going back to New York shouldn't seem like so much of a chore. It should be a relief, the thought of getting to sleep in my own bed, and that's how it has always felt, but the city no longer feels like home. My life is a mess, both work and personally since the two have always been tangled together.

Once again I've managed to let my personal and business lives twist together, the lines blurred until I don't know where one begins and the other ends. I could've stood in the middle of the Blackbridge office and ignored John, had my meeting with Deacon Black and acted like the prior night didn't affect me, but the hate and anger simmering inside made it impossible. I acted out like a scorned lover, a jilted woman who was wronged on the highest level when in actuality the man's wife held that title.

That poor woman. I feel so sorry for her. How many times has that man done that very same thing to her?

He picked me up in that bar with such ease, there was no way it was the first time. He was so smooth, not a hint of guilt in his actions. There was a tremble in his hands when he touched me, but not a single hesitation of guilt or look of remorse in his eyes. He was a god in that bed, owning me like he had every right to be there.

I shake my head, trying to shove those memories away. He could've at least had the grace to feel even a little bad at what he did, had the slightest of a stutter in the way his hips moved or a slip of his hand when he gripped me, but of course he didn't. He's skilled in his manipulation, in his betrayal.

I have to put it past me, pretend this weekend never happened.

His sins are not my own. Last night was his mistake, his cross to bear, not mine.

People bustle around me, the airport busy this Sunday morning as people rush around. I have time to kill, the airport bar calling to me as I try to ignore the urge to drink the horrific day away. I know the memories will still be there so there's no real point to flying with the possibility of getting sick in the air. I'd rather do that back at my apartment where there will be no witnesses to my downward spiral.

My phone rings in my hand, and just seeing my sister's name on my phone for a video call request makes my eyes burn with fresh tears. I let the call ring through as I search for a quiet place to speak with her. I know I have plenty of time to kill.

I curl up against the wall in the corner of an empty terminal, rolling my suitcase in front of me as a makeshift shield and call her back.

"I expected you to call me back sooner," she says once the video call connects.

"So you video call?" I mutter, my eyes scanning the airport instead of looking at her directly.

We're best friends, and I guess that's a good thing since we were born only eleven months apart. Chelsea was the loner, whereas I clung to Dad, needing to find love where I could. He didn't have much time to spare since he was always busy running Redmond Enterprises, so I found interest in what he was interested in, and there my love for consulting was born. As things go, I look like Mom, dark hair and eyes, and Chelsea, much to her dismay, looks like our father, light eyes and sandy blond hair. She says I'm mysterious and sultry. I argue with her, complaining that I'm plain and unapproachable. How I wish that were true after last night.

"Where are you?"

"The airport. I told you I was coming home. Blackbridge didn't work out. I think I'm going to have to renege on what I told Dad."

"That's going to be a problem." She sighs, her pretty face frowning, and I can tell she has bad news.

"Just tell me. It's not like my day can get any worse."

She scrunches her nose.

"That bad?"

"Dad was upset that you were upset," she begins, and my heart starts to race.

I'm expecting the worst. Pain lashes at me from the inside. My mother is hard. The one that has no feelings, the uncaring one. The one who probably regrets ever having children. My dad is a workaholic, and that probably has more to do with avoiding my mother and having to interact with her more than anything.

If he hurt himself because of something I said, I'll never be able to forgive myself.

"Is he—"

"He told Mom about the affair."

"He what?"

Chatter near me comes to a halt, but I don't bother to look away from my phone to look up at the people I know are now staring at me.

"Are you kidding?" I hiss at my sister.

I didn't think he had it in him. Now that she's telling me this, I realize I never expected him to actually do it, although I felt like she deserved to know.

"Not a joke," my sister deadpans. "And that's not the crazy part. He packed his things and moved in with Margaret."

My mouth is hanging open. I can see it in the tiny image on my phone, but I just can't bring myself to close it.

"And what was Mom's reaction?"

"I wasn't there, Leighton." She rolls her eyes, her tone dry as if she's relaying news about a discrepancy on her taxes rather than the crash and burn of our entire family.

"This is bad."

"Worse than bad. Mom shut down Redmond Enterprises."

Sound ceases to exist around me. I no longer hear people chattering. The baby that was crying disappears. The roar of the planes taking off fades away. Chelsea's face starts to blur. But it isn't until I drop my phone do I realize that the world does in fact keep on spinning despite my world imploding.

"Leighton? Leighton?"

I pick the phone back up, swiping at my eyes with the back of my hand. "She did what?"

"Shut the entire thing down. She went into the office, gave everyone an hour to clear out their desks, handed off envelopes with severance packages, and made them vacate the building."

"Everyone?"

"Every last person."

"Over a hundred people work there."

"I know."

"Technically, I work there."

"I don't know if you got a severance. You know she's a bitter woman. She probably thinks you knew the entire time. She sure as hell called me and accused me of knowing."

"What did you say to her?"

She scoffs. "I don't answer the phone when she calls. You know that. She left all of that on voicemail."

"She hasn't called me. When did all of this happen?"

I wipe at my eyes some more, but the tears won't stop falling. People are going to stare at me when I have to board my plane, and that thought makes me cry even harder. The idea of crawling back to my dad, effectively telling him that I was going to have to be okay with his affair because I couldn't make it on my own was going to be bad enough, but now I literally have nothing to go back to.

"Yesterday. I just got off the phone with Dad. I called you straight away."

"Mom hasn't called me. Dad hasn't called either," I mutter.

"He knows you're mad at him."

And I am. I'm so incredibly mad at him. I blame him, but I blame Mom, too. They're so miserable, a terrible couple, and so much of this could've been avoided if they had made a decision to split years and years ago. Yeah, my life would've been on a different trajectory, but at least I wouldn't be thirty years old having to reboot my entire life.

"I'm not going to call him," I say before she can open her mouth and insist that I do. I refuse to apologize for his mistakes. I have every right to be angry at him. His choices hurt more than just him.

"I know you won't. Maybe you should call Mom."

"I'm not going to do that either. You know better."

"I know you can run that company, and she knows it, too. You should call her and remind her of that."

"She'd like nothing more than to keep it shuttered just to spite me."

Chelsea has that look on her face like she knows it's true. Mom is the vindictive sort, and Redmond Enterprises, although insanely profitable for the family, isn't where the majority of the holdings are.

"If you need mon—"

"I will hang up right now," I growl, glaring at my sister.

Chelsea makes her own money working as a nurse at a pediatrician's office, but her husband Gabe is loaded. He's the owner of a tech firm and very good at his job and investments. She'd help me if I needed it, but much to my dismay, stubborn pride is one thing I did get from my mother.

"Then what are you going to do?"

I've asked myself this a million times since that unannounced visit to my dad's office.

"I don't know," I answer honestly.

"What happened with that job you're in St. Louis for?"

"It didn't work out."

Silence fills the line, and I know she's waiting for me to expand, to give her more information. I may one day, but sitting in the middle of the airport is not the place for me to make those confessions, not while I'm still feeling the misplaced shame for my actions.

"I hate all the lies," I mutter.

"I do, too," Chelsea quickly agrees.

"If they had divorced when we were kids, then maybe I'd be an architect."

"You can't draw a straight line without a ruler."

"Or maybe a nurse like you."

"Blood makes you gag."

"I could've been an accountant."

"You still count on your fingers."

"A veterinarian."

"You're allergic to dogs and cats."

"A marine biologist then."

"You have sensitive skin. The salt water would be too much of an irritant."

"I could've been an author."

"That's still a possibility," my sister says.

"Nah. It's too much work. My back hurts just thinking about sitting for so long."

"Is there a point to this?"

"The point is, my life could be different, but now I'm too damn old to have a different life. His lies and secrets have ruined my life." I grind my teeth, wanting to be angry instead of sad. Tears make me want to curl in a ball and eat ice cream. Rage would be better. It will make me want to take action, to take control and actually do something that will make things better.

"You're not old, and you can make a change. So I'll ask you again. What are you going to do?"

Secrets and lies.

That's all I can think of.

But neither situation recently has been my secrets or my lies.

They're Dad's secrets and lies. His affair was his lie. Telling my mom was his confession to make.

John's secrets and lies. Not wearing his ring last night was his lie.

So neither are my guilt to bear.

I stand from the corner with the phone in my hand, my spine a little more solid than it has been since last night.

My sister smiles a little. She can already see the hint of determination I'm trying to build.

I can work with Blackbridge and not even have to see John. He's an acquisitions expert for Blackbridge. The job I'd be hired to do—if Mr. Black is even willing to work with me after the way I acted today—will have nothing to do with the man. I can easily still perform and be able to use this opportunity to start over. Consulting and executive recruiting is what I do. It's what I know, and I'm very good at it.

"I have to go."

"Talk soon," Chelsea says. "Love you."

She ends the call as I grab the handle to my suitcase. They're finally calling for my flight as I walk out of the terminal.

I wait until I get to an even quieter spot in the airport to place a call to Deacon Black. I apologize for my earlier behavior, but I don't give him a reason or make an excuse for the way I acted. The behavior was unprofessional enough. I refuse to make it any more juvenile by trying to explain it away. I ask for another meeting, finding it mildly strange that he agrees quickly but insists that the meeting take place at his home tomorrow afternoon.

After jotting down the address he provides, I grab a cab and head back to the hotel.

I can do nothing but smile at the woman at the front desk when my company credit card is denied. It seems my mother was very thorough when she closed Redmond Enterprises. I spend a few moments on my phone, scouting a less expensive hotel because if I'm having to stay on my own dime, I know I'm going to have to pinch some pennies.

Chapter 7

Gaige

When I walked out of this place this morning, I told myself I needed to take the week before coming back so I have no damn clue why I'm leaning against the same damn bar I was posted against last night.

Okay, that's a lie, and when did I start lying to myself?

I know exactly why I'm here.

Deacon Black.

And that's another lie.

I'm here *mostly* because of Deacon Black.

And yet another lie.

I'm here *partially* because of my boss.

Mostly, I'm here because I want to see *her* again.

And it's not because of the constant pain in my foot that I can't seem to stop thinking about her. There's also that low throb a little higher north—in the area right around the middle of me—that serves as a reminder as well.

"How'd it go last night?"

I grunt at Sherman rather than giving him an actual response.

"She must've been a fucking wildcat. I saw your ass limp in here a few minutes ago."

I huff, lifting my tumbler of whiskey to my lips.

"I struck out." I nod, knowing he does often. The poor guy has no real game despite the fact that objectively he's a good-looking guy. The problem is, most of the guys here are, and the women have their pick of the litter so to speak. Without the charm, they just aren't interested.

"Maybe your friend from last night will be here again. You could introduce me."

A low growl erupts from my throat, and it shows my fucking hand.

Sherman raises an eyebrow, my behavior out of character. I don't do repeats. Not that I've had to outright say as much to him, but he's an astute guy. I don't really pay that much attention. I get in, get out and move on. The women I sleep with are forgotten by the time the hotel room door closes at my back, and I imagine I'm the same way to them. It's how it's supposed to be.

Sex is great. It's fun. It's a way to unwind and relax. It's an endorphin rush. Then it's over.

Or so I fucking thought.

"You're here waiting for her yourself," he surmises. "Pussy that good?"

The best I've ever had.

"Quit talking," I grumble.

She won't be here. She was leaving. She said as much before she stomped on my foot like a crazy woman, so there's no reason for me to be here. I take another long sip of my whiskey, my eyes scanning the bar, getting lost on the guy sitting in the spot she occupied last night.

There's no flash of red dress, no woman with long, dark wavy hair catching my eye. She's probably already back in New York by now, cleaning up the mess she left behind after discovering her father's long-term affair with a woman he works with. Wren was very thorough in his research.

I can't help but wonder if her actions last night had more to do with her needing to take her mind off what she was going through personally than wanting to have a little fun. The ring nestled safely in my pocket burns a little hotter at the thought. That news makes my actions even more heinous than I originally intended. No wonder she looked at me like I was the devil. No wonder she walked out of the BBS office without looking back.

I lost the hand in a game of poker I didn't even know I was playing.

"Good luck tonight," Sherman says with a quick slap on my back. He's got his eyes set on a cute blonde across the bar who he has absolutely no chance of locking down.

I don't try to stop him. I need the quiet. The bar doesn't offer it to me, but I can't leave just yet. The night is young, and I'm still holding out hope that Leighton might still be in the city. Maybe she changed her mind. If she found out about what her mother did in retaliation of her husband's affair, maybe she decided to stay and hole up back in her room. Maybe seeking the comfort of a man in her bed two nights in a row will cross her mind, and I'll be damned if that man will be anyone other than me.

I'll confess my lies. I'll tell her that I'm not married. I'll beg to get her back to the office if that's what it takes. I need to satisfy whatever this is that's burning inside to get her under me just one more time. I'm certain that's all that it will take. Once more is all I need. I should've stated that need last night. I could've avoided all of this shit. Had I just left that little golden band in my pocket and crawled up her delectable body, we could've laughed about having a great night at lunch while discussing her plans for building the secondary team for BBS, commiserating over good food and great sex.

We could go our separate ways with fond memories of each other rather than a burning desire on my part and hatred on hers.

I fucked it all up with my need to run, with my fear of that look in her eyes.

I spend two more hours at the bar avoiding eye contact with everyone, avoiding advances from several women whom I would've easily disappeared with were it any other night.

At some point, I pulled the ring from my pocket and put it back on my finger, hoping to avoid all advances, but this just seemed to draw out those women that were in the bar for trouble. I felt dirty and disgusted as they approached, their own bands and diamond rings glinting in the overhead lights. It takes a special kind of sleaziness to go trolling in a bar while wearing proof of your infidelity on your hand.

And as if the universe is out to prove me wrong on all levels tonight, I watch as Sherman walks out of the bar with that cute little blonde, a smug look on his handsome face, two fingers tossed over his shoulder in my direction, a smarmy peace sign not meant for use by anyone who is past hitting puberty.

I drain my glass of whiskey, realizing as I step away from the bar that I've allowed myself to be overserved for the first time in as long as I can remember. But the bartender has my back, telling me that he's called me a cab and it's waiting out front. I close out my tab, tipping generously for the discretion, and head outside. The intake of alcohol doesn't help the limp Leighton has left me with, but I manage to crawl into the back of the cab, giving the driver the address to work instead of to my condo. As much as I want to be alone, I just can't stomach the thought of it right now.

Feeling more than generous, and because I grumble about women being the work of Satan, I tip the cab driver well and climb out, saluting him stupidly as if he's a general in the military before stumbling into the elevator of the office building, thinking that a few hours of sleep on the couch may be just what I need to get my life back together. If I'm lucky, no one will be inside, and I can get through my shame without anyone noticing.

Of course, since I haven't had any amount of luck in the last thirty-six hours, why should I have any now?

Kit, Finnegan, and Brooks line the sofas, leaving me no room to stretch out.

"Did you leave any whiskey at the bar?" Kit asks as I fall gracelessly to the sofa beside him.

"Not much," I grumble, lifting my legs and dropping them to the table in front of me. My head drops back on the cushion, a low groan escaping my lips. I already feel hungover, and that means tomorrow is going to suck horribly.

"You don't normally get drunk," Finn says.

I keep my eyes and mouth closed. Maybe if I pretend to be asleep, he'll leave me the fuck alone.

Kit shoves my shoulder.

"Fuck off," I grunt.

"You drinking because of that woman?"

"Leave him alone," Brooks mutters.

And this is cause for me to lift my head and look toward the other man.

Brooks is normally the first one to get in the middle of someone else's business. He's almost as nosy as Wren. Maybe just as much so, only he doesn't have the tech ability to dig as deeply.

"What?"

Brooks shrugs. "It's clear you don't want to talk about it."

All eyes go to Brooks. He just made himself the center of attention, and honestly this is the best outcome for me.

"Fuck off," he hisses, looking across the room after realizing what he's done.

"You know," Finnegan begins, leaning forward, a slow smile spreading across his face. "He's been in a shite mood since he got bit by that dog. What case was he working when that happened?"

"You'd be in a foul mood too, if you got attacked by a damn dog," Brooks argues.

"It was a fucking chihuahua." Kit chuckles.

"It was a Bichon Frise and that little fucker was vicious."

We all chuckle with his statement.

"Aren't those the little white fuzzy dogs?" Kit asks. "The ones that look like little clouds?"

"Holy fucking terrors," Brooks mutters.

"But that case," Finnegan says again, unable to be deterred.

"The Bremen case," Kit fills in.

"That's the one," Finn says, pointing his finger. "What's going on with that?"

Brooks looks away again, refusing to answer.

"Kit, do you remember the details?"

Kit looks to the ceiling as if he's having trouble remembering the case, but we know the details. Most of the country knows the details about Archer Bremen. The rock god was recently found in a very compromising position with a bandmate, which isn't unusual. The only problem is that the bandmate was male, and his fans had no clue that he was gay.

Archer blamed alcohol and drugs at the behest of his manager and that caused another shitstorm from sponsors and the band's label. The tabloids are having a field day. BBS got involved for both image cleanup and security. The gossip around the office is that Archer Bremen has been a headache to deal with and has been giving Brooks a hard time.

"I'm not talking about the Bremen case. The man is a pain in my ass."

Finn's cheek twitches like he wants to laugh, and it makes me want to ask so many questions. Brooks looks at me, and it has that *go ahead, open your fucking mouth and I'll do the same* look to it. I just lean back against the couch and close my eyes again.

"I take it you didn't find Ms. Redmond," Finn asks when it's clear that Brooks isn't going to share about Archer Bremen.

"She went back to New York," I mutter. "Deacon is going to be pissed."

Three grunts of agreement echo around the room.

"You could always go there and try to convince her to come back," Kit offers.

My cock jerks with the prospect, but I doubt showing up at her place would yield the results I want.

"Something you need to tell us?"

Finn flicks my hand, and it makes me lift my ten-ton head, my eyes darting down to my left hand.

"Fuck," I mutter.

"I thought maybe you did the whole fuck and run on her. Please tell me you didn't elope with that woman."

"Jesus, fuck, Gaige. Really?" Brooks mutters. "I thought I was in the middle of some bullshit."

"I didn't fucking marry her," I snap, pulling the stupid band from my finger and stuffing it back into my pocket.

"You sure? You're pretty drunk," Kit argues. "I'll call Wren and have him trace your steps."

I smack the phone out of his hands before he can pull up the contact.

"I didn't marry the woman. I use it as a ruse when I can't scrape a chick off."

"That's kind of fucking ingenious," Brooks says.

"And a really dick move," Finn mutters.

"Super shitty," Kit agrees.

"Leave me alone. I'm too drunk for this."

I don't know if they actually listen to me, or if I just pass out, but I don't hear another word from them.

Chapter 8

Leighton

I angle my head so I can get a better look at the house. The GPS on my phone had no problem finding the place, but the man I met yesterday in the well-fitting suit didn't look like he belongs on a damn ranch. The huge porch is welcoming, the barn I'm certain housing beautiful horses and other farm life even more so.

Fresh air welcomes me as I open the rental car's door, and it makes me miss the city I left behind even less. I couldn't live in the country but spending a little more time away from the hustle and bustle doesn't seem like such a bad idea either. Things seem slower out here, as if taking a deep breath and just angling my head up to the sun is the only thing that really matters. I know I can't do that. There's a good chance the man I embarrassed myself in front of yesterday is watching me from the window, and since I made a horrible first impression, I have to do better today.

I straighten my spine, swipe my sweaty palms down the front of my dress, and walk with all the confidence I can muster to the front door. My first knock goes unanswered, and although there is an old looking dinner bell attached to the wall near the door, I'm not going to ring it. I rap my knuckles against the heavy wood once again, taking a step back when I hear footsteps inside.

Deacon Black answers the door, and the put-together man I met yesterday is nowhere to be seen. Gone is the nice suit, and in its place a wrinkled t-shirt and lounge pants. His hair, thankfully, is cut short because if it wasn't, I get the feeling it would be sticking up all over the place. He has a five-o'clock shadow on his jaw, eyes tired and rimmed in red.

"Mr. Black?"

"Shit," he says when his eyes focus on me. "Ms. Redmond."

It's evident that he forgot I was coming as he looks over his shoulder.

"Please, come in."

He pulls the door open further, but no sooner do I step inside, he darts up the stairs, leaving me standing in the entryway alone. I don't close the front door. Meeting him here was strange enough. If he didn't have such an upstanding reputation, I wouldn't have accepted, but I'll be damned if I'm going to close myself alone inside his house with him looking like there's a chance he's been up all night torturing people.

Minutes tick by, and I let my eyes wander, taking in the cozy home, memorizing details just in case I need to relay them to the police at a later time. A sound makes my ears perk up, but then more silence. Another sound, a soft whimper. Silence. A whimper. Silence. A louder whimper. A masculine grumble.

What in the hell is going on?

A woman's soft voice.

A man's terrified words.

A woman's frustrated sigh followed by a soft laugh.

Another round of masculine grumbles.

Then Mr. Black appears at the top of the stairs, a tiny package in his hands, and it all makes perfect sense. In one hand, tucked tightly against his chest is the smallest little bundle, a squeaking baby. Against his side, a smiling woman who beams up at him, the slightest hint of irritation on her lovely face as she looks from him to the baby.

He guides her down the stairs slowly as if he's torn between making sure she's okay and that the baby is safe as well.

This man is absolutely smitten with both of them.

She looks up, noticing me standing there for the first time. Awkwardly, I lift my hand and give her a little wave, feeling like a fool for invading their moment.

"Seriously?" she huffs. "You really just left her standing there in the middle of the room? You didn't even offer her something to drink? Or a place to sit?"

"He was crying," Mr. Black says like it explains everything.

It's clear the man would ignore the world burning down to tend to his family, and honestly that's how it should be. I'm not offended at all by his words. I smile at her.

Her eyes grow wide. "Please ignore my husband. He's a neanderthal. I'm Anna."

She slowly walks toward me, making it clear that she very recently had the baby. Anna holds her hand out to me.

I shake it once she makes it close enough. Mr. Black stays right beside her. I don't know if he thinks I'm a threat to either of them, but the man isn't taking any chances.

"Leighton Redmond."

"Let me take him," Anna says, her arms outstretched toward the tiny baby.

Mr. Black's body shifts, the baby held a few inches higher.

"Deacon," she snaps. "We talked about this."

"He's mine," he growls, his voice a low rumble.

I bite my lips to hold back a chuckle.

"We're not fighting over the baby. You have business to take care of. Hand him over."

Deacon looks from the little boy and back to his wife twice before he concedes, and even as he passes the child to his wife, he looks pained in doing so.

"I need to feed him," she says softly. "As soon as your milk comes in, you can take over doing that as well."

He huffs, and this time, I can't hold back my laughter.

He snaps his head up at me, confusion drawing his brows in as if he's only now remembering that I'm still standing there.

"I'm thirsty," Anna says softly. "Will you get me a drink?"

"Carrot juice," Deacon says.

"Water," Anna says as her nose scrunches up.

"Carrot juice is better for milk production.

"My milk production will be fine." Anna sighs again. I get the feeling the woman is going to be doing it a lot around this man.

"My son is going to need a lot of milk."

"*Our* son will get plenty. Water, please."

He hovers for a moment longer, looking between the three of us before hastily making it out of the room.

"I knew parenting wasn't going to be easy, but that man is exhausting."

"First-time parents?"

"Not even forty-eight hours. Is it that easy to tell?"

"Less than two days?" I don't bother to hide my shock. "How are you feeling?"

"I'm fine. He's the one who hasn't slept. I think he's terrified if he closes his eyes, it's all going to disappear. Please forgive the caveman act. I could lie and say he normally isn't like this, but he's always a little high strung. It's only gotten worse since I got pregnant, and he's in DEFCON 1 since Jr. arrived."

"Understandable."

"He's not going to be very focused today. So you'll probably have to relay everything you guys talk about to either Pam back at the office or to one of the other guys."

"Okay." So long as it won't be John, I'll be fine.

"No," Anna says, looking over my shoulder.

"It's water."

"It's tinted orange."

"It's water," Deacon argues.

"You spiked it with carrot juice. I'm not an idiot. Leighton, can you hold the baby? I'll get my own water."

Unsure how to really hold a baby as I've never done it before, I extend my arms, but Deacon is right there.

"I'll hold him."

Anna cradles the bundle back to her chest, eyes narrowed at her husband. "Step back."

Like a sulking child, Deacon obeys her. I seriously love their dynamic. This tiny spitfire of a woman has this behemoth of a man wrapped around her little finger, and from looking at the spark in his tired eyes, he loves his position there. His teeth dig into his bottom lip, and I can feel the heat rolling off him, the fire in his blood heating the air around us. I take a step back, feeling like an intruder in their space.

"Are you going to get me a regular water?"

"Yes," he grumbles. "But the carrot jui—"

She cocks an eyebrow, effectively shutting him up. He's gone mere seconds before returning with a glass of ice-cold water. I remain standing in the entryway as she follows him to the living room. He places the water on a coaster on the side table before helping her sit in a rocking chair, arranging a weirdly shaped pillow on her lap. He presses a soft kiss to her forehead, bending in the middle to whisper words in her ear before pressing his lips to his son's head.

When he turns back to face me, he motions to the dining table, taking a seat that still gives him a clear line of sight to his family. I envy what they have. I never pictured myself having such a life. I never really wanted a house with a wide front porch and a huge front door made more of glass than wood, but growing up in the city, those things aren't sought after. Real estate is expensive in the city and glass is too easily broken, making robbery too appealing. A family? No chance. It left you open for pain and having to do things alone. If my father's affair had come to light sooner, while Chelsea and I were still in our teens, what would've happened? We probably would've ended up broke and living with Dad. Or we would've been living with Mom because no doubt we would've been just one more thing for her to fight over, a battle to win rather than someone to love.

I'd never want to put myself or children in that situation, and since I'm in the camp that all men are dogs—except Gabe, my sister's husband and now Deacon Black—there's no doubt I would've ended up divorced and alone.

I smile at the man, waiting for him to pull his attention away from his wife and child. I don't feel an ounce of irritation at his lack of focus. Honestly, I feel like I should postpone.

Only two days since he became a father? I feel even worse for the way I acted yesterday. It means he left the hospital to keep the meeting with me yesterday, and I wasted that precious time.

I sit perfectly still, enjoying the sight of him as he enjoys the sight of her with his son, rolling my lips between my teeth to hide a smile when his jaw opens. I can tell he's either mimicking Anna or the baby when he opens his mouth, moving it this way and that as if he's trying to encourage the baby to latch onto his mother's breast. The child must be successful because a slow, prideful smile spreads across his handsome face. I don't know the man at all, but I can tell he's going to be a great father.

There's no shame in his eyes, not a hint of embarrassment, when his face angles in my direction. He doesn't make excuses the way most people would. I'm the one to open my mouth with apologies.

"Had I known you were—"

He holds his hand up.

"It's unusual to invite you to my home, but Redmond Enterprises comes highly recommended."

I clench my jaw, knowing I can't walk out of here letting this man think that I'll be operating under the umbrella of my family's company.

"Redmond Enterprises was disbanded recently."

"Recently?" Mr. Black looks down at the paperwork on the table. "The portfolio I have is from last week."

"Effective late Saturday," I confirm. I hold my head as high as the weight on my shoulders will allow. "A family matter seeped its way into the business, staining, well, everything, and—"

"So you're unable to work for BBS?"

"I can't work for Blackbridge under Redmond Enterprises. I can provide the same services under my own name, Leighton Redmond. I'm not currently incorporated, nor am I insured."

The more I speak, the more I realize how unprepared I am.

"We have our own insurance, Ms. Redmond," Deacon says. "There are measures we can take to make sure you're covered. We know your skill set. We know what you're capable of. The team we're trying to build is important to BBS. If you're willing, we'd still like you to come on board."

I give him a smile, emotions clogging my throat. Maybe my life isn't as torn apart as I let myself believe it was.

"It would be an honor to work with your team, sir."

"Perfect. I'll have Mr. Ward draw up new contracts to reflect the change of information. Please meet with him tomorrow."

"With whom, Mr. Black?"

"Deacon, please. Our attorney, Gaige Ward. I'll arrange a meeting at the office. Does nine in the morning work for you?"

"Nine is perfect."

I stand, taking his hand when he offers it. We shake, and then I'm forgotten. Deacon leaves me in the dining room to go to his wife. I give Anna a wave from the entryway before heading back outside. I got the job, and I don't have to meet with the acquisitions' guy. My life is already looking up.

Chapter 9

Gaige

"What's wrong?"

"Does something have to be wrong?"

"You don't call unless something is wrong."

I remain silent, waiting for my little brother to speak.

"Nothing's wrong," I assure him.

"Did the condom break again?"

I huff a laugh. "No."

"That's the last time you called me first."

"That condom broke over ten years ago," I argue. I cringe thinking back. I was celebrating my graduation from law school by banging my way through a vacation in the Caribbean when a rubber snapped. My life flashed before my eyes, first with images of my dick rotting off, then of little Gaiges running around. I thought my world was over. My brother, already on the path to being a doctor was the first person I thought to call. After a good laugh, he gave me all the information I needed to get me through it. Worst fucking year of my life.

"Same goes," Tyler argues. "I was still pre-med then. So is it crabs this time? Chlamydia?"

"I don't have crabs and I didn't get chlamydia last time, you asshole. I've never gotten a fucking STD."

"Only because you're lucky."

"I'm safe."

"Picking up hookers in bars isn't safe, Bro."

"They're not hookers."

"Any chick that you only sleep with once is a hooker."

"Hookers get paid, and if you open your mouth and call them names, I'll reach through this phone and snap your neck. Aren't doctors known for hooking up in on-call rooms and sleeping their way through the nursing staff?"

"Apparently you watch too much TV."

"So it's not true?"

"Not for everyone."

He doesn't tell me which direction he leans, but I know the man dabbles a little in the same direction I do. He's three years younger and living his best life as a hot, young doctor. The guy pulls plenty of tail.

"So why are you calling?"

"Can't I just call to check in on my little brother?"

"You can, you just never do. What's her name?"

"There's no chick."

There's a pause.

"There's no chick."

"Who's Leighton Redmond?"

"What the actual fuck?" I mutter.

"Wren," Tyler says, and I can hear the evil smile in his voice.

"I'm going to kill him." I type out that exact message in a text to Wren, only getting a full line of crying text emojis in return.

If I were at the office, I'd throw the breaker on the entire building just to fuck with him in hopes that he hadn't backed up his damn system in the last couple of minutes. Of course, it would only be a minor inconvenience, but still.

"Are you bringing her to Lala's birthday party?"

"No," I answer quickly.

"You should."

"I'll never see her again."

"You sound upset about that."

"I'm not talking about Leighton Redmond."

"Hmm."

I don't feed into his bait.

"You should bring someone."

"I'm going alone. Just like always."

"You're just going to get hounded like always. You're thirty-three and unmarried. They're never going to leave you alone until you settle down, get married and have kids."

"I know how to handle them. You should bring a date."

"I'm a busy doctor. I don't have time for a wife and kids."

"I'm a damn attorney," I argue.

"You hang out with your friends all day. I save lives. It's not the same thing."

Can't really dispute that.

"Then just tell Lala you're going to be a bachelor for the rest of your life. I don't know why you keep telling her that you just haven't found the right one yet."

"I don't want to break her heart."

Tyler snorts. Neither of us want to upset our paternal grandmother. She's an amazing, tell-it-like-it-is woman. She's hysterical, even more so the older she gets, uncaring who's watching or who's listening. If it's on her mind, it's coming out of her mouth. She's the center of attention wherever she's at, and we love her all the more for it. She's as fearless in her words as she is in her love, and we're all strong, better people because of her.

"I may skip it this year," I mutter.

"She'll track you down and skin you alive."

"I know she will." I smile at the image of Lala Ward shuffling my way, waving her fist at me, cussing up a storm for missing her ninetieth birthday party.

"I'll see you then?"

"What? Why are you getting off the phone?"

"One of the nurses just winked at me and disappeared into an on-call room."

The line goes dead.

"Asshole," I mutter as I slide my phone back across my kitchen counter.

My day started out better than it should've, after waking up on the BBS couch, curled in a ball like a little bitch. One of the asshole guys put a pillow under my head and covered me with a damn blanket—probably Kit because that guy is always looking for someone to take care of. I didn't have the headache I was anticipating.

If Jude hadn't disappeared the day before with Parker, I would think he started an IV with some sort of magical hangover cure. I came home and hit the gym to sweat out the rest of the alcohol, ate a hearty late breakfast, and have done my best to try to keep busy.

Working out doesn't help me keep my mind off her. The grunts while lifting weights? Yeah, I made some of those noises while we were together. I also discovered it's nearly impossible to hide an erection in basketball shorts. Sorry old man at the gym.

Eating only made me remember wanting to put my mouth on her, and how stupid I was for not kissing anything but her neck. Who the fuck is dumb enough to have a woman like that in his arms, her silky skin against his fingertips and he doesn't kiss her? I fucked up in more than one way that night.

I can keep my body busy, but my mind only has one focus. Nothing works, nothing helps, and I know it's because she got away. I don't mean it in the sense that I long for her. Deacon wanted that woman to work for BBS and she turned me down. I couldn't get her back. I couldn't *acquire* her.

That's all it is.

She was a great lay. I'll never deny that.

But sex is great more often than not.

Short of a woman just lying there—and that never happens with me.

I have lots of sex. I've had more women under me and on top of me, than I can count. It's not a flex. It's the truth, cold hard facts. It's the bachelor life, plain mathematics when you have rules about no repeats. I'm not sleeping with a different woman every night, but adding several new notches in my bedpost a week isn't unheard of. I'm a sexually needy guy, and sex is fun. I'm safe. I get tested. I don't put myself or my partners in danger. I don't engage in risky behaviors.

Besides, variety is the spice of life, right?

It just so happens that Leighton Redmond was a super spicy piece of ass. She burned the tip of my fingers, left scorch marks on my body lasting a little longer than the women before her. The sting is only lasting longer because she crossed that line from nighttime fun into professional when she showed up at a business meeting.

Those two paths aren't supposed to cross, but I guess my luck was bound to run out, eventually.

Frustrated, I pound my fist on the sofa cushion at my hip. *Jeopardy* was supposed to engage my mind, fill it with useless facts, but it too has not helped.

I glance up at the clock on the wall. Is three in the afternoon too early to hit the bar? Maybe a little afternoon delight is exactly what I need to get the last woman out of my head. And hell, if it doesn't work, at least my nuts wouldn't hurt as much as they do right now.

My phone rings, and at this point, I'm willing to talk to a telemarketer if it serves as a distraction.

Deacon's name flashes on the screen.

"Boss man," I say, answering the phone, hoping my jovial mood will make it less likely that the man fires me for fucking up.

I don't mention Leighton even though I know it's unlikely he's forgotten how badly I fucked up yesterday.

"I'm calling about Leighton Redmond."

"I went to her hotel, but she's just not interested. I can find someone else. I did a little research. There's a recruiting agency in Detroit that is—"

"She's going to work with BBS. She just left the house."

"What?"

News that she is, in fact, still in St. Louis floors me. Did I leave the bar too early last night? The prospect that she came down then left with some other asshole makes my blood run hot, and not in a good way.

"She's going to do the recruiting for us. Redmond Enterprises dismantled, and I have no clue what's going on there. Maybe get with Wren and make sure it's not some crazy shit, but I need you to draw up a new contract reflecting that she's the sole person we'll be working with."

I don't mention I know exactly why the organization split up.

"Okay," I say instead. "Let me grab a pen. What's the new business name?"

"You're just going to use her name. The itinerary we had will stay in place."

"We can't send her out on her own if she doesn't have the proper insurance. It's a liability to BBS."

"She won't be going alone."

I do not like the tone of his voice.

"Deacon," I groan.

"Gaige," he counters. "You fucked this up once. Don't do it again."

"You're not saying—"

"I don't have to say anything."

"This isn't a smart choice."

"You're going with her."

"The schedule is weeks of traveling."

"So I guess you need to clear your schedule."

"I handle all legal matters for the company," I remind him.

"Which you can still easily do from your computer while traveling. Any of the guys can drop shit off at the courthouse. We don't have anything on the docket schedule until the middle of next month."

"And if something is scheduled?"

"We'll address it if something arises."

"This is a really bad idea. The woman hates me."

"She's very good at her job, Gaige, and so are you."

Praise at this point means nothing.

"Keep things professional and both of you will be fine. I've made arrangements with her to meet you at the office at nine."

Silence fills the line, and I know there's no way to talk him out of this. Honestly, I don't have a leg to stand on. I have no right to ask him for favors right now. I should be grateful he found a way to get her back when I failed to do it.

"And Gaige?"

"Yes, sir?"

"Keep your dick in your pants. I need this to work out."

The line goes dead.

Chapter 10

Leighton

I've stood in front of surly, misogynistic men, boardrooms full of ancient people who would rather light me on fire than listen to what I had to say with a straight spine without feeling as nervous as I do right now, riding the elevator up to the offices of Blackbridge Security for the second time.

I'm in a weird state of elation and worry, a combination of fear and excitement. I hate that I might run into John, but at the same time, I'm incredibly excited that Mr. Black is giving me an opportunity to still work with his company even after hearing that my father's company no longer exists. It says a lot about my work as an individual, meaning he did very thorough research while he was vetting me. All this time I thought I was always shadowed by my father and his name. I've always worked hard, anticipating that the company would be mine, and only then would I shine, but it seems all that work is paying off now.

"Good morning," I tell Pam, the BBS office manager, once I step off the elevator. "I have an appointment with Gaige Ward."

Pam gives me a friendly smile. "Good morning, Ms. Redmond. Please have a seat. Mr. Ward is running just a few minutes behind. He'll be with you shortly."

I take a seat in the leather chair she directs me toward, placing my portfolio near my feet, hands clasped in my lap. The small waiting area is sleek and professional, the main marble wall etched with the business name. It's nothing like the ranch-style home I visited yesterday, and I kind of like the two different worlds Deacon and Anna Black seem to inhabit. It must be easy for them to keep their worlds separate.

The minutes tick by, Pam staying busy with the incessantly ringing phone, but her voice stays nice and polite with each answer. Her fingernails click over her keyboard when she isn't speaking. Her phone rings once again, and I wonder if it's going to be just one more person she has to tell that Blackbridge doesn't do that type of work, making me curious exactly what the requests are for, but she looks up at me, another smile on her face. She hangs up the phone.

"Ms. Redmond?"

"Yes," I answer.

"Mr. Ward is ready for you. If you'll follow me?"

"Of course." I grab the strap of my portfolio and follow her.

Several guys are in the breakroom areas we walk through, and my cheeks heat as they watch me. I know conversations were happening before I entered, but they all cease as they notice me. It feels like walking into the cafeteria in middle school all over again. I wait for the burst of laughter that happened that day, but I know for a fact that my skirt isn't tucked into the back of my tights this morning. I'm not wearing tights, but just in case, I sweep my hand over the back of my left leg just to make sure. Pam doesn't bother knocking on the door before opening it, and as I step in, I realize the sterile office is empty.

"He'll be right with you. Please make yourself comfortable."

She closes the door behind her, and silence surrounds me. I quickly take a seat across from his desk, resting my portfolio in the empty chair to my left and press my hands to my face. Being escorted in here felt like a walk of shame, and my cheeks are on fire.

Taking calming breaths, I look around the office, noticing nothing personal aside from the various diplomas hanging on the wall. There isn't even a potted plant in the corner. I'm not a psychologist, but it's clear the man this space belongs too has serious commitment issues.

The door clicks open, and I rise from the chair, a professional smile on my face, but it doesn't last long. Gaige, or should I say John, enters the room, a look of boredom on his stupidly handsome face.

"Ms. Redmond, good morning."

So it's going to be like that is it?

"Please have a seat."

He angles his hand back to the chair I'm holding on to for dear life. I'm only half standing, my jaw fully hanging open. My eyes dart to his left hand, but the damn thing is stuffed into the pocket of his slacks, and I don't miss the little smirk on his face. He noticed me looking.

I narrow my eyes, seconds away from blowing this for a second damn time. This man has the ability to piss me off in seconds, and I hate that power he has over me.

I take a deep breath as I sit back in the chair. One deep inhalation. One slow exhalation.

But it isn't enough, so I do it again.

And again.

And then for a third time.

When I open my eyes, I find him watching me, his head tilted a little to the side, his eyes watching me the way a scientist would watch a caged animal, trying to decide if it is going to lunge or settle.

Both hands are on his desk, but I refuse to look.

"May we get started?" He moves his hand, the left one purposely drawing attention as he places it on top of the folder in the center of his desk.

He wants me to look, but I studiously refuse.

The folder opens.

"I have a copy here for you."

He offers me a copy—with his left hand. Yep, there's the ring.

I take it—and another quick glance around his office. There isn't a single picture of his wife or children. There are no pictures colored from a child's wild imagination. There aren't accolades or certificates. No pictures from youth league teams. Nothing. Not a single hint that this man is a father. That there are people at home that he's supposed to love. It makes him all the more despicable.

"As you can see, Redmond Enterprises has been fully removed from the contract. The itinerary has remained the same. Blackbridge is responsible for returning you back to home base of St. Louis every Friday and the work week will begin again Monday morning. Blackbridge is not responsible for travel expenses accrued over the weekend but will pay for hotel expenses if you prefer to stay in the city rather than going home. Ms. Redmond are you paying attention?"

I look up at him, blinking. "Excuse me?"

"You look lost. Are you paying attention?"

I clear my throat. "Please continue."

This time, I manage to look down at the contract instead of watching him while he talks. His wife got the short end of the stick where fidelity was concerned, but the woman won the genetic lottery with her kids. The man is smoking hot.

"Page two, Ms. Redmond," Mr. Ward says, a hint of amusement in his voice.

I flip the page on my copy of the contract, and if he's looking at me, I know he can see the tips of my ears turning red.

The bastard.

"As I was saying, you're more than welcome to stay in St. Louis on the weekends if you don't want to return home, and Blackbridge will cover your hotel costs. Strategy dinners each evening while traveling are required, and—"

"Through Zoom?"

"I'm sorry?"

We look at each other.

"The meetings." I point down at the line in the contract. "Will those be conducted by video?"

I like to eat, and I don't feel exactly comfortable stuffing my face while chatting with my client on video.

"They will be in person."

I tilt my head, unable to hide my confusion.

"You'll have a travel companion."

My shoulders slump because I know my day just got worse.

"I'll be traveling with you."

Make that terrible.

"Like hell."

"It's the only way we can do this."

"I'm capable of doing this alone."

"Perfect. Let's flip to page five."

I do as he asks, looking at the list of requirements—all the things I have in my portfolio that have the Redmond Enterprises letterhead on them. Insurance, tax identification information, and half a dozen other things I don't have. Things that will take me weeks if not months to procure.

He picks up the receiver of his phone. "I can have Pam make copies for you."

I vowed to be professional today no matter the outcome, but that doesn't stop me from flopping back in my chair and crossing my arms over my chest like a teen that just got into trouble at school.

Gaige steeples his hands in front of his face, resting his fingers against his mouth. I can't tell if he's trying to hide a smile, but the look in his eyes says *your call*.

It's a challenge. He's daring me to run, and I have no idea why he'd even want to travel with me. His words to me before he left the hotel room that night were literally *thanks for the great lay*. Then he walked out—with his fucking wedding band on.

That goddamn thing is staring at me right now.

Surely, he doesn't think it's going to fucking happen again. The man is a psycho if that's the case.

I should walk out and leave. I could be any of those things I listed to Chelsea yesterday while we talked at the airport. Only I can't because she was right. Plus, I'm good at this. I like doing this. I'm good with people. I like herding cats. I love the sense of accomplishment I get when I get a job done, and I like a challenge.

I should make him wait.

They want me to work for him. Deacon sounded relieved when I called yesterday. The man had me come to his house. Didn't hesitate for a second. Didn't tell me to give him a few days until his world got back to normal after the birth of his son. Hell, he left the hospital to meet me. All of that adds up to tell me that they *want* to work with me.

I watch him watching me for another few minutes, and I hate the silence between us. My anger shows my hand. It's a confession that he affects me. Instead of reaching across his desk and wrapping my hands around his throat, I lean up and grab the contract, reading through it on my own.

He sits as still as a statue, thankfully not disrespecting me further by trying to read it to me like a toddler at bedtime. I sign it, flipping to the next page and completing the information with my hotel information so a car can pick me up in the morning. I tear off the pages with my itinerary on it and pass the completed pages back to him.

He reads over everything, making sure he has everything. He frowns when he sees what I've written, but he doesn't say a word.

I stand when he does.

"Welcome to the team, Ms. Redmond."

I stare down at the hand he's offering me and back up at his eyes. I'll never touch this man again.

"Good day, John." I turn and walk out of the office, head held high. I manage to make it back to my hotel before a single tear falls. I feel like I just sold my soul to the devil.

Chapter 11

Gaige

I'm smiling when Leighton walks out of my office. She doesn't slam the door like I expected her to. It closes softly, and I wonder what the guys are thinking as she walks past them. Like a coward, I hid out in Wren's office when she entered, watching her on the camera.

Of course, I first watched her sitting in the waiting area, a small smile on her face as she watched Pam work with Puff Daddy, Wren's obscene African grey parrot, shouting all the things he wanted to do to her in my ear. Now I know how Deacon feels about the things he says about Anna, only Anna is the man's wife and Leighton is just a woman I fucked once.

I wait an ample amount of time for her to get out of the office before I stand from my desk, realizing I have to wait another minute for my erection to go down. It started the second I walked in and the scent of her perfume hit my nose. It wasn't an overpowering scent, just the slightest hint of vanilla, but that was all it took for the memories to flood back. God, the way her hair teased her back before she turned around, the reminder of what it felt like in my fist as she bounced on my cock.

I clear my throat and crack my neck as I walk to the huge window in my office. The sight of St. Louis calms me some, at least enough to not draw attention to the front of my slacks.

"Her hair wasn't even a mess," Kit says with a grin when I walk into the breakroom.

"If you need some pointers," Finnegan says.

I ignore them both as I head into Wren's office. Chuckles follow me inside.

"Where's my bitch at?"

My head spins on my shoulders as I glare at the bird.

"That's taking it a little too far, Puff," Wren chides, but there's humor in his voice. The man loves being in the middle of everyone's shit.

"Bring her to Daddy!" The ignorant bird spreads his wings wide, head bopping up and down.

"What else have you found?"

"Since you left my office twenty minutes ago?"

I just glare at the man. "You could take over the world in five, so don't give me that shit."

"I have no desire for world domination, Gaige." He sounds bored, but I know he's anything but.

"We have different plans!" the bird screeches. "Like Daddy's pussy!"

Wren points to his feathered friend in agreement.

The IT guy has never been normal. He's always had weird proclivities, but they've only gotten worse and more vocal since he stalked and finally started a relationship with his girlfriend Whitney. The man is a slave to his sexual desires, but I guess most men at his age are.

"Wren," I growl. "Information."

"I'm still working on it," he says as he leans back further in his office chair, arms crossed over his chest.

"Perfection takes time," Puff Daddy squawks.

"I don't know how her personal life is going to affect her job performance."

"Job performance is always affected by what's going on in our personal lives. You know that."

"You mean like coming to work drunk because you can't get someone off your mind?" he challenges, making my eyes narrow.

"Or like pulling your dick out and watching your girl masturbate on video?" I return.

"Touché."

"And it was after hours. I didn't show up to work intoxicated."

"My work was already done."

"Not always!" the bird supplies helpfully. "An hour ago—"

"I'll let Simon eat you!" Wren threatens. Puff chuckles like he doesn't believe Wren.

"What have you found?"

"Nothing good, but I doubt Leighton knows just how deep it goes."

I sigh, pulling the other chair in the room away from the wall so I can sit down. Wren will give me the finer details I'll need instead of having to wade through all the information.

"Her dad is having an affair with a woman at work which you already know. The woman also happens to be the CFO, Margaret Winston. It's been going on over fifteen years. He confessed his discretions to his wife over the weekend. She didn't take it well. I'm sure the wife knew of the affair long before he actually said the words, but once they were out of his mouth, she couldn't just sit around and do nothing. She shut the company down."

"I know all of this. Deacon made me change the contract to reflect only working with Leighton. What else?"

"Margaret, I'm sure at Mitchell Redmond's request, has been skimming company funds for many years."

"Embezzlement," I mutter.

"Estelle Redmond owns the entire corporation. The money is hers. She brought everything into the marriage. It's why she easily shut it down in a matter of hours. From what I can tell, she hasn't notified the authorities, but the hasty way she discarded everyone, there's no doubt eyes are going to be on her. She literally started the storm. Investigations are going to happen. It's only a matter of time."

"And how is Leighton involved?"

Wren watches me, his eyes darting between mine, and my heart is in my throat. I don't know a single thing about that woman other than the way she feels coming on my cock, and although that's not enough to determine whether she's a good person, I don't want to believe she's the type of person to steal from her own family.

"I'm still digging. I have a few programs running, but I haven't found anything that makes me believe she knew anything about it. I know she didn't know about the affair." He sighs as if his heart is a little broken with what he's discovered. "I procured a couple of text threads, one from Mitchell's executive assistant and another person in his office about when she walked in on him and Margaret on Friday, catching them in a compromising position. She was devastated. It seems many people knew, and she didn't. They like the woman, felt really bad for her. Oddly enough, they like him, too. Seems Mommy Dearest is the devil incarnate, but the fact remains, the man and his mistress are corporate criminals."

"That sucks."

"Big time."

Even Puff Daddy must sense the change in atmosphere in the room because he keeps quiet rather than squawking some shit about bitches and hoes.

"She's a hard worker. Leighton, I mean. I don't think she's going to let this affect her work ethic. If anything, it's probably going to make her work even harder. She doesn't have anything really to go back home to. According to her financials and spending reports, all the woman does is work. She's got a pretty good nest egg built up because she doesn't spend her money. She doesn't have a pet, probably because she doesn't have time for one."

"What else?" I ask, praying the man doesn't make me actually ask the questions I'm dying to know the answers to.

"She doesn't own a car. The company provides a driver, but she insists on an economical car, a Camry, I think. She makes a weekly trip to the local coffee shop near her apartment—a one bedroom, eleven hundred square foot if you're wondering—on Saturday mornings, but during the week, she drinks coffee at the office. Her clothes come from a monthly subscription box, but from the looks of it, she sends eighty percent of it back."

He spins around, facing his computer again, and I wait him out. He knows what I want, and he's either going to give it to me on his own, or he's waiting for me to ask. I don't have anything else on my plate today, and that means I have time. I'll wait him out if I have to.

"The company has a small gym on site which she uses religiously four days a week according to her office badge scans, mostly the elliptical. I imagine she'll begin to use the one at her apartment complex now."

He grows silent as his fingers work over the keyboard.

Puff seems agitated, and it's possible the bird may ask the questions I need, so I look in his direction. The stupid thing chuckles. I guess he's not on my side either this morning.

"She doesn't go out very often. If she does, she's not the one paying the tab. White wine is her drink of choice."

I already knew that from the night we met.

"Red is her favorite color."

She looks fucking amazing in it.

"But I guess you already knew that."

I lift my eyes, wanting to smack him in the back of the head at the video playing on the computer screen but I can't pull my eyes away. It's from the bar that night.

There's no soundtrack, but I don't need it for the memories to recreate it in my head.

Her eyes on me as I approach.

Her body language, open and welcoming.

My fingers tingle when I reach out for her on the screen.

My cock threatens to thicken.

"Wow," Wren mutters. "Now that is some serious heat."

"Yeah," I mutter before I can stop myself.

"Forty-five seconds," Wren says in awe.

"What?" I ask as I watch the two of us walk toward the elevator.

"That's all it took for you to cross the bar and walk away with her. Who has that kind of skill?"

I don't brag. There's no point. It's not normally like that. It was different that night. So many things had to line up for it to happen the way it did. Chemistry. All the stars in the universe. Karma. So many things had to be perfect.

And it was an epic night.

Until it wasn't.

"She doesn't do relationships."

His statement stops me before my memories take me from the elevator to me kissing her neck in the hotel room.

"She works too much. Her dedication is to her job—was to her job, I guess. She's never dated from what I can tell, and with all the shit going on in her life, I don't see that changing now."

It sounds like a warning, and I don't know if he's telling me all this to try and protect me or because he's trying to protect her.

What he doesn't understand is that I have no intention of doing anything with Leighton Redmond. She was a great fuck, and my cock knows that, but I'm a man fully in control of my body. She signed a contract earlier with BBS. That makes her one hundred percent off-limits.

Chapter 12

Leighton

If anyone ever needed an example of Murphy's Law, they could easily use today's date and fully understand the definition, meaning if it could go wrong, it has.

I planned for today. I knew it was going to be stressful. It's my first day on my own. At thirty years old, I'm experiencing the real world, one not proctored by my father, for the very first time. It's terrifying. More so than I imagine it would be at sixteen. At that age, you have rose-colored glasses, and a filtered look at the world. You're ignorantly unaware of the shitshow the world actually is. As an adult, you know firsthand just how awful things can be.

So I prepared, not just emotionally with two tiny bottles of wine I got at the grocery store while buying a prepared salad for dinner, but also with a handful of tasks to make my morning easier. I plugged my phone in and set my alarm thirty minutes earlier so I'd have time for a little stretching and stress-relieving yoga.

Since Murphy is a total dick, I didn't realize my phone charger wasn't plugged into the actual wall. Not only did my alarm not go off, but my phone died in the middle of the night. I didn't wake up thirty minutes early but an hour and fifteen minutes late.

I couldn't *not* take a shower. I slept horribly last night, tossing and turning of course until the last three hours where I fell into a coma-like state, leaving my hair in a knotted mess. The less-than-stellar hotel I'm staying at decided today was the day the hot water was optional, but awesome for me, the cold shower perked me right up.

The hasty packing I did in the hotel room to get away from Gaige "John" Ward left my clothes wrinkled and the iron in the room doesn't work. The call to the front desk went unanswered.

The car that was supposed to be waiting for me out front had already left because I was so late and unreachable by phone. Thankfully, I managed enough charge to order an Uber to get to the airport. I didn't email Deacon to apologize, figuring if I made my flight, it wouldn't matter.

Traffic was horrific, because why would anything possibly go right, but breathing a sigh of relief as I finally made it to the airport was premature.

The link sent for my flight was wrong, or the terminal changed overnight, and I didn't have the wherewithal to check. I lost valuable time finding the correct one.

Side note, huffing at TSA while they dig through your suitcase because your leave-in conditioner is a half-ounce too big will not make them work faster, and they have perfected the *failure to plan on your part does not constitute an emergency on mine* look. They must teach it in orientation.

They are calling my name over the intercom system as I run through the airport, waving my phone at the gate attendant as she steps away from the desk to close the door.

"I'm Leighton Redmond!"

It feels like a million eyes turn in my direction, but I'm not worried about these people. I'm more worried about the irritated people I'll have to spend the next five hours on a flight to San Francisco with.

"Bad day?" she asks as I approach.

"The worst," I tell her, holding up my phone.

"Can you unlock the screen for me?"

I turn it over. The screen is as black as night. I tap the thing but nothing happens. Tears well in my eyes, and I curse technology not for the first time today.

I have to tap the screen twice more before it comes to life. Finally managing to unlock the screen, she scans the barcode and urges me to hurry. The flight attendant isn't as welcoming when I finally arrive, and the glares I get from the passengers cause physical pain in my chest. I keep my eyes down. The high I was floating on two days ago from landing the job with Deacon Black's company was nearly crushed with being forced to work with Gaige Ward, and this morning took every gust of wind out of those sails.

Then I get to my seat, finding him with the same frown as the other passengers. Disappointment, as if he has any right, creases his forehead as he stands so I can take my seat against the window. His fingers brush mine as he reaches for the handle on my rolling suitcase, and I just let him have it. If I have to open my mouth and speak to him, I'll cry, and I hate myself from so easily turning from the confident woman who strutted from his office yesterday to the blubbering mess I am right now.

My eyes are focused out the window where I plan to keep them the entire flight by the time he takes his seat. I won't talk to him, and I damn sure won't apologize for a bad morning. He cheats on his wife for fuck's sake. Being late pales in comparison.

I feel him settle back in beside me, his eyes burning into the side of my face. I guess I should be thankful that I'm hidden from the agitated glares of the other passengers. It's an early morning midweek flight, probably filled with business professionals like us. They have places to be, schedules to keep, and the fifteen-minute inconvenience I caused is just long enough to irritate them enough to form hatred. People are so petty these days, forgetting that they've probably also had bad days.

My throat burns with emotions, and I will them down as best as I can.

"Ma'am?"

I don't look over. I don't want nor need a drink or snack. I need to be left the hell alone, a few minutes reprieve to get my shit together.

"Ma'am?" The irritability in the flight attendant's voice doubles.

Gaige nudges my arm, and when I turn my head, I glare at him first for having the audacity to touch me before looking up at me.

"We can't take off until you have your seatbelt on. I think we've been delayed enough already." She cocks an eyebrow at me.

I scramble for my seatbelt, hearing a man mutter, "Stupid bitch," in the seat behind me.

Gaige turns, glaring between the seats.

My fingers tremble as I struggle to clasp the belt, swallowing repeatedly before I can get the thing to lock in place, but once it's done, my gaze goes right back out the window.

We taxi, take off, and reach altitude quickly. I guess I can be thankful we don't have to wait in line behind a slew of other planes because of my delay. It's the only thing that has gone right today.

Gaige pulls out his computer, lowering the tray table and begins to type away. Curious, I look over, but he has one of those privacy screens on his computer that makes it impossible for me to see what he's working on. Feeling like he's purposely trying to one-up me, I decide maybe I should look busy too, but doing so would mean I have to stand and get my own computer out of my carry-on.

I could sleep. Closing my eyes would probably be the best thing right now, but that attempt makes me all too aware of his presence beside me. The brush of his arm against mine occasionally feels like a branding iron to my skin, my arm bare, his covered in a long-sleeve button-up that has no business looking so good on him.

Maybe it's my mind playing tricks on me, but it's almost as if I can *feel* his presence beside me.

"Excuse me," I say suddenly, standing in my seat.

We're not in first class, but business is roomier than coach. Gaige lifts his computer, flipping up the table tray, but he doesn't stand, forcing me to practically straddle his legs to get by. His eyes drift to my stomach, tongue sneaking out to wet his lower lip as I move past him. I don't meet the eyes of the other passengers as I pull my suitcase from the overhead bin and quickly get my computer out. Of course, I have issues trying to decide what to do with it while also needing to return the damn thing to the bin.

"Let me help you," Gaige says as he takes my computer from my hands and places it in my seat.

He stands, his body practically aligning with mine in the narrow aisle, his chest brushing mine. I take a step back, my ass hitting another passenger.

"Sorry," I mutter, turning around to face the man I hit, gaining a sneer from the woman sitting beside me.

Gaige chuckles at the man when he smiles and says, "No problem."

I rush back to my seat, nearly crushing my computer, making sure to snap my belt back in place. The very last thing I need is another damn warning from the fucking air sheriff for not wearing it.

Gaige doesn't try to talk to me when he takes his seat. He simply goes back to work, pulling a pair of glasses from his computer bag, and I hate myself for noticing how damn handsome he looks with them on his face.

Work doesn't take precedence over creating a résumé, something I've never had to do before.

I connect to the in-flight Internet and research what elements a résumé should have. I wasn't part of the hiring committee, so I'm not familiar with their format.

I spend the rest of the flight building it from scratch, hating how anemic it looks once I'm done. More than once I had to fight the urge not to wipe my face in order to keep tears from welling on my lashes, knowing it would draw unwanted attention. If this day is a warning of how my time doing this job will be, then it's going to be horrible.

I sigh, closing my laptop and letting my eyes flutter closed.

A warm hand covers mine on the top of my closed computer, and I just let it stay there for a second, getting lost in the comfort. A hug from my sister would be amazing right now. The second I open my eyes and look down, it's that damn hand, wearing that stupid ring, and I nearly lose it.

"Don't fucking touch me," I snap, jerking my hand away. "Don't ever touch me again."

That ring is just one more reminder of just how messed up my life is. How people are truly disappointing. How people can hurt others, betray people without guilt or remorse. It's so disgusting. I feel nauseated with the part I played in it.

His eyes look down at the hand still resting on the top of my computer and he frowns, as if that gold band is the only problem, as if it wasn't there, then there wouldn't be an issue at all. Slowly he pulls the hand away, his thumb rubbing the metal on the underside.

He doesn't say another word as I turn my head and focus my attention out the window.

Chapter 13

Gaige

If I had any doubt that she wanted to put physical distance between the two of us, the demand that I never touch her again washed all of that away.

I should be grateful for the clarification. I did make the declaration to myself just yesterday in Wren's office that she was off-limits. I meant it. At least, I think I did.

I really wanted to.

I affirmed that vow this morning when I got the notification that the hired car waited for her, and she didn't show. I was sure she'd tucked tail and went back home. Deacon wouldn't hold her to her signed contract if she changed her mind. He isn't the type of man to force a scorned woman to work with a man she regretted sleeping with. It tows the line of sexual harassment, and he wasn't going to bring on that sort of trouble. Or maybe he would since he's forcing me to be her shadow in this endeavor even though he's well aware we've been intimate. Who knows where the man's head is at these days?

As we walk through the airport, I can tell she's trying to get away from me, but her heels just can't carry her as quickly as she wants to go. Honestly, I'm not walking as fast as I can because I don't have a problem keeping my eyes on her ass from a few feet back. If she wants a little distance, this works just fine for me.

I can tell she's had a bad morning. There's no chance in hell she would willingly show up for her first day at a new job looking disheveled the way she does right now.

Unless...

My feet misstep, and the blunder is so unnatural for me, I have to look back to check for the imperfection in the flooring. Finding none, I continue to walk.

Did she hit the hotel bar last night?

Did she find another man to warm her bed?

Was she late this morning because he wasn't the type to leave right after?

Did she get out of the shower, get dressed in that sexy-as-hell blouse and pencil skirt and he just couldn't take it and hiked it up her thighs, bending her over the bed, fucking her until she came on *his* dick?

Did I have to wait on a plane while someone else got her off?

A low growl escapes my throat as I reassess her in a new light. She does look freshly fucked—her clothes wrinkled, hair a little ratty. She's walking with confidence, but the woman takes cock like a goddess, so that's not exactly evidence either way.

My cell phone chimes with a text, informing me that our hired car has arrived and is waiting outside for us. I don't bother telling Leighton because I'm pissed while fully understanding that I have no right to be.

"Blackbridge?" Leighton asks the man standing beside a sedan before I can do just that. The man smiles and nods, opening the door for her.

Leighton smiles, climbing inside as I walk around to the other side. The driver loads our luggage into the trunk before climbing inside.

I give him the address, and Leighton immediately corrects him. He finds my eyes in the rearview mirror, and a slight nod of his head tells me that we'll be heading to my address first.

She turns in her seat, eyes pissed, tiny little lasers that would cut me in half if she possessed the power. "We have a meeting in an hour."

"It's been postponed."

"By the prospective client?"

"By me."

"It's in poor taste to reschedule. It looks bad for Blackbr—"

"It's in poor taste to show up for a meeting looking like you just rolled out of bed." My eyes sweep the length of her, and honestly, if I were the one who caused the dishevelment, I'd be all for it, but I hate the sight of her, knowing I didn't have a hand in making her this way.

I look away, barely restraining myself from shaking her and demanding that she tell me who she met last night.

My jaw clenches as we pull away from the airport, and it hurts, the tension stirring the beginning of a headache by the time we reach the hotel.

"You have two hours to put yourself together," I tell her as we inch toward the valet area. "Showing up to work looking like this again is unacceptable. It doesn't meet the expectation Blackbridge had when they hired you, Ms. Redmond."

Her eyes are straight ahead, refusing to look in my direction, but I don't miss the tiny quiver of her chin. I'm an asshole, but I'm normally not with women. You get more bees with honey as the saying goes, and maybe I should apologize. Hell, I probably shouldn't have said it at all, but I just can't get the mental image out of my head that she spent the night with someone else.

I'm pissed that I had to wait for her. Irrationally angry that it wasn't me making her late.

I told Deacon this was a bad idea, but I can't imagine sending any of the other guys to do this. They know how hot she is. I love them like brothers, but I'd strangle any one of them for even thinking about her the way I do.

Shit.

I just need to stop.

The car rolls up to the front, and I climb out the second I get the chance. Not waiting for the driver, I grab Leighton's suitcase from the trunk along with my own. The sooner I can get us checked in, the quicker I can put some distance between the two of us.

Leighton waits off to the side while I flirt with the front desk clerk. She tells me that it's another two hours before check-in, but she finally manages to find two rooms side by side, blinking up at me when I assure her that we in fact don't need to stay in the same bed and that I need a room with a king because I sleep alone.

Unlike Leighton, the desk clerk doesn't seem to notice the ring on my finger, and if she does, she doesn't care. I give her a wink that makes me feel dirty and not in a good way before turning back to Leighton. She seems to have better control over herself now. The tears I was certain were going to fall have been replaced with sheer revulsion and anger. She snatches the keycard from my hand when I pass it to her.

"An hour and forty-five minutes."

"You said two hours."

"That time started when we pulled up. Don't be late."

She steps away, the heels of her shoes on the carpet making it impossible to sound as angry as I know she truly feels. I make arrangements with the concierge to take my suitcase up to my room because even sharing an elevator with her right now would be dangerous. Being on the same floor with her while having her spare keycard in my pocket is trouble. Knowing she's in the shower? There wouldn't be a damn thing that would keep me out of her room, and getting arrested in California over two thousand miles from home wouldn't put Deacon in the best mood.

I take a seat in the luxurious lounge area that's clearly meant more for aesthetics than comfort and wait, trying to look interested in things on my phone when really, I'm antsy about how the rest of this trip is going to go. I have no real worries about the job. Deacon is a master at picking people. He built Blackbridge from the ground up, and although the guys, me included, fuck around a lot, we work our asses off when the situation calls for it. We get the job done every single time. If he has faith that Leighton Redmond is the right person to build the female team he thinks the company requires to meet the needs being demanded, then she's the one.

I'm more worried about the working and personal side of it. I can't think straight around her, and that compromises my ability to get shit done. Like right now. I have a list of things that need to be taken care of—all the things Deacon assured me that I could take care of while traveling, and I sent my fucking computer up to my room with my suitcase. I'll have to work later tonight to not fall behind, all because I can't focus.

That's the working side of things.

The personal side has me even more confused. Don't get me wrong. I'm not misogynistic. At least I didn't think I was, but more than once since she walked into the BBS office, I've thought, *I can't work with this woman. She doesn't have any business working in the damn office.*

And that's more on me than on her.

I know it's not her fault that my cock gets hard nearly every time I see her.

That's my lack of control.

And it seriously pisses me off, and that makes me hate her a little, makes me want to be mean to her.

I'm not that person.

I'm not a man who is mean to women.

Women are meant to be teased and pleased, pleasured and aroused.

And fuck if I don't want to do that to her over and over and over again.

And now we've come full circle.

Right back to the anger and inability to control myself.

Which of course I blame her for.

See? Misogynistic.

The discomfort that begins to settle is more than just the weird chair I'm sitting in, and the bar has too great of an appeal to avoid any longer, so I make my way in that direction. I order a soda when I really want a whiskey, but more than rescheduling, showing up a little buzzed would definitely look bad for the company. I'll have plenty of time to drink this evening.

You'd think sitting at a bar in the middle of the day midweek would be lonely, but you'd be wrong. The women sucking back Cosmos on a Wednesday are more trouble than those enjoying a girls' night out on Saturday. They're lonely, waiting around for husbands to get out of business meetings and looking for trouble.

I ignore their blatant staring, hating the luck I have with women, and feeling even more like an asshole for even realizing that I'm a handsome guy. I guess being one of those fools who doesn't realize he's good looking wouldn't bring me any more favor at this point in the game so who really cares?

It's only been an hour when Leighton steps off the elevator looking like a million damn dollars, and once again I forget why we're even in San Francisco to begin with. I stand, a wide grin on my face, throwing down a twenty on the bar before walking toward her as if I've been waiting to take her out on a date. The scowl on her face brings me right back down to reality when she sees that fucking ring on my hand again.

Chapter 14

Leighton

"Just a few more minutes, promise," Mila, the receptionist behind the desk assures us with a polite smile.

"It's fine," I say from my seat in the small waiting area across from her desk. "We're so sorry we had to reschedule. We appreciate the flexibility."

Miller Inc., run by attorney Janine Miller, is a very small consulting firm that is growing by leaps and bounds on the west coast. Deacon is a smart man to try and scoop her up while she's still building her empire.

Gaige is antsy beside me for some reason as if he's a toddler needing to use the restroom or something.

His normal cool and calm demeanor flew out the window the second I stepped off the elevator.

Mila's phone rings. "Ms. Miller. Yes."

Her cheeks turn pink as she listens, her head lowering as she whispers into the phone, and I have to roll my lips between my teeth to keep from smiling.

"She's ready to see you now," Mila says as she returns the receiver. She clears her throat, pointing to the closest door behind her.

We stand, walking in that direction, and I knock on the door, waiting for permission to enter before turning the knob even though we've been announced.

Janine Miller stands behind her desk, an imposing woman in an impeccable suit, and for the first time today, I'm glad Gaige insisted that we go to the hotel for me to shower and change. He was right, although I'll never tell him so. Ms.—I look down at her left hand—Mrs. Miller would never have respected me had I shown up the way I had originally planned.

"Mrs. Miller," I say as I cross the room, not even giving Gaige the chance to shake her hand first.

"Ms. Redmond."

"Leighton, please," I tell her as I shake her hand. She doesn't offer me the same informality, and I find that I like it. She demands respect, and I fully plan to give it to her. "My colleague, Gaige Ward."

"Gaige."

Mrs. Miller shakes his hand, and I smile at the tic in his jaw with her choosing to use his first name before it was offered. I love her already.

"Please, have a seat."

We both sit, chatting at first about the weather and differences between California and Missouri. Gaige, of course, not missing the opportunity to insert comments about the beach and how we should all be in bathing suits in the sun instead of business attire in an office. It's sneaky of course, nothing too trashy or sexual, but we're all educated enough that we catch the flirting. I want to throw up in my mouth. Mrs. Miller raises an eyebrow, looking over at me as if to check and see if she's hearing me right. My cheeks flame in embarrassment. We're losing her, and we haven't even started discussing the possibility of wooing her to work for Blackbridge.

"I don't know how much Deacon Black shared with you when the meeting was arranged, but—"

"Literally nothing," Mrs. Miller interrupts. "I only accepted because the company is held in such high esteem."

Her eyes dart back to Gaige as if she no longer believes what she has heard.

He gives her a quick grin, and if her desk wasn't made of transparent glass, I'd kick the hell out of him and tell him to read the room. Was he not watching when Mila answered the phone and was talking to her boss?

I give her a smile, darting my eyes in Gaige's direction, letting her know I'm just as frustrated with him as she is. It seems to calm her a little.

"I've been brought on by Mr. Black as an executive recruiter for Blackbridge Security."

"A third party?"

"That's correct."

This seems to help even more to know that I'm not a direct employee of the company, but it doesn't really bode well for what we're trying to do.

"And Blackbridge is recruiting for what?"

"They're looking to build an elite female team. They have so many requests for—"

"No."

My mouth snaps closed.

"Blackbridge is—"

"The answer is no," Mrs. Miller says, now interrupting Gaige. "I've built this company from the ground up. I've worked my ass off to get what I have, and I won't work for anyone else ever again."

"The benefits package alone is—"

"Gaige, I'm not interested." She gives him a condescending smile, and once again I roll my lips between my teeth.

I hate that we won't even get a maybe from this woman, but man do I love seeing him get put in his place.

Acquisitions expert my ass. Maybe he only goes after a sure thing.

And that has a little sourness settling in my gut because wasn't I one of his sure things not long ago?

Mrs. Miller picks up her phone, pressing a few numbers. "Mila, could you bring in a slip to validate their parking please?"

Twenty seconds later, Mila walks in. Mrs. Miller stands from her desk to meet her near the door, but before the woman can get away, Mrs. Miller stops her, bending low to whisper in her ear. Of course Gaige and I both watch, and I laugh when realization washes over his face.

"Oh," he says, nodding as Mila giggles before shuffling back out of the room.

"My wife," Mrs. Miller says as she passes the parking validation slip to me on her way back behind her desk.

"Fuck." Gaige slaps his hand over his mouth, pulling a smile from Mrs. Miller for the first time since we entered her office. "Sorry. I mean, yeah, sorry for the slip, but also the flirting."

"I'm sure it normally works," she says. Shaking her head at his ridiculousness, I know that I could easily be friends with this woman.

"What about contract work," I spit before she can dismiss us, all the while hoping I'm not breaking any Blackbridge rules.

This wasn't covered in the contract, and it definitely hasn't been discussed between Gaige and me since we've said as little to each other as possible. Maybe this is why Deacon insisted I have someone with me for liability reasons. But Gaige doesn't speak up.

"In what capacity?" Mrs. Miller asks, leaning forward with her elbows on the desk, genuinely intrigued.

"Blackbridge Security gets calls from all over the world. Financially it would make more sense and also for timeline and expediency purposes to have people the company trusts to handle issues in California. Also, Gaige hasn't passed the Bar Exam here yet."

I feel his eyes burning into the side of my head, but hell, that's a matter of public record and literally everyone has access to Google.

Her smile widens.

"That *is* something I would consider."

"So I have a maybe?"

She nods. "You have a maybe."

I stand, holding my hand out. I know when to exit a meeting.

"We'll have something drawn up for you to take a look at. Thank you for your time, Mrs. Miller."

"Janine, please," she says as she releases my hand.

I'm on a damn cloud when I walk out of the office, but I don't know how long the high will last. I may have very easily overstepped my bounds with what I just pulled in there. My first job lasted fourteen years. There's no reason why my second shouldn't last less than fourteen hours.

"You did good in there," Gaige says once we're settled back inside of the hired car. "Thinking on your feet. Good call."

I breathe a sigh of relief. I don't need his praise, but I do need this job, so I'll take the win any way I can get it.

"Did you know she was gay?"

I huff a laugh, shaking my head at his ridiculous question as I watch the buildings pass by, but I keep my mouth closed.

"One hour until dinner?" he asks as the driver parks in front of the hotel.

"Excuse me?"

"Dinner. It's required."

I clench my jaw.

"We discussed this. It's in the contract. We need to be better prepared for tomorrow's meeting."

"I was prepared for today's meeting," I counter. If you don't count my wrinkled clothes and bad attitude from the horrible morning I had. "I'm not the one who thought I could flirt with a woman, thinking it would change her mind."

"Jealous?"

I huff, climbing out of the car and racing to the elevator. The man is infuriating.

Chapter 15

Gaige

I take my time while showering, needing the solitude as a distraction, but it doesn't keep my mind from her. Nothing seems to be able to do that these days, and I kind of hate myself for it. I feel manipulated somehow. I'm a smooth talker. Always have been. Most lawyers are. I've perfected the skill over the years, honed those talents long before I ever stepped foot my first day into law school. It aids me daily in my tasks of acquisitions for Blackbridge.

Those skills were on hiatus today, nowhere to be found. It seems I left them in the back of my closet in St. Louis. I shave after my long shower, deciding to be fashionably late to dinner. She kept me waiting on the plane, so it only serves her right to sit waiting for me a few minutes this evening. I spend a few minutes longer than necessary shaving, then even more picking my favorite shirt and denim jeans that I know look amazing on me. By the time I'm riding the elevator down to the restaurant, I'm ten minutes past the time I told her to be here. She's not waiting up front, but as I'm pulling out my phone, thinking she's stood me up completely, I see her already sitting.

Only she isn't exactly waiting. Leighton Redmond is already halfway through her meal. From the looks of it, she rode the elevator up to her room, dropped her work portfolio off, and rode the damn thing back down and was sat at a table. She's eaten an appetizer, a salad, and has consumed more than half of her entrée already. I'd frown if she didn't look like she was in hog heaven with all the food and empty plates surrounding her. I know they're still there to prove a point. She had to have told the waiter to leave the empty dishes. The hotel is too upscale for the waiter to leave them on the table as the next course was delivered.

"You couldn't wait?" I ask as I take the chair across from her, needing to rile her up, because that little fire she has when she's agitated gets me going more than any other emotion she has.

"I was hungry," she says after swallowing a bite of steak.

She sips on a glass of water, a challenge in her eyes. I demanded this dinner, wanting to spend more time with her when I should've just let her off the hook. It was her ability to think on her feet, to attempt to get some form of agreement out of Janine Miller when the meeting was doomed from the second we walked into the office that made my dick hard. I liked how she commanded the room, taking charge even though she was possibly offering something she couldn't back up. She did so as if she had all the power of Blackbridge behind her.

"Sir?"

I look up, blinking and wondering how long the waiter has been standing there.

"May I get you something to drink?"

"Whiskey. Neat. Grilled Salmon. Steamed vegetables."

"Very good, sir," he says before walking away.

I should've ordered a double even though it looks like she's choosing not to drink at all tonight. Does she not trust herself to consume alcohol around me?

"This is a working dinner. Do you not plan to work?" I ask purposely as she takes another bite of food.

She chews slowly, making me wait, in no rush to answer me, and I find that I like that too.

Damn this woman.

"Yes, I do."

I pull my laptop, clattering her empty dishes into a pile on one side of the table so I have space to open the thing as she watches just as the waiter brings my drink. We switch out, me handing him the dirty dishes, him handing me the whiskey, his eyes going to Leighton before he carries them away, confirming that she wanted them left on the table.

She shakes her head, her eyes darting away from my ringless hand. Maybe if I were really married, I would actually have missed the fact that I didn't put it back on after my shower, but I've worn the damn thing more in the last couple of days than I ever have my entire life, and I seriously hate the foreign feel of it on my hand.

"We'll drive up to Santa Rosa tomorrow morning and then to San Jose on Friday."

"I'm well aware of the schedule, Mr. Ward."

"Vic—"

"Victoria Nadir, twenty-eight, lives in Santa Rosa with her parents because she's still on Federal parole after serving eighteen months in prison for hacking into several federally protected databases where she funneled funds from the government and funded a local library. While the thought was nice, it was still illegal. She's a criminal, and although I'll recruit her the way BBS wants me to, I honestly don't understand why the company would want someone like her working for them."

"All IT specialists are criminals."

Her morality and opinions on Victoria Nadir just confirmed that she has no idea what her poor father has been up to.

"They are not. Are you saying the man you guys currently have working for you is a criminal?"

I hold my hands up. "I don't ask Wren questions I'm legally bound to report."

"Plausible deniability?" She snorts. "Attorneys are snakes."

I give her a wink. A small smile plays on her pretty face.

"I'm sure there are things you do that are against the rules, but you do them anyway. Or things you know about but don't report."

"Nothing," she says easily.

"You don't have a dog, take him for a walk without picking up after him?"

"I don't have a dog. They aren't allowed in our building."

"No one in your building has a dog?"

Her mouth snaps shut, and I raise an eyebrow at her.

She leans in close. "Mr. Sniffles is an emotional support animal, and it's not the same as stealing money from the government. Clarice is eighty years old and gets lonely. She always picks up after him."

"Victoria diverted five hundred dollars from ten different agencies that spend a hundred times that on overpriced copy paper and Post-it notes to help fund a literacy program for underprivileged kids."

"So long as it's some Robin Hood shit, it's okay?"

"I'm not saying that," I argue.

"Then what exactly are you saying?" she snaps, leaning in closer.

"Not everything is black and white."

"Sir, your meal."

The waiter waits for me to lean back, making me realize just how close we'd gotten over the table before he places the plate in front of me. The grilled fish and vegetables don't look nearly as appetizing as the steak she's eating, but I can enjoy watching her eat it, licking my lips as she takes another bite.

"I'll be honest. I don't think BBS needs another IT person anyway. Wren can handle anything we can throw at him."

She laughs like my statement is ridiculous.

"What?"

"Only a man would say something like that."

"It wasn't a sexist remark."

"You even thinking that is sexist."

"How do you figure? Online information is linear."

"Research isn't linear. How a person approaches a problem isn't the same. People don't think the same. I didn't go to law school, but surely they taught you that men and women think differently, even if it was to explain simple things like motives for murder or say cheating."

She raises an eyebrow, I guess, thinking that this subject should make me uncomfortable. I guess in a way it does, only because she thinks I'm a cheater, but since I'm not, this is a conversation I can have with her.

"Lay it out for me."

"If men think a woman is cheating, they're going to have their wife followed, or they're going to put up hidden cameras. They want to catch her in the act. It's mostly actions going forward. A woman will work retroactively. She will dig so deep into a man's past she's going to find out about the medical bills unpaid from the time he got alcohol poisoning freshman year in college."

I swallow thickly, straightening up in my chair, the perfectly cooked salmon suddenly dry in my throat because I was certain I paid that bill in full.

She chuckles. "It was just an example, you idiot. The point is, men and women think differently. I'm not saying all men, or even your guy Wren isn't going to go back and look, maybe he does. Experience teaches a lot of stuff, but genders think differently. Having two different people who do the same thing on a team is always beneficial. Different approaches to the same task are always better than one when they're working together."

"Another whiskey, sir?" the waiter asks as he approaches, and our conversation must've looked intense because he already has the glass in hand.

I nod, looking to Leighton. "A white wine?"

"No thank you," she says to the waiter even though I'm the one who asked.

"And San Jose," I say, getting us back on track. She's already floored me with how prepared she is despite not having a computer in front of me.

"San Jose brings us to Dr. Phoebe Cox, surgical resident at San Jose Regional. Top of her class at St. George. She chose San Jose to be close to her elderly parents. She was adopted at the age of ten by Thelma and Peter Cox," she says, frowning before taking another bite of steak.

"Why that look?"

"What look?"

"The frown."

"She's not going to work for Blackbridge."

"You don't know that."

"I do know that. Did you not just hear me?"

"I did. She attended medical school at a prestigious university at a gorgeous island location. The woman isn't afraid of a little adventure. A female doctor on staff is very important for the comfort of our female staff."

"I don't disagree, but she had her pick of residency all over the world and she went right back to California to be close to her family. Her mother is going through chemo treatments for breast cancer. She's not going to pack her things in the middle of that and her third year of residency to tend to battle wounds in St. Louis, Missouri." She holds her hand up before I can even open my mouth to argue.

"I'm not saying I won't go through the motions. I get paid either way, but it's a waste of time."

I nod, having nothing else to say.

"Are we done?"

"Yes," I say as I close my laptop.

Without another word, she scoots back from the table, stands, and walks away. The woman didn't even change out of her work attire for the day, and I can't say I'm disappointed. I don't take another bite of food, watching her ass until she disappears out of the restaurant.

Chapter 16

Leighton

I'm cursing stupid, handsome men with quick smiles and fingers that can't decide if they should wear wedding rings or not. The face mask I've applied forces my face into a frown, but I know I'd be angry even if the mud mask wasn't doing it for me.

His ability to draw out my worst emotions is uncanny, and I hate him for it. I'm not an angry person, or at least I wasn't a week ago. Hell, six days ago, I had a smile on my face. Life was wonderful. Work was fast-paced as always, and I loved every second of it. I helped organizations, big and small, find the people they needed to take their companies to the next level. I take pride in my work, and I tell it like it is, but he just wouldn't listen tonight. He has to know that we're wasting our time. The women we have lined up to meet are all like Janine Miller, the woman we met today. They've each busted their asses to get where they are, and they're not going to be the least bit interested in throwing that away to work for anyone other than themselves. And if they aren't already independent contractors with their own company, then they're situated in life exactly where they want to be. If we get lucky and find one person willing to uproot and move to St. Louis, that's not enough to make the team Deacon wants.

But being angry doesn't solve anything. My mud mask cracks, flaking, tiny pieces dropping to the towel in my lap when I try to set my face into a calmer position.

The television is muted, and I could argue that I have a headache and noise will only make it worse, but I don't have a headache. In fact, I'm listening for Gaige's door to open, waiting to shower so I don't miss his reentry to his room. He was dressed to the nines tonight—looking like a man who had more on his mind than a casual work dinner—in a shirt that hugged every muscle across his chest and stomach and jeans that were too sinful for public viewing if kids were around. His cologne had me shoveling food in my mouth like a starving woman just to keep from breathing in the scent over and over.

As much as I'm starting to hate him, I hate myself even more because I know the man is married, and I'm still attracted to him, still thinking about the night we shared. I'm an awful human being, an awful woman, a disgrace to womankind in general. On principle alone, I should've kicked him in the nuts instead of stomping on his foot, forcing him to come up with some excuse when he went home to his wife that night, and refused to work with BBS.

I chose myself. I chose to further my withering career.

If I weren't already in my pajamas, with plans to shower in the morning since I already showered earlier today, I'd go down to the little store in the hotel and buy them out of chocolate to eat my feelings, but I deprive myself that luxury, a penance for being so horrible.

I've been back in my room for nearly an hour, and he hasn't even bothered to return long enough to drop his messenger bag off, but it doesn't surprise me that he's willing to troll the bar and pick up women with it. There's no telling what kind of supplies he keeps in there.

I grow increasingly angry as I sit in the dark, knowing it'll be easier to tell when he returns from the light under the door linking our two rooms. Of course, we ended up with adjoining rooms, but I made sure the damn door was bolted on my side.

A noise in the hall stops my breathing completely, and it makes me feel like I'm doing something wrong, as if I'm some sort of stalker. Then his door opens, the light from the hall casting a dull shadow into my own room. His room light comes on, but no other sounds are made. I'm frozen on my bed, but less than five minutes later, his door opens, and he's gone again.

I move from the bed to my peephole, but I'm not fast enough to catch him as he walks past. What a damn snake.

I wash my face, turn off the television, and go to bed, tossing and turning before rolling over and double-checking to make sure my phone is not only actually charging this time, but the alarm is set.

I'm exhausted, but I just can't find sleep. Every noise bothers me, and that says something about how stuck in my own head I am. I live in the middle of New York City. Noise is a requirement to me. Silence is what usually causes problems. Tonight, it's a combination of the two, everything getting on my nerves.

It's over an hour later when his door opens for a second time, and I squeeze my eyes closed. I will lose my mind if I have to listen to him entertaining another woman in his room, and not because I'm jealous or want to be in there myself. Yeah, I know what it's like to be under that man. I know how skilled his fingers are, how easy my body was able to bend to his will, but he's a dirty dog. I want nothing to do with him that way, and if I ignore the throb in my body when I think about that night, I can almost convince myself that those aren't lies.

Listening to him cheat on his wife, now knowing he's married? There's no way I could lie here and not bang on that door and tell the next unsuspecting woman what he's up to. I never would've led him up to my hotel room that night if he had that ring on, and I know it was missing from his finger tonight at dinner. I knew then he had plans.

No sounds come from his room. There aren't any grunts or whispers. I don't hear him asking a woman what she needs to get off. I don't hear commands for her to lift her ass in the air or press her forearms to the wall.

A shadow crosses in front of the connecting door, still right there instead of just a hesitant break in the light. Oh my God. Is he pressing his ear to the fucking door trying to figure out what I'm doing in here? What a creep.

I turn over in the bed, doing my best to ignore all thoughts of him. Eventually, I manage to fall asleep.

***

Like it always goes, I wake before my alarm goes off, still exhausted from two nights of horrible rest. My body aches, more from tossing and turning all night than anything else. My eyes feel like sandpaper, dry as if I stood in the sun for hours without proper hydration. Even my throat is a little scratchy as I sing in the shower to music playing on my phone, an awful attempt to lighten my mood.

I'm fully dressed, applying eye makeup when the knock hits the door connecting our rooms. I ignore it. It's not appropriate for that man to be bothering me before eight, and he sure as hell has no right to interlope on my semiprivate current residence.

He knocks again.

"What?" I snap from in front of the bathroom mirror.

"Can I come in?"

"Absolutely not," I hiss, my words a little skewed from the position of my mouth as I line my eyelid.

"Leighton."

"What do you need?"

"Can I come in?"

I slap the eyeliner on the counter and go to the door, opening it just enough to see his face. Of course, he's already ready. Men have it so damn easy. Shower, get dressed, brush hair, done.

"What do you need?"

He doesn't answer as his eyes go over my shoulder, scanning the room.

"Can I help you?" I'd stand on my toes to keep him from seeing behind me, but I'm not big enough that it would help much.

"I heard you open your door early this morning."

"Okay. What business is that of yours?"

The sun wasn't even up when I grabbed the newspaper from the hallway, but I won't tell him that. He has a wife at home. He doesn't need to worry about what I'm doing in my hotel room.

"I don't want your extra-curricular activities interfering with your job like they did yesterday morning."

Is that what he honestly thinks? That I was too busy getting fucked to make it to work on time? I wish... I fucking wish an orgasm was the reason I was late.

"I'll try to do better," I say instead of telling him the truth before closing the door in his face.

The day doesn't go any better than I expected it to. Blackbridge is too organized and regulated for Victoria Nadir. She'd never consider working for The Man—her words not mine—and we didn't even make it off her mother's front porch before she told us to kiss her ass and leave.

We return to the hotel with our tails between our legs. I'm feeling like a failure, wondering if taking this job was a big mistake for more than the reason sitting beside me at the bar.

Chapter 17

Gaige

"She's probably going to hire a team to sweep her front porch for bugs," I tell her, as I lift my shot glass.

Her brow creases in confusion, but she lifts her shot glass as well.

We tap the bar top and toss them back. I don't recall when we went from her sipping wine and me drinking whiskey, but here we are, laughing and joking about the unfruitful day and slamming tequila. It's the most fun I've had in as long as I can remember.

"The porch looked pretty clean." She shudders, her gorgeous body giving a sexy little wiggle from the disgusting taste of the alcohol.

"Like digital bugs, not the creepy crawly ones. Hackers are notorious for being paranoid."

She tilts her head in that knowing way of understanding.

"She really got in to trouble for helping out a library?"

"Yeah," I answer. "And she was completely unremorseful."

Her face grows somber. "Redmond helped a lot of people."

Her eyes drop to the empty glass in front of her before she lifts her fingers to wave over the bartender for another round.

"The company donated a lot to non-profits. Those people won't get that help any longer. I bet my mom didn't even take that into consideration when she—" She clears her throat, making me want to reach out and press my palm to her back.

I want to tell her that things will be fine, but lying to her wouldn't solve anything. Shutting down the company is only the beginning of the shitstorm coming for Redmond Enterprises. When the investigations start, her dad is going to be in serious trouble— prison time sort of trouble. I feel like a fraud for not bringing it up.

The bartender pours two more shots, and Leighton immediately holds her shot glass up between us.

"Blackbridge donates to a lot of non-profits as well," I tell her with a smile, hoping that it will help to know that she's once again involved with an agency that helps in a good way.

She smiles, her attitude improving.

"To charity." She clinks my glass before taking her shot.

I hold mine still suspended between us and watch her lips on the glass, her neck working on the swallow. She has to be the most gorgeous woman I've ever met. Even in her no-nonsense blouse and black slacks, her three-inch pumps and sophisticated pearl necklace, she's sexy, understated in a classy way. Modest and appealing in a way that makes me want to dirty her up, corrupt her until her makeup is running down her face and she's begging me for more.

She likes bossy and a little rough, and I want to give that to her for hours. My cock thickens when her eyes find mine again.

"Are you going to drink that?"

I nod, tilting the shot to my lips, and then I see it, the same look in her eyes as I swallow.

She may hate me, but she still wants me. She doesn't want to, but she can't help it. I'm in the same damn boat, a slave to my body, a captive to the urges I can't seem to control around her despite knowing just how terrible an idea all of this is.

"I want to fuck you again," I whisper, the bar not busy enough to speak those words at full volume.

Or maybe I'm hoping she won't hear me in case I'm reading the situation wrong, and we aren't on the same page. She doesn't slap me. She doesn't stand and storm away. She flags the bartender down again, asking for two shots each this time. I don't argue even when the alarms are going off in my head, telling me that there's a reason she's needing more alcohol to end up in my bed tonight. That she's going to regret it in the morning and Gaige Ward doesn't deal in regrets. Good times and pleasure are what I'm about, but my mouth stays closed, lips firmly locked tight because I want her so badly, need her like I've never needed anything more in my life.

There isn't a ceremonial lift of the glasses when those shots are poured, nor a toast. She lifts one in each hand and throws them back, one right after the other, and I have to lift each of mine quickly when she starts to eye them, looking like she wants to take them as well. Drunk sex is one thing but having her pass out before we get to the room is another.

"Okay," she says.

"What?" I shake my head in confusion.

"I want to fuck you, too."

She's steadier on her feet than I feel when she stands, and much like we did on the first night we met, I place my hand on her back, wanting to fist pump the air when she doesn't cringe away from me. I'm counting it as a win as we walk to the elevator. We don't make out on the ride up to the rooms, but I want my hands and mouth all over her. I wonder if she can feel the sexual tension floating around us because my cock is straining in my slacks, knowing the zipper is going to be imprinted on the length of my cock.

My room is closest to the elevator, so that's where we end up, as if walking the additional four feet is just too far. I unlock my door and guide her into the room. I stumble just inside, wondering if turning on the light would be too much. Would it break this spell, make her change her mind? I probably should. Maybe being a gentleman would tip the scale in my favor, gain a little credit in the plus column.

I don't turn on the main light, opting to flip the switch in the bathroom instead because not seeing her at all isn't an option. She's too fucking glorious in nothing but her skin to miss.

She's not even close to changing her mind, I realize as I stand near the door watching her fingers work open the button of her silky blouse, revealing the lace that has been teasing me all damn day when her shirt shifted just right and teased the fabric with whispers of sexiness.

Her teeth dig into her bottom lip, more in an effort to concentrate as she tries to kick off her shoes and unbutton her slacks at the same time than trying to be sultry, but it works both ways. I take a half-step toward her before stopping. I want to peel every piece of clothing from her body, but even in my muddled state, I know I need her to be the one to do this.

In what seems like years but is probably only a few minutes, she's standing in front of me in nothing but lace panties and that sexy bra. She's mouth-wateringly beautiful. My eyes sweep her from head to toe, cock throbbing with each pulse of my rapidly beating heart.

"Can't fuck me if you're clothed," she says, a teasing lilt to her voice.

I toe my shoes off, working open my own shirt and cursing the man who invented buttons and zippers and clothes in general. She giggles when I have to lean against the wall to pull my slacks off, getting tangled in the damn things. I send up thanks for not falling on my ass, still knowing that unless I ended up with a major head injury, it wouldn't stop what is going to happen tonight.

"You look fucking amazing," I tell her as I somehow remember to grab a condom from my wallet before tossing my slacks completely away. "Take the rest of it off and get on the bed."

She licks her lips as she does my bidding, and as much as I like the sight of her ass, that already slick pussy of hers, I don't want her like I had her the first time. I need to see her face, need to check in with her and make sure she's okay the entire time.

"On your back," I say, when she attempts to position herself the way I had her that first night.

She turns over, her face angling toward the wall away from me. That just won't do. I need her eyes on me. She may regret this in the morning, and that makes me the biggest asshole in the world, but I don't want her feeling it right now.

"Eyes on me," I tell her as I stroke my cock, condom wrapper between my teeth.

Her jaw is slack as I run my thumb over the tip of my dick.

"How greedy is your pussy, Leighton?"

She gives me a little moan, her hips shifting just an inch or so.

"Think I can make that pussy purr for me tonight?"

She swallows, her throat working.

"Spread your legs. Wider, Leighton. Don't be shy. There you go. Mmm. Look at you." Her eyes start to flutter, and I have to pinch the tip of my cock. If I don't get better control of myself... "Eyes open. Show me your clit. Perfect. Is it tender? Does it ache?"

Another swallow but no answer.

I peel open the condom, rolling it down my cock before crawling up her body. My mouth starts on her ankle, the first brush of my lips making her body jolt, and I slowly make my way up. Her skin is soft and warm, just another part of her that's perfect, another thing I missed out on that first night, another thing I can kick myself for later.

I have to slow myself down when I reach her knee, lifting her leg over my shoulder to nip at the back of her thigh. She moans, her hands falling to the sheets to grip the fabric.

"Keep that pussy open for me, Leighton."

She groans, but her hands move back into position. I blow cool air on her center, making her hips flex up. I anticipate the move, keeping my face away, not giving her what her body is demanding until it's on my schedule.

"Naughty girl. Keep still."

I want to tease her to keep her right there on the edge of expectation for hours, but I find that I'm the needy one and I cave, placing my mouth over her, my lips brushing her fingers as my tongue presses against her clit. She's sweet and slick, the tang of her arousal lighting up every single tastebud, making me want to drink from her forever.

I groan against her, feeling the vibration of my own pleasure erupt from her throat in a needy whimper. Her hips roll, fingers no longer splaying herself open for me as they tangle in my hair, and I'm desperate for more, burying my face against her as I devour, tongue swiping, lips moving. I suck and nip.

"G-Gaige," she pants.

"Come, Leigh—"

I can't even get the words out or my fingers in her pussy before the pulsing against my mouth begins. I lick and suck her through it. My cock is pissed and hard as stone for missing out as I press against the mattress. My fingers dig into her inner thighs, struggling to keep her thighs open when she tries to clamp them over my ears. She has a mouth. If she wants me to stop, she's going to have to use it.

I don't lift my mouth from her until her body melts into the mattress, her chest heaving up and down, those perfect breasts bouncing with the force of her breathing. Only then do I continue the kissing up her body, my lips on her hips, her abdomen, her glorious tits, spending some time on her nipples, that dip in her throat where her erratic pulse is still pounding out a rhythm, and I don't stop there.

As I line up, my cock ready and knowing exactly where it needs to be, I press my lips to hers for the very first time, using the gasp she makes as I slide inside of her to gain access to her mouth. The slow roll of my hips feels incredible, but I know the sweep of my tongue against hers is what makes it otherworldly. I grip her around the back, my fingers of one hand digging into the top of her shoulder as the other presses into the mattress at her hip so I don't crush her. Her legs are wrapped around my back, opening herself up to me perfectly as I move inside of her. Utter. Fucking. Perfection.

Her breaths escape through her nose, uneven gusts on my cheek as I angle my face just a little more, the swipe of my tongue tasting the tequila on hers. It's a reminder of what tomorrow brings, but I can't focus on that right now. Nothing can ruin this moment.

Those fingernails, the ones that left the still healing marks on my back a week ago, dig into me again and my nuts draw up. I groan into her mouth, and she smiles, her lips curling against mine.

"You're the fucking devil," I whisper. "Harder."

Ten fingers curl into my skin, her mouth hanging open, eyes rolling back when I shove into her harder, my hips snapping forward.

"Your clit," I hiss.

She shakes her head, her dark hair a mess on the stark white sheets. God, I love mussing her up.

"I'm going to come, Leighton. If you don't—"

"Me, too," she pants. "Oh, God. Me, too."

I fuck her harder, pulling my arm out from around her shoulder. Pressing both fists into the mattress, needing to see our connection, I sit back on my calves and draw her body higher up on my thighs. I don't know if changing her position will ruin what she was building, but I'm a greedy bastard right now, and this gives her access to her swollen clit.

Her back arches as I slam into her, eyes closed, mouth hanging open, sounds I've never heard rumbling out of her each and every time I press into her. God, the way she grips me. If I thought it felt good... seeing it is on a whole other level. Her pussy, the greedy thing that it is, slides along my length as if it's desperate to not let go, slick and smooth.

Heaven. This is absolute heaven.

My balls tighten, detonation imminent when I press my thumb to her clit, and that's all it takes.

Her core locks down on me. There's no pulsing, no rhythmic clutch. It's a fucking vice grip. It's crushing, a clamp.

I freeze, my body getting with the program faster than my brain. Her mouth hangs open on a silent scream, and I'm pretty sure I do the exact same thing. It's like the black hole of orgasms. One second, we're close and there's all this activity, then we tip over, cross the event horizon and then nothing exists.

I crash down beside her, balls empty, eyes filled with wonder, body unable to move or function. I blink at her. She blinks at me, and all I can do is pull her close, kiss her forehead, and close my eyes.

I've never felt better in my entire life.

Chapter 18

Leighton

There are a few things I learned in my twenties.

Heavy drinking during the week is never a good idea.

Tequila is never a good idea.

Sex with incredibly charming men will most often always be extremely good. They've sort of earned that charm from somewhere, right?

Those three theories still hold as true this morning as they did many years ago. Usually, only two of those lead to regret.

I'm zero for three this morning.

I hiss, sore as I climb out of bed, more parts of my body aching than I'm willing to admit. I use the bathroom, only turning on the light so I can try to determine what sort of mess I'm going to be forced to deal with this morning. I can hide the bags under my eyes with a little concealer, but the tequila still swimming in my gut may be a problem with the hour-long drive to San Jose. I doubt the driver is going to be impressed if he has to pull over if I need to vomit.

I lean in close to the mirror, my palms flat on the countertop. My makeup is streaked down my face, a small smile playing on my lips at the memories of last night until the overhead lights reflect off the ring sitting on the counter. The gold band is a little innocuous thing, a harmless band if it weren't for its symbolism.

My stomach rolls, and swallowing doesn't help. Regret washes over me, and I barely make it to the toilet before getting sick. Anguish mixed with bad choices from last night burn my throat as I heave, my eyes stinging with tears I have no hope of holding back, my sobs causing even more pain and grief.

I never forgot that he was married. I glanced down at that ringless hand of his with each shot I tilted up to my painted lips, but with each swallow, I cared less and less, telling myself that if he didn't care, neither did I. I have no claim to the humiliation I feel in this moment, and my awareness of it deepens the betrayal.

I wipe my mouth with the back of my hand as I stand, flipping the light off, unable to look at myself any longer before rinsing my mouth with cold water.

I stumble back into the bedroom, my legs unsteady, my body wanting to revolt as I look for my clothes, each item scattered like we were wild last night, ripping at our own clothes and throwing them everywhere.

Tears continue to run down my face as I pull on each article of clothing, the fabric abrading my skin just as I deserve, each breath getting caught in my chest.

Even Gaige couldn't stick around this morning. I'm sure he has no regrets. He didn't the first time, but facing me wouldn't be part of his plan either. He probably paid for another room just to get away the second I fell asleep, despite the serenity in his eyes when it was all over, the press of his forehead to mine, the gentle kiss to the tip of my nose all a part of his game.

How did I let myself feel so valued through all of it? How did he give me exactly what I needed? The rough and dirty before the soft and tender, a combination so rarely found in casual sex.

The tears fall harder, faster, fat drops staining my wrinkled clothes. I don't bother putting on my pumps. I just scoop them up from the floor.

Then as if the morning couldn't get any worse, the electronic lock on the door whirs, and I freeze.

Gaige walks in, a misplaced smile on his stupidly handsome face, a cup of coffee in each hand, a paper bag hanging between two fingers. His smile fades away in an instant.

"What's wrong? Did you get sick?"

My stomach threatens a second revolt at his words, and I know I may never be well again.

"This was a mistake," I hiss.

The first time was on him, and I refuse to feel that guilt I've felt for the last week because of that. I probably would've never been able to let it go had last night not happened, but I release it now that I have my own choice to dwell on. Last night was on both of us, and that guilt will swim in my stomach for the rest of my damn life.

I made that choice knowing of his commitment. Even drunk I knew he had a wife—a family—back in St. Louis, and it doesn't matter if she's perfect or a bitter unhappy woman like my mother is. She's still his wife, a woman he made vows to. He betrayed her, and I've played a part in that for a second time.

He opens his mouth, the coffee and bag lifting a few inches in the air, but I can't listen to excuses. I refuse. There isn't a single damn thing he can say that will correct our behaviors, our sins.

I storm past him, a pained cry escaping my mouth when I drop one of my shoes on my way out of the room and have to use precious seconds of my escape to bend down and retrieve it. I enter my room, chest heaving with sobs as I lean against the closed door of my room, but I can't spend eternity drowning in my guilt because we still have a job to do. If I can make it through the day, I can spend the week deciding whether I'll be able to keep working for Blackbridge or if I'll break my contract and slink back to New York.

Five minutes later, my tears are mixing with warm water from the shower, and I can't even give in fully to my pain because I'm afraid he's going to hear me. I don't want him to know how much my mistakes are costing me. It gives him too much power, and he has already had enough over me. I obeyed every word last night. It was as if once we closed ourselves into that room, I was his to command.

Eyes on me. Spread your legs. Wider, Leighton. Don't be shy.

I want to bang my head on the shower wall, needing physical pain to detract from the emotional stuff I'm suffering from, but that would draw attention too.

After the shower that brings no real relief, I apply more makeup than usual in an attempt to hide the destruction on my face, and dress, wearing clothes that will end up being too warm for the California weather, but they're a shield against accidental brushes if we get too close.

As I'm pulling on my shoes, my phone chirps with a text.

Gaige: Dr. Cox canceled. Her mother took a turn for the worse last night. She's no longer interested. I've made arrangements for an earlier flight. Meet in the lobby in twenty.

Knowing the text will show as being read, I don't bother to reply.

I finish getting ready, pack my suitcase, and head down the second I'm done. The last thing I need is to be stuck alone with him in an elevator.

The car doesn't arrive early like I was hoping, and he finds me outside waiting near the valet stand.

"Leighton," he huffs on a sigh as he approaches, his tone making it sound like I'm being unreasonable.

"Mr. Ward," I return, my eyes focused on my phone.

I owe the man nothing, and that's exactly what he'll get.

He doesn't try again, and thankfully the car arrives. We don't speak as we ride to the airport or as we make it through security. He doesn't hover or attempt to place his palm on my back. It's like he knows I'm a ticking time bomb, and he's being cautious. I've also spent enough time with him to know that he's biding his time, waiting until what he thinks is the right moment to broach the subject. I know it won't be to ask for forgiveness. He's waiting to make sure I know to use discretion. He doesn't want his colleagues to know about what happened.

I can't imagine Deacon isn't suspicious with my behavior that first day at the office from the way I acted when I stormed out of there, but the man is so protective of his family, I can't see him being okay with a man on his team cheating repeatedly on his wife.

We settle on the airplane, taking off right on time, and when I hear him sigh, I know what's coming. I glare at him, daring him to open his mouth. He looks away, and the flight is spent in complete silence, him with his eyes facing forward and me stewing in guilt and animosity for the entire world.

The hired car at the airport in St. Louis doesn't take me back to the hotel I was staying at before flying to California but to the hotel I met him in to begin with. Instead of arguing, I decide that I can just get out of the car and catch a cab to a different place. It beats having to argue with him about it. Wasting my breath on him isn't worth it. Only he doesn't stay in the car like I expect him to.

As if he knows I have no intention of going back to New York for the weekend, he strides inside, takes his company-issued credit card from his wallet, and reserves a room in my name. He doesn't hand me the room key when the desk clerk offers it to him, and it makes me so angry I can feel the heat in the tops of my ears and on my cheeks. I'm seconds away from losing my shit right in the lobby of this five-star hotel.

He gives me a passive look before turning away from me, heading toward the bank of elevators. I follow him because murder is looking like the perfect way to spend my afternoon. Not for the first time, we ride the elevator in this hotel together, only this time it's filled with hatred, bitterness, and disgust. I keep my eyes on my feet, unable to even stomach the sight of him in the mirrored walls.

He walks off the elevators without looking back. He knows I'm going to follow him, and to make things even worse, he unlocks the door, pushing it open as he stands to the side so I can enter first. I stomp inside, hating that my suitcase doesn't run over the tips of his expensive shoes. I'm not above stomping on the damn thing again.

"You can leave now," I snap, shoving my suitcase until the thing tips over and crashes to the floor. The thick carpet keeps it from making the angry noise I was hoping for.

"You may not want to talk to me, but you're going to fucking listen," he says, his voice low and angry.

I swallow. I've been angry with this man almost every second since I've met him, but not until this very second have I ever been afraid. Gooseflesh crawls over my skin, my eyes darting to the door as I assess the situation. He's blocking my path of escape. I'd have to jump on the bed to get past him, and that would be impossible in these shoes.

He must sense my unease because he takes a step back, his hands clenching and unclenching at his sides.

But then something snaps in him, and I'm pinned against the wall. I turn my head when he leans in close.

"Look at me."

I obey, hoping that it will help his anger, only to find that gold band right in front of my face. Tears begin to track down my face, and the guilt I've felt all day would double me over if his body wasn't holding me up.

"I've done a lot of fucked-up things in my life." He swallows. "I've been a complete asshole to many women. I was a complete asshole to you that first night. I saw you lying in that fucking bed with little hearts in your eyes, all fucking sexed-up and needy. You looked like you wanted me to stay in bed with you forever. So, I pulled this ring out of my pocket and fed you some bullshit about a wife and kids. You want to know why?"

His hips flex against me, his erection digging into my belly.

"Because I wanted to fucking stay, Leighton. I wanted to crawl back into that bed so fucking badly my balls still ache when I think about it. I wanted to spread those milky thighs of yours and lick every inch of your body. I wanted to spend years inside of you."

His nose nuzzles the side of my face.

"I don't do years. Hell, I don't do days. I don't do repeats. Ever. There are too many different women in this world to waste my time on leftovers."

I can't help the cringe on my face at his honesty. What a horrible thing to say.

"I'm not fucking married, Leighton. I don't have kids. I use that ring to scrape off women when they get clingy." He takes a step back, and I feel relieved and desperate all at the same time. "I saw clingy in your eyes that night, but more importantly, *I* felt that tug of clinginess myself. I had to get away from you because I knew how goddamned dangerous you were. So get over that guilt you're feeling from last night."

I do the only thing I can in this moment. I slap the shit out of him. His eyes go wide, palm reaching up to his cheek.

"You egotistical fuck! The only reason I wanted a repeat was because you know how to fuck. I didn't want to waste my time at the bar a second night in a row. You didn't see hearts or clinginess in my eyes because my heart is as black as a moonless night. Now get the fuck out of my hotel room."

He stands there, stunned.

Then he kisses me, hard, tongue tangling with mine, cock pressed into me, and fuck if I'm not a fool and let it happen.

"There's my girl," he whispers against my lips before turning around and leaving.

Chapter 19

Gaige

"Things must be going well," Deacon says as I drop into the chair across from his desk.

"They aren't," I assure him.

"Yet, you're smiling."

I let the grin fall from my lips, and he chuckles.

"We haven't been able to get one person on board, and as you know, Dr. Cox wouldn't even take our meeting."

"Her mother is gravely ill. Family first. You know that."

"This female team isn't going to work."

"It'll be a great addition to BBS."

"I'm not saying it won't be. I fully understand your vision but building it will be impossible."

"I believe in you."

"Just hearing those words from your mouth sounds patronizing, Deacon," I say with a groan as I rub my hand over my face.

Walking out of that hotel room after confessing my lies to Leighton was extremely difficult, but I needed to give her time to work through what I told her. She may never want to touch me again, but I couldn't keep dancing around her with her thinking I was an adulterous piece of shit.

"I don't mean it to be." My boss leans back in his chair. "I want BBS to be as diverse as possible. Tell me more about Leighton Redmond."

"She likes white wine and steak. Weird combination, right? She chews on her bottom lip when she thinks something is funny and she's trying not to laugh."

Silence fills the room, making me realize that's not exactly what he was asking for.

"I mean, red wine with beef."

He shakes his head.

"She's tenacious. A hard worker. We almost lost Janine Miller."

"We don't have a signed letter of intent from Mrs. Miller."

"We don't, but there's a possibility for a contractual agreement. Mrs. Miller isn't going to give up her company or uproot her wife to move to Missouri, but right on the spot, Lei—Ms. Redmond—asked if she'd be willing to handle some jobs we get on the west coast. I'm going to pull some stuff up this afternoon."

He nods his head. "That could work."

Mentioning this to him makes me want to grin. Leighton specifically told Janine that I didn't pass the bar in California. What she failed to say, no doubt in her attempt at a jab at me, is that I've never even tried to take the bar in California. It's never been on my radar. That's just one more thing we can talk about the next time we see each other. That is if she ever shows back up. I don't know if the news I shared with her earlier is going to scare her away or make her want to stick around.

My cheek still stings from where she slapped me, and that little hint of pain makes my cock ache. I shift in my seat, trying not to think about how amazing we were together last night. I went to sleep with no regrets, only waking up with the one that I wish we'd done it completely sober so there were no hazy parts.

"What are you thinking about?"

"Nothing," I say a little too quickly not to be lying.

He raises an eyebrow.

"I like her," I blurt. "I think she was the right pick to get this job done, but the list you created is elite, man. Possibly a little too upscale."

This is the same thing she told me.

"Possibly, but I still want you two to try. It's a long list. You're bound to find the people we need."

"We'll keep on it."

I get up and walk out when his phone rings, grateful I was able to catch him. I know he isn't spending much time in the office since the baby was born. I'm also glad for the escape. I have a million questions I want to ask him, but I also want to point fingers and place blame. I'll lay that accusation on his feet or even Wren's or Flynn's. Hell, Jude and Ignacio can get in line. All of those fuckers have brought that feral possessive love shit into the office and it's leaking off of them. That has to be the only reason for me feeling any sort of way for Leighton. I don't love the woman. That mess isn't for me, but I'm also not eager to see the back of her either unless she's on her knees looking over her shoulder and begging me to pound into her harder.

Fuck, my life. I should probably turn back around. Walking into the breakroom with a semi isn't the best thing to do, but it's one hell of a conversation starter. I'm already committed, however, and Flynn has noticed my approach. Luck must be on my side today because he hasn't noticed the situation in my slacks. I'm able to face the coffee pot and get myself under control before I turn back around to face the small group of guys.

"How has it been?" Flynn asks as I settle in beside him.

"Can't complain," I say, keeping the smile off my face that Deacon noticed a little too quickly earlier.

"You're back sooner than expected," Wren says. He's the one who created the itinerary for travel.

"Complications on today's trip."

Wren nods. "No luck with Nadir?"

I look up at him, analyzing his face, trying to figure out which way he's leaning in regard to the female hacker. He gives nothing away.

"She wouldn't even let us in the house."

He smiles. "Doesn't surprise me."

"Trust no one, right?"

"That's the motto," he confirms before walking back into his office.

"How are things with Leighton?" Kit asks, his eyes curious.

Several of the other guys perk up with the question including Brooks who is smiling, clearly in a better mood than he was earlier in the week.

"What do you mean?" I lift my coffee cup to my mouth.

"Is she doing a good job?"

"Deacon did a good job picking her. She's very thorough."

Finnegan smiles, his red-topped head tilted a little to the left. "That's one word for it."

"I'm pretty sure the woman has an eidetic memory," I say, not playing into his trap. "She did a lot of research on each person. More than what was supplied by BBS. She knows exactly which subjects to bring up in small talk, and she—"

"Looks amazing in a skirt," Kit says.

"That, too," I agree, also not taking his bait, but I barely manage to keep the growl out of my voice.

"So no hardships working with her?" Brooks asks, his question the only genuine one so far.

"Not really." I shake my head.

Professionally, it's been great. Other than her tardiness the first morning—and the longer I think about it, the more I'm convinced it wasn't because she picked a man up in the bar—she's been on time. It's all the other shit that's made it difficult.

Her scent, that light vanilla on her skin, the flex of her calves when she walks, the way her hair brushes her back, the column of her neck when she moves her hair over her shoulder... those are things that make life difficult.

"But no one has accepted yet?" I move my eyes to Flynn.

"None."

"Are you broken?" Kit asks, his fingers cleaning a gun with expert precision even when his eyes are on me.

I huff a laugh. "I'm beginning to wonder the same thing."

I failed at getting Leighton to join the team. Deacon managed that on his own, and now I've failed at getting both Miller and Nadir to work for BBS. That's three strikes. I don't know how many more my ego can take.

"You two must be lost!" Flynn says as he stands from the couch.

We all look, seeing Quinten and Hayden walk into the room. The newly married couple both have wide smiles on their faces and freshly tanned skin.

"We just got back," Quinten says as he shakes Flynn's hand, growling not so playfully when Flynn tries to kiss his bride's cheek. "Had to grab a few things from my office before heading home."

"How was the honeymoon?" I ask, shaking his hand as well. I don't even attempt to touch the man's wife.

"It was lovely," Hayden says, her eyes beaming as she looks up at her husband, both of her arms wrapped around his.

"I thought I heard your voice!" Hayden squeals as she runs down the hall and into her friend's arms.

Hayden hugs her friend, and a look of pure confusion draws her brows in when they separate.

"Parker? What are you doing here?"

I take a step back as Jude walks closer, a wide grin on his face. He and Quinten do that handshake, back-clap thing all guys do. They're best friends, have been forever, but it's clear the couples haven't spoken since the wedding.

The girls have no damn clue what has happened in the last week.

Instead of using words to explain, Jude steps up behind Parker and presses his lips to her throat. A slow smile spreads across Hayden's face. "Really?"

Parker grins before nodding.

"Like for real?"

Parker nods more, and then they're squealing again.

"Too much estrogen," Finnegan mutters before walking out of the room.

"I think it's kind of sweet," Kit says, his voice a little dreamy.

"Not all best friends are happy when their friends get into relationships," Brooks says, his voice marked with bitterness as he walks away. There goes the good mood he was in.

"We have so much to talk about," Hayden says. "You should come to the condo."

Quinten leans in close, his lips brushing her ear as he speaks.

Her cheeks turn pink, and they get redder the longer he whispers in her ear. Her face is flaming by the time he pulls his mouth away.

"Maybe tomorrow. I'll call you," Hayden says, her voice low and a little hoarse.

Jude chuckles before shaking Quinten's hand again.

Parker smiles, knowing or at least assuming what Quinten just said to Hayden.

The newlyweds turn around and head straight to the elevator. I don't know what was said, but it was distracting enough to make Quinten forget that he came to the office to get something.

"What's that?" I ask, noticing the black leather bag in Jude's hand.

Like a child getting caught with something he's not supposed to have, Jude shifts it so it's further behind his back.

"Nothing."

"I think they're planning to play doctor," Flynn says, his British accent making it sound even dirtier.

Jude's mouth hangs open in shock. Parker shrugs. The two make such an oddly perfect pair.

"Don't you have a teenager to get home to, old man?"

Flynn narrows his eyes. "Remington is twenty-one, you arsehole."

Parker leans in, her mouth to Jude's ear much the same way Quinten did to Hayden, and it only takes a minute before those two are walking quickly to the elevator.

"Where are you going?" I ask Flynn when he heads that way shortly after.

"My girl is home alone," he says with a smile.

"Those lucky, fucks," Kit mutters, making me realize that we're the only two left standing in the middle of the room.

Chapter 20

Leighton

I'm antsy, bored, tired of sitting in my hotel room. I did it all damn day yesterday. I should be touring the city, taking in the sights, doing anything but staring at mindless television and thinking about *him*.

It's Sunday, the day of rest, but every muscle in my body is telling me to get up and move. I haven't been to the gym all damn week. I'm out of my routine, haven't been on the elliptical since catching my dad with Margaret, haven't felt an ache in my muscles since waking up Friday morning, and that pain had nothing to do with traditional exercise.

I climb off the bed, needing to move around, to do something to release all of this pent-up energy.

I get dressed, pulling on leggings and a loose t-shirt. I know I can do all of my work sitting comfortably on the hotel bed, but I need a change of scenery or I'm going to go mad. I order an Uber, and head to the lobby. Deacon offered office space at BBS, providing the elevator code and access to the building in my contract, and seeing as it's Sunday, it's very unlikely that I'll encounter a soul there today.

The drive over is slow, traffic heavy for midday, but I'm in no rush. I'm not as nervous as I was the second time I arrived. If anything, I'm a little excited, a little hopeful at the prospect of running into him even though the chances are slim. There hasn't been any contact, not a text or call, not even a business email sent in my direction from him.

Complete silence.

And I don't know if I should read anything into that.

I don't know if he left the ball in my court with his *there's my girl*.

Hell, I don't even know if there is even a ball in play at this point.

I stood in my hotel room with my jaw practically on the floor when he told me he wasn't married and didn't have kids. Slapping him was a visceral reaction. At the time, all I heard were his conceited words about how he thought I was practically in love with him. Yeah, the sex was good, but hell, in love? Get a fucking grip. It took minutes, maybe hours for all of it to sink in, for me to understand that he didn't betray anyone. It didn't get rid of all the anger. I had cried too many tears for me to just smile and be okay with what had happened between us. I had felt too guilty for too long to just be okay with his lies, but by the time I went to bed Friday night with a wine buzz, despite my tequila hangover, I was mildly better. At least I didn't hate myself any longer. I didn't want to throw myself in front of a train as an apology to all women for being a horny slut who willingly slept with a married man because he's charming and good at laying pipe.

I cringe, hating the way that sounds even in my head.

The elevator dings my arrival on the BBS floor. I'm grumbling to myself for once again getting lost in thought on a man I'm not certain deserves a second of my time when I enter the breakroom, stopping dead in my tracks when three pairs of eyes look up at me.

"Umm…"

"Hey there," a redheaded man says with an easy smile, his hands buried in a black box on his lap, some complicated looking metal contraption on a towel on the table in front of him.

"Hi."

"Finnegan Jenkins," the man says, pointing to his chest, his accent either Irish or Scottish. I never can tell.

"Brooks Morgan," a very handsome man says from the other sofa. He gives me an incredibly charming smile—one I'm sure works well for him very often.

"Kit Riggs," the third guy says, and it isn't until he stands that I notice the gun in his hands.

I take a step back as he places it on the table. New York is one of the states with some of the toughest gun laws, and it's like we've been conditioned to hate them from birth.

"Don't be alarmed. I'm just cleaning it."

"Kit is the BBS weapons expert," Brooks explains. "You're safe. I promise."

"If you're afraid, feel free to come sit by me, gorgeous." Finnegan places his huge hand on the sofa next to him, his flirtatious tone clear and easy.

I huff a laugh.

"Can I get you something to drink? A snack?" Kit offers.

"We have white wine," Brooks says, and I snap my eyes to him.

Has Gaige been talking about me to these men?

"We also have red, and I think there's some blush and possibly a bottle of champagne from Quinten's wedding if that's your thing."

"A bottle of water would be great," I say, thinking I reacted too harshly.

"How are you liking working for BBS?" Finnegan asks as I take the seat he's offered.

"With," I correct, and he gives me a soft smile. "I'm enjoying it."

Kit hands me a bottle of water.

"Gaige isn't driving you crazy?"

"Nothing I can't handle," I answer diplomatically.

"Have you had a chance to see the city?" Kit asks, his eyes following the tip of my finger as I absently trace the label on the bottle.

"Not yet. Maybe next weekend."

"I can show you around," Brooks offers, stealing his friend's thunder.

Finnegan snorts. "If you want hoity-toity, go with him. If you want to get a little dirty and eat the best food, I'm your best bet.

"Does she look like the type of woman who wants to get her clothes dirty in a filthy bar or play pool?" Kit points at me. "Even in leggings and a t-shirt, she looks like a million bucks."

I blush, taking it as the compliment I'm sure he meant it to be.

"I could do both," I say. "I like nice restaurants and playing pool."

"Yeah?" Finnegan says, sounding confused. "You can do that?"

"Of course."

"Nothing holding you back?"

I tilt my head. "No. I mean, I have a little work to do today, but I'm free next weekend."

Brooks clears his throat, and Kit and Finnegan both inch back.

"Do you know why you're here, Leighton?"

"I got bored in my hotel room, figured I could get some work done."

"No, I mean why Deacon brought you in?"

"I'm tasked with building a female team for BBS."

"Flynn Coleman is why you're here," Brooks says as he sits back on the couch, crossing one ankle over the opposite knee. "He took a trip to New York awhile back. He had a job watching over Remington Blake."

I nod. It was all over the tabloids. I wouldn't have to be the rag-mag junkie that I am to have seen the handsome man's face on the cover of those magazines. They were everywhere—lined the newsstand streets, at the grocery store checkouts, on the desks of some of the employees at work. Every social media platform had #BlackbridgeSpecial tracking. I'm guilty of typing it into a search engine more than once, although I didn't take it so far as to dig into the company. I have a rule about going in blind and not wasting time and energy on companies before they hire Redmond Enterprises. Before that rule, I lost so much precious time that could've been spent focusing on other things that mattered.

"They fell in love," I say.

"They did, and they're happy. That popularity drew a lot of attention to BBS, and Deacon feels like we have a gap in services. He feels like we should be able to provide the same services to men that we're able to provide for women."

My nose scrunches. "It sounds like an escort service."

"You would not believe how many times someone has said that in this office," Finnegan mutters.

"Don't check Wren's computer history prior to Whitney," Kit warns on a laugh.

"Men can provide security for men," I argue, playing devil's advocate.

"They can," Brooks agrees. "But sometimes discretion is needed."

"Sometimes men are victims and are more comfortable around women," Kit adds.

"Sometimes men are devious and are lying when they hire a company and plan to do harmful things." I swallow after speaking those words. You aren't in the business as long as I have been without being fooled once or twice.

"True," Brooks quickly agrees. "We vet each and every one of our clients, something that has become even more tedious because of our growing popularity. It's one of the reasons we need another IT specialist. It's one of the reasons the list Deacon provided is the best of the best. We could easily hire anyone, but we need people with that sixth sense, that gut feeling people get when they first meet people that tells them whether they're good or bad, and we need people that listen to that instinct."

I nod in understanding.

"We want to help people, but we need people willing to help themselves as well," Finnegan says.

"So, I must've been picked because I'm as much of a workaholic as you guys?" I give them all a wide smile as I meet each one of their eyes.

They all chuckle, the sound surrounding me easily. Kit goes back to cleaning the gun, the unease I felt earlier no longer making me want to run away. Finnegan starts digging around in the black box, what I realize now is filled with bits and pieces of nuts and bolts and various other mechanical parts. Brooks just sits and smiles, his eyes darting between the three of us.

"We're not workaholics. We just haven't managed to find a life yet," Kit argues.

"Speak for yourself," Finnegan huffs. "I'm avoiding whatever chaos is going on next door. I think the man is raising wild animals or something in his condo. It's ruined my entire routine."

A door down the hall closes, and all three of the guys look in that direction. I'm shocked to see Gaige walk into the room. Not one of these guys mentioned that he was here. The man looks just as shocked to see me as I am him. His eyes light up at the sight of me, and I feel it a little too much. Then they narrow at each one of his smiling friends.

"Ms. Redmond," he says, as if he hasn't had his mouth on my pussy.

"Mr. Ward," I say in a way that says he never will again.

Brooks chuckles like he knows we're both full of shit.

"What brings you into the office today?"

"Thought I'd try to get a little work done," I answer.

"How's that working out for you on the sofa?"

I roll my lips between my teeth when Finnegan gives a husky laugh.

"Oh don't go, mo stoirín," Finnegan says when I stand.

Gaige narrows his eyes at his friend.

"Deacon assured me I'd have office space available."

"Right this way," Gaige says, turning around without another word to his friends.

Their laughter follows us out of the room.

Gaige doesn't lead me to a different office. He opens the door to his own.

"My own space," I clarify before walking inside. "It's in the contract."

I can't remember it word for word, so I'm grasping at straws.

"We're kind of limited on space, Leighton. The couch is comfortable. I assure you. Plus, it's Sunday, and you don't get paid overtime for work you weren't able to get done during the week. That is also in the contract."

I huff, not exactly hating the idea of spending time around him now that I know the truth, but I won't speak those words out loud. I settle in on the sofa, choosing the end that gives me the best view of him and pull my laptop out of my bag. I situate it on my lap rather than being uncomfortable bending over the table.

He walks across his office, that swagger he had the first night back in his step now that he isn't limping from the damage I did from stomping on his foot a week ago. I manage to pull my eyes away from him just in time for him to turn around and take a seat in his office chair.

"Can we just move past all of this animosity and work together?" I ask without pulling my eyes from the computer screen. "Just forget about what happened and be professional?"

I look up. His jaw is ticking as he looks at me, the silence between us thick and heavy.

"Forget?" I nod. "You want me to just forget that I know what it feels like when you come on my cock? On my mouth? What my name sounds like when you whimper it? What your pussy tastes like? That's impossible, Leighton."

I blink, my ears not believing what I just heard.

"Are you going to work or not?" I swallow. "Because I have shit to do."

His tone is bored not angry, and I jerk my eyes back down to my computer screen, my fingers suddenly forgetting how to work.

It takes me over an hour to do the research on our next round of interviewees I'm sure it would take Blackbridge's IT specialist seconds to do, but I'm in no position to ask that of Wren Nelson. The man is probably at home with his significant other, Whitney, the woman one of the guys mentioned earlier.

I'm in the zone, not liking what I'm finding on Sandra Halen, a woman we're scheduled to meet with later in the week. She's good at the work she does, but she just seems... mean. Movement at Gaige's desk startles me, and I look up to find him with his desk phone's receiver to his ear.

"Hello, Penelope. Gaige Ward. I'm well, and you? That's great. Listen I need a table for two at Paragon. Yes. Tonight. Private. Yes. That's right, as intimate as you can manage on such short notice. Eight? That's perfect. Thanks, sweetheart."

I snap my eyes back down as he hangs up.

Paragon.

That asshole.

It's the restaurant in the hotel I'm staying at. What a bastard.

I manage to work for a couple more hours, but my heart is just no longer in it. I'm prepared for the first three appointments we have this week, and I know I'll have a chance to get the rest of it done before those later meetings. I close my laptop, standing from the sofa.

"See you tomorrow," I tell him with more cheer than I actually feel.

"Goodnight," he says without even pulling his eyes from his own computer.

I leave, waving at the guys as I walk back through the breakroom.

Chapter 21

Gaige

The feisty woman that slapped me Friday afternoon was not the same woman that walked out of my office earlier today, and I spent the better part of an hour sitting at my desk wondering if I fucked things up too bad. But as I walk into Paragon, I realize I shouldn't have bothered with worry.

She couldn't resist being here, and I can tell from the flush in her cheeks in the reflective wall décor that she has already had more than one glass of white wine as she sits at a table, dining alone. She listened intently while I made reservations, stewing all the while thinking I was making them for me and another woman. As if I'd want to spend a single second with anyone but her. I'll worry about that little fact at a later date.

Her flawless back is facing me, her spine open to the cool air of the restaurant in that very same devilish dress she was wearing on the night that we met. Then, I anticipated that she'd be trouble. Tonight, I know it for a fucking fact, and my cock makes himself known in anticipation, pulsing twice with eagerness that makes me wonder if the planned meal is even worth the bother.

She startles when I step up behind her, not wasting a single second before pressing my lips to her throat.

"You're at the wrong table, Leighton." I run my fingers down her arm, clasping her hand in mine. "This way."

Confusion draws her brows in, but it doesn't stop her from standing and letting me guide her across the room to the more private table I reserved.

"What's going on?" she asks as I pull out her chair and help her into her seat.

Unable to resist, I press my lips to her skin once more before taking my own seat across from her.

"Do you really think the reservation I made earlier was for anyone but you?"

Her eyes narrow, but they also sparkle with relief. "You're such an asshole."

"I think we already established that. Have you already eaten?" I tease, referring to last week when she was more than halfway through her meal when I arrived. "Or will we be able to do that together this time?"

She grins as she picks up her menu.

"A drink, sir?" the waiter asks as he steps up to the table.

"Sparkling water, please."

"More wine, ma'am?"

"Water for her as well," I interrupt, gaining a look of disgust from her. "I want you sober."

"I want wine."

The waiter, ever professional in this establishment, takes a half-step back. His eyes are focused elsewhere, but I'm no fool. I know the man will be able to hear every word from my lips. The deal is, I don't give a shit.

"You're riding my cock sober tonight."

"I may not be—" Her eyes dart to the waiter, but I pinch her chin delicately, telling her I own her attention. "I may not be riding your cock at all."

I smile at her, my thumb tracing her bottom lip before dipping it in her mouth. She nips the tip before pulling back and clearing her throat.

"Diet soda, please."

The waiter nods before walking away.

"That was embarrassing," she hisses, her cheeks a little flushed.

"But I bet that sweet pussy of yours is wet."

Her eyes dart around the room, but there's no one around. This is a very private table, and I'm paying handsomely for it. It's going to be worth every single penny.

"What exactly are you doing?"

"It's called foreplay, Leighton. Ever heard of it?"

She slaps her menu on the table, opening her mouth to say something, but the waiter returns with our drinks.

"We'll need a few more minutes with the menus," I tell him.

"Listen, Gaige, I—"

"Leighton, the sex is off-the-fucking-charts hot. We work well together, both professionally and in the bedroom. We're going to be traveling together for weeks until we can build this team. I'm not looking for anything serious and neither are you. Why not have mind-blowing orgasms and a little fun along the way?"

She blinks at me, and just when I think she's going to throw her drink in my face and storm away, her mouth curls into a smile.

"Yeah?" I ask.

"Why are we wasting time on eating?"

"Because I like to watch you squirm. How slick are your thighs?"

"They're—"

"Ready to order?"

I could cut this man right now.

We both place our orders, Leighton getting the upper hand when she orders her steak medium well instead of medium rare like she did before, knowing it'll take longer to cook.

"Tell me about yourself," she says, the bread basket in the center of the table going untouched by both of us as we chat.

"I have a younger brother. Tyler is a doctor."

"A doctor and an attorney. The family must be proud."

"Very," I tell her. "What about you?"

"My sister is older by eleven months. She's a pediatric nurse at a doctor's office, happily married to a tech mogul."

"Fancy."

She smiles.

"You never got close to getting married?" I ask because these are things I'm not already supposed to know, and I find myself a little sad that I'm not learning these things for the first time directly from her.

"Never." Her body gives a little shake as if she just can't imagine doing something so awful.

Conversation and jokes continue. Dinner is served, and we lose track of time. She doesn't say much about her parents, and I'm careful not to let anything I'm not supposed to know slip out. I tell her stories about my childhood, keeping it light and easy, trying not to brag because I know how good I had it growing up. My family was and still is amazing and supportive, even now as an adult. Lala would welcome this woman with open arms. She would smother her in all the love she missed out on as a child. I'm certain of it.

"Dessert?" the waiter asks as he lifts Leighton's plate.

"Oh, no," she says with a laugh. "I'm so full."

"Chocolate Crème," I tell him, finding her eyes as he walks away.

Ten minutes later, despite her saying she's full, I watch with a slack jaw as this woman licks creamy chocolate off a fucking spoon. The noises coming from her lips make me want to dive under the table and have her for dessert.

"Enjoying it?" I ask, my voice thick and raw.

She nods. "It's so good."

"Wanna bring it back to your room? You can suck it off my cock."

"I'm going back to my room alone tonight."

"Like fuck you are."

Her top lip twitches. "No?"

I shake my head, my eyes still drawn to her perfect mouth.

"Because you bought me dinner?"

"Dinner has nothing to do with it."

"Because I made your dick hard?"

"You always make my dick hard."

"That so?"

Another lick of that damn spoon.

"Is your pussy wet."

"Soaked."

"Why are we still sitting here?"

"You haven't taken care of the check."

"The waiter hasn't brought it yet."

"I wonder why?" she whispers.

"His dick is probably too hard to walk if he saw what you were doing to that spoon."

"I'm being naughty."

"So fucking bad." I lift my arm up, knowing that the guy can't be too far away. "Put the spoon down, Leighton."

Thankfully, she listens and is wiping her mouth with her napkin, an innocent smile on her face when he arrives. He hands me the check and I pass him cash, not having the patience to wait for the swipe of a card.

In the next second, I have her hand in mine and we're speed walking out of the restaurant.

"Do you want me to get a different room?" I ask.

"Really?" she scoffs. "Get real, Gaige."

"What? I don't know if you're going to have a problem with staying in there after we're done. I'm just trying to be courteous."

"I'm not some teenage girl with an obsession. I'm not going to roll around on the bed smelling the sheets when you leave. My room is fine."

I smile as I lead her to the bank of elevators.

As if the fun we had at dinner was washed away by one simple question, she heads straight for the minibar once we're inside her room, and just like the first night, my lips can't seem to stay off her skin. This time, she actually finishes the drinks, handing one to me and sipping on the other.

Her eyes fall to my lips, and she's the first one to move, licking away a drop of whiskey, and then the real fun begins.

Chapter 22

Leighton

I've tasted a lot of great things from all around the world, but I don't think there's anything better than chocolate and whiskey from Gaige Ward's lips. If there is, I haven't experienced it yet.

I lick into his mouth again, arching away from the chill of his glass when he presses it to my exposed back. He grins against my lips.

"Cold?"

I nod, unwilling to pull my lips very far from his.

"What do you want tonight?" he asks.

"Everything," I confess, unwilling to lie.

I do. I want it all.

"Greedy girl."

He takes a step back, his gaze raking over my entire body as he lifts his glass to his lips.

"You want me to strip you?"

"Slowly."

"You want me to taste you?"

"Every inch."

"You want to taste me?"

"Please."

"What else?"

"Fuck me."

"And?"

"Tease me."

"And?"

"Make me beg."

"It's going to be a long night."

I swallow. "I'm ready when you are."

He drains his glass, the ice clinking as he sets it on the dresser.

"Pull up your dress."

My fingers tremble in anticipation, the fabric silky against my thighs as I tug.

"No panties? You little minx. What if I had made plans with someone else tonight? Would you have brought someone else up here and showed them that perfect pussy?"

I don't answer because I don't really know. It's possible, I guess, because seeing him with someone other than me would've hurt, and I lash out when I'm in pain. He must see that answer in my eyes, but he doesn't press me further. It tells me that he takes some ownership in the lies he told.

"Mmm. So wet. Is it throbbing?"

"Yes."

I nod, and it looks like he physically hurts not touching me, regret in his eyes from putting his glass down now that he has nothing to do with his hands.

"No," he scolds when I reach between my legs. "Don't touch it."

I groan my disappointment, drawing a sly grin to his handsome face.

"Take the entire dress off."

The hem drops around my thighs again as I work open the top at the back of my neck and there's no grace as I drop it, the slinky thing sliding down my body to puddle at my feet. A bra is impossible to wear with this backless number, leaving me completely naked except for the heels on my feet. He doesn't seem disappointed at the sight of me, his eyes taking their time, slowly scanning me up and down as if he can't decide where he wants to focus.

"What now?" I ask, not because I'm nervous standing in front of him or uncomfortable, but because I'm anxious to get this night started. I know what his touch feels like on my skin and need it desperately.

"Come here."

And I do. I walk toward him, my feet carrying me closer with little to no seductive sway to my hips, too quickly to be coy, so fast he chuckles at my eagerness.

"Enthusiastic," he whispers as I step close, his fingers brushing my hair off one shoulder without actually touching my body. "I like it."

I'm trembling at this point, my skin on fire, the tips of my fingers cold and needing the warmth of his own body.

"I want you to ache for me."

"I do," I assure him.

His lips brush my jaw, his breath floating over my cheek, and it's the only point of contact as he steps back when I try to inch in closer.

"Don't move."

I love his bossiness. I even told him that the first night, but damn I really want to disobey right now. The gentle fingers that moved my hair now tangle there, the tenderness turning feral as he tangles them in the strands, gripping a handful so he can angle my chin to his liking. His mouth is on my throat, on my collarbone, tongue licking at that triangle where my pounding pulse takes a deeper dive into my chest.

I feel him everywhere even though he's only touching a small part of my person, and I moan with both satisfaction and need.

"You have the softest skin," he says, and I smile with the praise, raising my hands to his hips.

My own hands brush fabric, and I despise his clothes right now, wishing to touch his bare skin.

He doesn't correct me, doesn't command me to drop my hands, doesn't threaten to tie me up, and just the thought of that sends a tremble up my body. I've never experienced that, being restrained while with a lover. I couldn't chance it before. Putting faith in men I just met for sex is never smart, but my body is fully on board to let those things happen with Gaige. Hell, I slicken with just the prospect of doing it with the man lowering his mouth over the top swell of my breasts. I had no clue when I told him everything that it would include things I had never imagined before.

I groan again when the heat of his mouth surrounds my nipple, the lash of his tongue evolutionary. I'm a changed woman because of this experience, and this is only the beginning.

His breaths are as harsh as mine, and it thrills me that he's taking pleasure in doing this as well. Touching me isn't just a task for him, and it turns me on even more.

"How are your legs?" he asks against my skin.

"Weak," I respond truthfully.

"On the bed." He steps away, breaking all contact with me. "On your back."

I scamper, once again too excited to worry about trying to look sexy. His lips are swollen already from licking, sucking, and kissing my skin, and I know I'm going to have to sit with him in a meeting tomorrow, trying to concentrate on work with marks from tonight on my skin. I already know it's going to be impossible, but that's tomorrow, and there's nothing that's going to stop this tonight.

Gaige must be just as eager as I am because he doesn't laugh as I hastily crawl up the bed.

"Open for me, Leighton."

Just like he commanded the night we were drinking, I spread my legs wide, lowering my hands to open myself further.

"Perfect," he whispers, his eyes locked on the center of me.

I swallow thickly, my eyelids heavy with lust and need.

He starts to climb up the bed fully clothed, and I want to beg him to strip, but I know this man is methodical. He puts too much thought into his actions. He's not forgetting that he's dressed. He's not going to spend all of this attention on me to just shove his pants down a few inches and fuck me with his cock barely out.

I have to find patience. God give me strength.

My back arches off the bed as his hands float over my legs, his eyes still locked at the apex of my thighs. I'm a quivering mess, knowing what it feels like to have that sinful mouth there, and the man was right to have stopped me from drinking more alcohol. The experience with him while intoxicated was incredible. Tonight, I get the feeling, is going to be unforgettable, a *ruin me for other men* kind of occurrence.

"You have the prettiest pussy I've ever laid eyes on," he says, his voice gruff as he traces a finger down the line where my leg meets my torso. "I'm such a lucky man."

I'm torn between watching his teeth dig into his lip as he watches me and keeping an eye on his finger as it wanders toward where I'm the most tender.

"Touch me," I beg. "With your mouth."

His head lowers, tongue licking where his finger was, and it's just not enough. He's a bastard because he knows it isn't exactly what I need. His strong hands hold my hips in place when I try to move them to reposition his mouth.

"Don't be impatient," he says, swiping his tongue over me once before pulling back.

That's all it takes for his lips to glisten with me, and the look in his to eyes change.

It's like a shark getting the scent of blood. One second, he's fine and the next, he's a savage, his mouth attacking me in the best ways. His fingers grip, the curl of them pressing on those tiny bruises that were left behind from the last time he did this, and I revel in the dull ache.

The buildup, the anticipation is just too much. I want to draw this out. I want his mouth on me for an eternity. I never want this to end, but he's too good.

"Gaige, slow down."

His head shakes back and forth and back and forth, and I have no idea if he's telling me no or if it's just another part of his assault, but it doesn't matter, the result is the same—blinding light behind my eyelids before utter darkness and then splashes of color with each erratic pulse of my heart. My core throbs, and then I feel it. His mouth stops, his finger or his teeth, I don't know what, but it's the pinch, that perfect clamp on my clit and I nearly die. The man gives me exactly what I need.

My body seizes, locks in place and I'm on a different plane of existence for what seems like days. Everything that makes up happiness and perfection is here—beaches and fruity drinks, sunshine and worriless days, hot oil massages and fluffy puppies with no allergies.

The return to regular life is slow and calm, easy and welcomed with the brush of his mouth on my stomach and across my hip bones. The man is obsessed with my skin, and as I lay pliant, boneless, and spent, I just grin lazily down at his wet mouth like I should've been the one to pay for dinner after an experience like that.

"Thank you," I whisper, my fingers sweeping through his hair.

"My pleasure," he says.

And I believe him as he licks his lips. He did enjoy it. I read people for a living, knowing when to switch gears and when to bring up certain topics and when it's best to avoid something altogether is a skill I honed many years ago. Gaige Ward legitimately likes getting me off with his mouth.

"I think you broke me," I whisper as he sits up on his knees and begins to unbutton his shirt.

I rest my hand on his thigh as he shrugs out of it.

"Yeah? That's not good. Kind of ruins the plans I have."

My eyes lower to the bulge in his pants before roaming up the ridges of muscle to his eyes.

"Were you going to share these plans with me or am I supposed to figure them out on my own?"

He shrugs, his fingers working to open his belt and then the button and fly of his pants before dropping his hands.

"I can't decide which one would be more fun."

"I've always been a fan of discovery," I say, my teeth digging into the corner of my bottom lip. "I'm okay with surprises."

Having most of my control back over my body, I sit up, grabbing the waistband of his pants and boxers in my fist. I pull them down past the curve of his delectable ass, revealing the root of this thick cock.

"Wait," he says, reaching into the back pocket and pulling out his wallet.

He snags a condom, tossing it toward the headboard before shoving the wallet back into the pocket. His hands fall back to his sides, giving me all the power once again. I keep my eyes off that single condom. This will be the third time we'll hook up, and I heard him when he said he doesn't do repeats. Obviously, that doesn't apply to what we're doing, and I'm not a fool. I know it doesn't pertain to us right now, but a single condom also means not doubling up tonight. It shouldn't bother me, but it niggles just a little in the center of my chest.

Although we aren't standing, I try to do the very same thing to him that he did with me. I press my lips to his jaw, enjoying a little too much the way the scruff there feels against my lips. I want to rub against him like a cat, purring my pleasure in his ear until he pets me and calls me a good little kitty. My pussy seems to like the idea of that as well.

My mouth roams down his neck, tongue tasting his skin, but I make sure not to suck too hard. Hickeys are for teenagers needing to mark their territory. Not only are we adults, but I have no claim to this man.

I lick at his collarbone, pulling a rumble from deep in his chest, and a hiss of pleasure when I sink my teeth into the muscle between his neck and shoulder.

"Fuck," he moans. "Again."

I pull back, looking him right in the eyes. That first night he asked what I liked, and I never reversed that conversation for him, but he wants it rough too. This man likes a little pain. When I lean in again, teeth bared, his exposed cock brushes against my stomach, the wet tip of him leaving a trail of arousal on my skin. When I sink my teeth in on the other side, much like I did, his hands just have to find my hips.

"Leighton." My name sounds like a plea.

I pull away before I do end up marking him like a possession.

"Lie back," I urge, pressing my palm to his chest.

He crashes to the bed, more his doing than mine because the man is a brick wall. At some point, he kicked off his shoes. Hell, my heels are gone too, and I have no damn clue when they disappeared, and that says a lot about how distracted I am around this man.

I tug his pants and boxer briefs the rest of the way down, uncaring of where in the room they land, grateful for his help to lift his legs because I couldn't have done it myself.

I kiss up his legs, letting my fingers roam, noticing that he likes it when my hair sweeps over his skin almost as much. I change the routine from what he did to me, bypassing his cock to kiss and lick the rippling muscles on his abdomen, letting my long tresses tease his cock instead of touching it with my mouth or hands.

"You're going to give me a heart attack," he complains when my teeth nip at the skin near his belly button.

"Don't be impatient," I mock, repeating the words he said earlier.

He flexes his hips, his cock shifting between my breasts, and a slow smile spreads across his face. He does it again and again, the pre-ejaculate leaking from his tip, making the glide easy. I angle my head, looking down at the action, and snake out my tongue.

It's like he's been popped with a branding iron when it makes contact with the head of his cock. I look back up at him, giving him a wicked grin. He groans in frustration.

"You want my mouth?"

"More than anything."

Cold chills swim over my skin with the huskiness in his tone.

Leaning back, I lick the length of him, swirling my tongue against his tip. Who needs alcohol when I can get drunk on this man so easily?

His hips flex again, his need to go deeper in my mouth clear in the action. I give him what he wants because I need the very same thing. With cheeks drawn in, suction tight on his tip, I lower my mouth. His moan of pleasure is better than any song I've ever heard, the clench of his hand on the back of my head the exact pressure I need to keep going.

"Leighton," he complains when I pop off and run my tongue back down his shaft.

Then there are no complaints grumbling from him when I suck one of his balls into my mouth. He makes no noises, his shock and pleasure keeping him silent. I never knew I could feel so much pleasure in doing this. Giving head isn't something I do very often. With the encounters I normally have, getting to the actual deed of sex is usually quick, a fast orgasm and then getting away from my partner is the goal. But I want to spend hours, days even, worshiping this man.

But even as I think that, I'm desperate for more of my own pleasure. I suck on him one last time before wrapping my lips around the head of his cock again, sucking him down as far as I can take him before letting my lips run back up. His grip tightens, the tug on my roots a pain I welcome. I get lost in him, in the teasing, the sucking, the licking, the sounds he's making.

He presses harder, urging me to take more until I lose my breath. He urges me deeper, his cock head pressing against the back of my throat, and I find myself wanting him there, wanting to gag and choke, and he seems all too willing to give that to me, to take that from me, but then the pressure eases, but I don't pull away.

"Leighton," he hisses, and I hear it as the warning it is.

I don't listen. I grip the part of him I can't manage and squeeze, my other hand cupping his sac and tug. His hips jolt, cock jerking, and all I can do is swallow, repeatedly as he explodes.

And there's regret in the moment because he's so far, so deep that I barely get a taste of him because his orgasm is all the way at the back of my throat, past my taste buds. I attack the head, needing more when I pull back, licking at him, sucking him eagerly.

"Fuck," he snaps, his fingers still tangled in my hair as he urges me away. "You're dangerous."

I smile up at him as he drags me, using that grip in my hair, up his chest, his mouth meeting mine, uncaring that his taste is still on my tongue. It's so fucking sexy, a man who doesn't care that his cum is on a woman's lips.

I'm a little disheartened as we explore each other's mouths. My orgasm was spectacular, and as his hands wander down my back, I know his was too, but sex with him is also amazing. I'm terrified that I took things too far sucking him off, and now I'm going to miss out on that. Not all men have it in them to go so soon again after something like that, but as hands roam and tongues tangle, I find myself not needing to worry as his cock thickens against my hip.

He nips my chin, pulling his face back to just look at me. He looks sex-drunk as I lick my lips, his eyes taking in every action.

"You said I was going to be riding your cock tonight," I whisper, my hand resting on his chest.

He shakes his head. "Not tonight."

Maybe I was wrong. My face falls, a smile tugging at his lips as his thumb traces my frown.

"There's so much expression in your face. Are you disappointed?"

"Yes," I confess.

"Next time, okay?"

I nod, shifting back to get off him, but he doesn't unwrap his arm from my back. Instead, he sits up and flips me to my stomach. A giddiness, something akin to a child walking into an aquarium and seeing underwater sea life for the first time fills my veins and washes over me. I shift my body so my ass is in the air.

"Nope," he says with a quick slap to my ass.

I yelp, the action surprising me more than hurting.

He chuckles as he leans over my body, reaching for the pillows at my head.

"Like this." He presses his huge hand to my back until I'm lying flat, and then he stuffs two pillows under my pelvis. "Keep your legs together."

I cross my arms under my head and wait, wondering how I look from his vantage point as I hear the crinkle of the condom wrapper. Another rush of cold chills sweeps down my spine when I feel his hand on my ass, and then he's spreading me open. I told him everything when he asked what I wanted, but now I'm not so sure I actually meant it.

"Gaige?"

"Do you have any idea how fucking sexy you are?" His thumb sweeps over my pussy. "I haven't even fucked you yet, and you're swollen and needy."

My breaths grow shorter, more erratic. Anticipation has to be the best and worst thing ever created.

"Think you can take my cock like this without spreading your legs for me?"

"I want to," I confess.

"I want that, too." He presses his thumb into me, my body so ready for him he sinks in easily. "Ready?"

"So ready," I pant.

He covers me like a blanket, his warm skin melding to my back, his cock hotter than any other part of him.

I moan with the sensation, my breath getting caught in my throat when the tip of him dips inside.

"Gaige."

He presses his cock forward, slowly, his mouth right near my ear.

"Let me in, Leighton."

My first instinct is to spread my legs and lift my ass, but I hold steady and whimper as he shifts, nudging forward another inch. It's a tight fit, and I love that it is. I feel all of it.

"That's it," he praises with a slow, delicious roll of his hips. "God, that's fucking perfect. I know you want to come already, but that isn't how tonight is going to go."

I groan, not knowing if I want to love or hate that he can read me so easily.

He chuckles, a low sound in my ear.

"I think this pussy was made for me, Leighton. Fuck, how did I ever walk away that first night." He shifts back, the drag of his cock through all that sensitive tissue makes my head come off of my arms, exposing my neck to his mouth. He takes advantage, sucking on the skin there. "If you could have seen how fucking creamy you were after coming on my cock... Jesus, I'll never forget how it looked. Your panties were still pulled to the side. Those perfect pussy lips of yours dark pink. I bet they tasted amazing. Need to taste you after you've been fucked, Leighton. I bet it's better than you tasted before."

I whimper, my hips needing to move, but it's impossible with his weight pinning me to the mattress.

"Do you know what you taste like before getting fucked?"

"Yes," I whisper.

"Dirty fucking girl," he hisses in my ear, teeth digging into the lobe. "But I knew you would. How often do you dip your fingers into that tight little hole and lick them clean?"

"Oh, God. Gaige."

His hips move faster, his filthy words having as much of an effect on him as they're having on me.

"I wanna fuck you raw, make this pussy sore. Wanna watch you walk into the meeting tomorrow, knowing my cum is dripping down your thighs."

Harder thrusts, more powerful.

It's all fantasy. He's wearing a condom, and we'd never do something so risky, but fantasy is just that.

"Yes," I moan. "Fill me up."

"Bitch," he grunts, and I smile, knowing his balls are getting tighter.

He wants it to last. Hell, I do too, but we're both already teetering on the edge. It's always just too good to last for hours and hours. Stamina is nonexistent where we're concerned.

His hand moves, leaving his grip on my shoulder to drift down between my body and the pillow. I almost open my mouth to tell him I'm not going to need it, but I know the orgasm will be more powerful with his touch there, so I keep my mouth closed. The first brush is almost enough, but I hold off as best I can, clenching my jaw, which in turn tightens every muscle in my body.

"Not yet, you evil woman."

"Hurry," I beg.

He doesn't hurry because the man can't be commanded.

"Wait," he warns again when my body begins to tremble.

A shuddering breath escapes my lips, and I'm doing my best, but my restraint only goes so far when his cock is magical, and his fingers are working me over so expertly.

"Gaige."

"Wait," he hisses.

"Can't."

"Leighton." It's a plea.

"I need your cum."

He freezes, cock kicking inside of me, and then I feel the pinch on my clit. It's a little tighter than I probably need, but somehow, it's also perfect, and I detonate.

I come back to reality with his cock still in me and his tongue tracing my lips.

"Hey," he whispers against my mouth.

"Hi," I tell him with a smile before deepening the kiss. "Thank you."

He chuckles, but he doesn't give me hell for showing gratitude for good sex. Maybe he's feeling it, too.

His hands trace the curve of my hip after he pulls out and we face each other. I try not to smile like an idiot at the fact that he doesn't immediately just pop out of bed and run away.

"Oh!" he says his eyes going wide. "I almost forgot."

In the next second, I'm on my back, legs over his shoulders, and his mouth on me. My fingers are digging into his scalp, my pussy incredibly sensitive as his mouth tastes me. He doesn't torture me long, and he's smiling as he lifts his head, eyes shining.

"Just what I thought, fucking delicious." He nips the inside of my thigh before crawling out of the bed.

He's gone maybe a few minutes, and I give him the privacy everyone deserves after great sex before he returns with a washcloth. He doesn't toss it, hitting me in the face with it this time. He crawls up the bed, spreads me wide and wipes me with the warm cloth. I've fucked this man three times, let him come down my throat, orgasmed on his mouth more than once, and I've never wanted to cover my eyes until this moment. It's more intimate than anything else we've ever done.

He kisses the inside of my thigh before carrying the washcloth back to the bathroom.

I feel the need to cover myself when he walks back out into the bedroom.

He doesn't crawl back into bed with me. We both know what this is, but he keeps his eyes locked on me as he dresses. He doesn't hide the fact that he wants me, his cock still half erect as he pulls his clothes on.

"The car will be here in the morning to take you to the airport," he says as he sits on the end of the bed to tug on socks and shoes.

"Okay," I answer.

He stands, the night over, but instead of heading straight to the door, he leans over me, pressing a kiss to my temple.

He nearly straightens completely before bending over once again, sucking a nipple in his mouth, releasing it with a loud pop. Then the man winks at me and leaves.

And like a sex-drunk fool, I do exactly what I told him I wouldn't do before we came up here tonight. I roll over and bury my nose in the sheets, looking for the scent of his skin.

Chapter 23

Gaige

"We're doing something wrong," Leighton mutters as she sinks back into the plush leather of the back seat.

She won't even look at me after the last meeting. We've met with three women already this week, and that makes five total if you count the hacker from Santa Rosa that looked at us like we were aliens.

"We're not doing anything wrong," I tell her, my fingers brushing her wrist. "We're adults having fun."

Her head snaps in my direction as she jerks her head away.

"I'm not talking about that. Is *that* all you think about?"

I wink at her, letting her see my eyes travel down her legs. Houston is nearly as warm as California was, and the humidity has made sure Leighton hasn't covered her legs with anything as ridiculous as pantyhose.

"I'm talking about work, Gaige."

I back off a few inches. We can talk about work for now if that's what she needs.

"We're doing the best we can."

I'm not surprised by the roll of her eyes. I knew when the words left my mouth how bad they sounded.

"These women aren't going to be interested."

I can only listen to her. We've had this conversation repeatedly, and she grows more agitated each time we walk out of a meeting with another no.

"They've fought the glass ceiling all their lives. They're not going to roll over. Men coming in wanting to drop them down a couple of levels and hire them isn't a good thing."

"BBS isn't trying to do that."

"We know that, but that isn't how they see it."

I whip my arm out in front of her when the driver has to hit the brakes when another car cuts us off in traffic.

"Sorry," he apologizes.

I use the opportunity to trace Leighton's bra line down her blouse before pulling my hand away. We haven't touched each other since Sunday night. A ridiculous rule she came up with was that while working, we don't fuck. The weekends are ours to do with what we want, but it's all business when we're traveling.

It hasn't been a total waste. We've had dinner together the last two nights since we arrived in Texas, and I swear she masturbated loud enough last night just so I could hear her through the interconnecting door to our rooms. I came in my fist when she moaned my name. We didn't talk about it this morning.

"Are you listening?"

"I wasn't," I admit.

"Maybe if you stop staring at my tits, you'll actually hear me."

I'm slow to pull my eyes away and look at her face, my gaze getting lost on her mouth.

"Gaige," she whines, and I know she's had as much trouble with her work rule as I have, but I won't push her. She set a limit, and I'm trying to respect it.

"You were saying?"

"Deacon is awesome. We all know that, but these women are past the point in their lives where they need validation from anyone, much less a man. They don't need these jobs. They've already carved out their perfect spot in the world."

"I agree."

"We have to look elsewhere."

"We only hire the best of the best."

"The best are already doing what they love, and they won't be swayed. They don't need BBS."

I shrug because if that's true, there's really nothing that we can do. Leighton doesn't seem impressed with my response. She smacks her back to the seat, her eyes looking out the window.

"I need a glass of wine and an orgasm."

"Wanna suck me off while we wait for room service?"

Her head rolls on the leather until she's looking in my direction, cheeks pink. The driver doesn't even flinch. There's no telling what this man hears on a regular basis.

"We need a different approach."

"We've tried different."

The women we've met with this week are so busy they wouldn't even entertain the idea of contract work. I wish they wouldn't have wasted our time with agreeing to meetings in the first place. We're burning through BBS resources and money for no good reason.

"Then we need to just give up."

"I don't give up."

"We can't just badger them until they agree. It doesn't work that way. Even if you stopped flirting with them, I still don't think they'd agree."

"Jealous?" I waggle my eyebrows comically.

She scoffs. "Hardly. It makes you look like an idiot. Not every woman wants to jump on your dick, Mr. Ward. It's rather disgusting to watch. Men and women alike have been using sex to get what they want for hundreds of years. Do you really think you're the first? Do you think that any one of the women we've met with hasn't had some man walk in her office and try to use his dick as an offering to get something from her?"

I frown. Her saying it like that is kind of disgusting. I'd never actually pulled my cock out to score something for BBS.

"Jealousy is hot as fuck on you, Leighton," I say to lighten the mood, because her getting all growly on the topic really is turning me on. I lean in close so the driver can't hear. "Especially knowing just how pretty your pink puss—"

"Finish that sentence and you'll never see it again," she snaps.

My jaw clamps closed of its own accord. At least some parts of me are smart.

My dick?

Still hard and begging me to do something about it.

Her fingers are tapping on her thigh as she chews on her bottom lip. She doesn't do this often, but I noticed she does this when she's working through thoughts in her head.

"Just spit it out, Leighton."

"I want to see Sandra Halen alone tomorrow."

"No." My answer is immediate. I could catch a lot of shit if it goes south and I'm not with her. "We approach this as a team. That was the deal."

"I think I can get her on board if you aren't there flirting with her."

"I can go and not flirt."

She scoffs. "Impossible. It's innate. You couldn't manage it."

The rest of the car ride back to the hotel is silent, and I hate it. The banter between us has sort of become our thing. We don't touch each other or have sex while we're traveling, but that never stops the innuendo. It's like we're both letting that sexual tension and anticipation build during the week, so it'll be explosive once we get back to St. Louis on Friday.

The atmosphere in the elevator is weird, but thankfully, we're alone.

"I'll let you go alone tomorrow on one condition."

She turns her face in my direction, eyes narrowed. "I told you shower sex isn't my thing. Hard limit. I nearly drowned in college. You've got to respect my boundaries."

Okay, we've talked a lot about sex in the last three days. Evening meals with her have been a blast. It's the parting ways without touching that have been hard. My hand will have blisters by Friday.

I laugh. "Not shower sex, but I swear, Leighton, I'm strong enough to keep you standing. I'm not some college fuck boy."

She crosses her arms over her chest as if she's anticipating something even worse than a hard limit.

"I want you to attend a function with me."

"What is it?"

"Doesn't matter. If you want to go alone tomorrow, you go with me on Saturday."

"If it's black tie, the answer is no. I'm not going to be another Remington Blake and end up being the next front woman for #BlackbridgeSpecial."

"It's not black tie," I assure her.

The elevator dings the arrival on our floor, and I hate that we're not having dinner tonight. She asked earlier if room service was okay because her sister needed to chat about something personal going on with her family, hence, the joke about the wine and orgasm.

"You didn't give me an answer, Leighton." I brush my fingers down her arm, my eyes begging her for way more than just a yes or no about Saturday.

"It's not a wedding?"

"Not a wedding."

"Because I can't handle some big family event."

"Not a wedding," I repeat.

"Fine."

"Okay."

"See you in the morning."

"I'm sleeping in if you're going to see Sandra Halen on your own." I lean over, inches from kissing her, but pull back once I realize how close I came to fucking up. "Goodnight, Leighton."

She nods, disappearing quickly into her room.

I don't hear another peep from her for the rest of the night. I still come in my hand because of her.

Chapter 24

Leighton

If I had anyone to compare Sandra Halen to, I guess she'd be like Quinten Lake of BBS. If there's a problem with the appearance of image, Sandra is the one to call. She's poised perfection, smiling for the camera, but she's also a bulldog, able to put someone in their place with a few sharp, well-educated words that leave many people standing with their jaws hanging open, wondering what just happened while she strides away on red-soled shoes.

My research told a different story. Gossip sites and digging through hashtags revealed that Sandra is a prima donna, a little crazed when she doesn't get her way and a total bitch when she's seriously inconvenienced. I took a lot of what I found online with a grain of salt because so many people online hide behind their keys, but I'm approaching this meeting today with unease in my gut. Maybe coming alone wasn't such a good idea. If I ever needed a flirty man, this is probably the best one to bring Gaige to. The research also depicted Sandra as a cougar. In her late fifties, the woman has been married four times, and it's reported that she's on the prowl for number five.

The lobby of her organization is glamorous sparkling gold and accented with turquoise. I expect nothing else from a southern woman with style. The slender man at the front desk gives me a smile that doesn't reach his eyes as I approach.

"May I help you?" He blinks up at me, and the redness around his tired eyes is the first indication that things aren't rosy in his world.

"Good morning, Dustin," I say after looking at the nametag pinned to his chest. "I'm Leighton Redmond. I have an appointment with Ms. Halen."

He cringes, looking over his shoulder at a semi-open door.

"My apologies, Ms. Redmond. She—p-we're running a little behind this—"

"David!" The screeched voice comes from the office behind him.

Embarrassed, I look back down at his nametag, but I had the correct name.

He looks even more embarrassed, but also on the verge of tears, or more tears, because although it's only ten in the morning, I have a feeling that this poor man has already shed a few.

"David!"

"Please excuse me for a moment."

Dustin takes a long calming breath, the air shuddering through his nose before slowly releasing from his mouth as he stands. He gives me another smile and walks into the office, closing the door behind him. She screams at him so loudly, there was really no point in pulling it closed, but I understand not wanting to have witnesses to such things.

I should immediately walk out and leave. There is absolutely no way in hell I'd ever work with this woman.

But I don't turn around and leave.

I pull a slip of paper out of my purse, making a mental note to order business cards and wait for poor Dustin to return to his desk. He's shaking, tears tracking down his cheeks. His lower lip wobbles as he takes his seat. He tries to smile, but the man just can't manage it. My eyes sting in misery for him, but crying doesn't solve his problems.

"I need your personal cell phone number," I say and shove the slip of paper across the low counter toward him.

He shakes his head. "I apologize for being unprofessional, Ms. Redmond."

"Dustin, I need your number. You're going to get a phone call from another local business, from a boss that will respect you, treat you better, and will never make you cry at work. Trust me?"

His eyes search mine, and I can tell this man has been beaten down so much by the woman in that office he doesn't know if he can trust me or not. Eventually, he caves, writing his number down.

"Answer the phone when it rings, Dustin."

"Yes, ma'am. What do I tell her when she asks where you went?"

"Tell her that I said to go fuck herself."

A wide smile reaches across his face as I walk out of the building.

I felt great when I walked out of the building, but as I rode back to the hotel, I imagine I fucked things up royally. Deacon handpicked that woman. There must've been something about her that put her on the list.

I made a call to the office of the woman we first met with this week. She had a level head, and was so busy she was a little scattered, saying more than once that she had trouble finding good help to keep everything straight. I give her front desk clerk Dustin's information, praying they'll give him a call and bring him in for an interview. It's the best I can do for the beaten down young man.

The ride back to the hotel is too fast, and I have no idea what I'm going to say to Gaige once I get back to my room, but I can't put it off as long as I'd like because I find the door connecting our rooms ajar. It doesn't feel like a violation. The man has spent too much time inside of me to get offended that he accessed my room and unlocked it from my side.

I walk toward it, pushing it open to find him still sprawled on his bed, covers up around his waist with his laptop on his lap.

He gives me a lazy grin.

"Look at how the other half lives," I tease as I lean against the doorjamb.

"You're back earlier than expected. I was trying to talk myself into going down to the gym but now that you're here, I can get in a whole other kind of workout. Come jump on my dick."

I shake my head, my lips automatically turning up into a grin. The teasing between the two of us is so easy. I actually find myself liking this man.

"Did she cancel last minute?"

I shake my head. "Sandra Halen would not be a good fit for BBS. She's a total asshole."

"She was who Deacon wanted."

"She isn't. Trust me. The way she talked to her desk clerk, there's no way he would want someone like that working for him."

He just nods, and I beam internally that he's so quick to have confidence in me.

"Come here." He crooks his finger, urging me forward, but my feet are glued to the floor.

I shake my head. I made a rule, and more than once, okay many, many times, I've regretted it. Not having sex when we have so much free time in the evenings was stupid, but we've gone this long, I might as well stick with it. I don't want to look weak. Plus, I don't want to be weak, and that's exactly what this man makes me. It's bad enough that I think about him constantly. Keeping my hands to myself is nearly impossible. Having that access? He'd see just how frantic I am most of the time. We'd be late for work every day, and that's if I allowed him out of bed to show up at all.

"You sure?"

"I'm sure," I say, my voice soft.

He flips the covers back, his golden skin missing those tan lines I noticed the first time we were together on full display. His thick, proud cock reaches for his abs with just the right amount of curve that drives me wild no matter what position he puts me in. Knowing I haven't truly ridden him yet is driving me crazy. I want to know what the burn in my thighs feels like, what his hands on my hips feel like when he's urging me higher, making me go faster or slowing me down because he's just as crazed as I am when we're together that way.

"Still sure?"

I shake my head, my body's answer not matching my words. "I have to pack."

"We have six hours until we have to head to the airport."

"I feel dirty," I tell him, my eyes locked on his magnificent cock.

"I'll lick you clean."

I huff, meeting his eyes. "I hate the way that woman made me feel.

"We can just watch a little TV," he offers, pulling the sheets back up to cover his lower half.

This isn't something that we do. We haven't talked about that part, but it's one of those unspoken things that goes along with two people who are only hooking up. That's part of being in a relationship and neither one of us is interested in crossing those lines.

Even knowing I shouldn't, I tell him this. "We don't do the cuddle thing."

"We could try." He shrugs. "It could be fun."

He looks away from me, and I can't get a good read on him. Is he regretting his words or feeling a little exposed? I honestly can't tell, and for some reason that makes me feel a little dirty too, and not in a good way.

Sandra Halen ruined my good mood, the one that started Sunday with him in my bed and began to dwindle with the first meeting of the week. It's been slowly draining as the week progressed, only getting slightly recharged each evening by having dinner and conversation with him. Maybe I shouldn't have canceled dinner with him by lying and saying I needed to have a serious conversation with Chelsea last night. I didn't speak with my sister yesterday. I just needed a break from looking at his handsome face before I opened my stupid mouth and said something reckless that would make him rethink this whole just hooking up thing.

What the hell would Gaige Ward do if he found out that I was starting to get ideas about more than just wanting to hook up with him?

He'd probably run a mile in the other direction, and that may still be the case since I can't seem to do the damn job BBS hired me to do.

"It would be fun," I tell him. "Then your hands would wander down my spine."

"Probably."

"And then my knee would hitch up over your leg."

"You'd have to take that skirt off. It's too tight to get comfortable in."

"Of course," I agree.

"That would put that fire-hot pussy of yours on my leg."

"I'd likely burn you."

"I'd have to cool you off with my mouth."

"See?" I tell him I as I push away from the doorjamb and stand to my full height. "Cuddling would never work."

"I agree." He flips the blankets back once again, fisting his cock.

His arousal is already beading on the tip when I turn around and close the adjoining door. He's muttering about hard cocks, a perfectly wet, unused pussy and throat as I click the lock into place.

I press my forehead to the door because he's right. I'm fucking soaked, and I have no idea where I found the strength to leave him naked in that room. I don't think it's bravery or willpower. Maybe it's stupidity. Possibly self-preservation because I can picture myself with my head on his chest just resting in his arms while pretending to watch some dumb show on television.

It's already going to be hard enough to walk away from mind-blowing sex. The last thing I need is my other emotions getting tangled up in Gaige Ward. The only problem is, I can't be a hundred percent that they aren't already.

I rush to the other door when I hear his door open, watching him stride past with gym clothes on. He doesn't even glance at my door on his way.

Chapter 25

Gaige

Lifting weights doesn't ease the tension.

The treadmill doesn't come close to touching the strain in my muscles.

It's an unfamiliar feeling, something deep but also on my skin, and I don't know the cause or how to treat it. I head outside, thinking a run in the Texas humidity will fix the problem, but that doesn't help either. I'm drenched in sweat by the time I make it back to the hotel, killing three hours of the time left before we have to head to the airport, but unfortunately, that still leaves three more to go.

I spend an hour in the shower, wondering if the weekend starts tomorrow. Even though it's Friday, we aren't working. Well, we don't have meetings scheduled. My cock swells with just the thought of being back in St. Louis, knowing what her rules are. I think about ignoring it, but I know how that ends. I've tried it before. Ignoring it doesn't work. It used to. Before Leighton Redmond, I had control of my life and my body. I no longer have power. She has that, and she doesn't even know it.

I stroke myself to completion, biting my lip to keep from saying her name, and press my forehead to the shower wall. If the guys back at the office could see me now, they'd all give me shit. Oh how the ladies' man has fallen. I wouldn't say I'm in love with Leighton. I'm far from it. Like she said when I told her I wasn't married, she doesn't do love either. I have no interest in it. It's not love, but it's definitely obsession. I'm infatuated with her. Captivated. Enthralled. Haunted with thoughts of her.

Maybe that's what this feeling is that I can't seem to get rid of.

Climbing out of the shower, I dry off, shave, and get dressed in clothes I know will get her attention. My long sleeves are rolled up my forearms because I caught her looking at them the other day at dinner. I'm wearing those jeans I had on for the first dinner we met for in California. I find myself wanting her to notice me, to catch her looking at me with that same gleam in her eye she has when we're alone and about to get naked.

Then I wait, sitting in the room with my eyes locked out the window on hazy Houston until it's time to leave, that heavy feeling in my chest not easing the slightest until she's standing at my side, waiting for the hired car to arrive in front of the hotel.

Then I know I'm in trouble.

The flight back to St. Louis is much like the one to Texas after we made our deal about hooking up for fun. It's light and fun, more stories about our lives, places we want to travel to, but there's also an undercurrent of something else in her tone. Something is bothering her. There's a hint of distance between us. I have no clue what it is, and I have no right to ask her about it. We're colleagues, two people who fuck on occasion. I wouldn't even call us friends. We have dinner in the evenings because it's in the contract she signed. We travel together for the same reason.

We fuck because we're so good at it.

Friends?

I wouldn't call us friends despite the conversation coming so easily. Has she told me anything she wouldn't tell others in casual small talk? I smile during a break in topics and think back.

We talk about siblings, my brother and her sister, our stories—surface stuff—matching almost point for point. She's allergic to small animals. I'm allergic to cedar and other seasonal things. We talk business.

I don't know her fears. She hasn't mentioned the problems with her dad or his affair. She hasn't mentioned that her mother never attended her school functions growing up, not even her high school or college graduation because the woman is always traveling and just happened to have schedule conflicts. I know these things because Wren researched them.

I haven't told her about how I was gutted and missed a semester of college when my grandfather died because it devastated me, and how just the thought of losing one of my parents could possibly send me over the edge. I would never tell her about Freckles, the stuffed rabbit I had as a child—and slept with until I was twelve—that is still somewhere in my room at my childhood home.

We aren't friends. It's not my place to ask her what's wrong if it isn't something she's willing to open up and speak about on her own.

The shift continues, her mood changing even more as the plane lowers in the sky, getting closer to landing. By the time we're pulling up to the terminal, she's silent, giving me small smiles and blank eyes. I keep my distance even when I want to back her against the wall, tilt her chin up and demand she tell me what's wrong. I don't get to tell her that all I want is her pussy in one breath and then demand she open up in the other. It's contradictory, and I know I'm not ready for the fallout. What if she rejects me and I never have her that way again? What if she gives me exactly what I ask of her, and I'm not ready for that either?

We slide in the back of the hired car, our bodies as far away from each other as the seat will allow as the driver takes us to her hotel. Instead of getting out with her when he pulls up to the front, I lean over, brush a kiss to her temple and wait for her to climb out. He helps her with her suitcase, and I can't watch her walk away.

I easily go after what I want in life, but right now I have no idea what that is. Normally I'm a sampler, a little of this, a little of that, but there is no little of anything with her. I want it all, but I know I don't deserve a damn thing. I'm grateful for what she's given, but that emotional shit, I just can't handle right now.

The deal was her body, her pussy, her mouth. Fun. Fucking. That's what we agreed to. Now she's got me tied up in fucking knots.

Granted, I was tied up in knots before I opened my mouth with the stupid suggestions, but that's beside the point. Maybe we took it too far. We touched too much. Spent too much time together outside of fucking. Hell, maybe I've been the clingy one, and she's the one trying to pull back.

Fuck.

Is she the one backing away, and I'm the one too stupid to read the room?

Son of a bitch.

I'm the damn clinger here.

Everything is fine.

If I can just go back to the original agreement, then there's no longer a problem.

I have the driver take me to BBS because going home to an empty condo sounds like the worst idea ever.

Most of the guys are in the office, but it looks like the majority of them are getting ready to head out. I get waves and greetings as I swing through, Ignacio telling me that Deacon is in his office when I ask on my way through.

I knock gently on his door, waiting for approval before opening his door.

My boss looks exhausted, shadows under his eyes when I step inside, but he also looks like the happiest man in the world.

"Fatherhood looks good on you, Dad," I say as I sit across from him. "Except that." I point to the stain on the shoulder of his shirt. It has to be spit up from the baby. He looks down, flicking at it with lazy fingers, missing it completely before looking back at me. This once completely put-together man doesn't even seem bothered that another human has regurgitated on him.

"How was Texas?"

"Another shitshow."

He nods as if he expected as much.

"I sent Leighton to the last appointment alone." I leave out the fact that I used it to my advantage in order to get her to go with me on Saturday.

He doesn't give me a hard time about liability because he trusts me.

"She said Sandra Halen is a horrible person and was actually surprised she made your list."

"Hmm," he says, nodding.

"I feel like you're sending us on a wild goose chase."

"There's a reason for every meeting, Gaige."

"And if you told me what the end game was, maybe we could get to it quicker without wasting our resources." As I say the words, I realize I don't want faster. Ending the traveling means bringing Leighton's time with BBS to an end, and that's the last damn thing I want.

"Just stick with the itinerary. Georgia is next. Maybe you'll have better luck in the south."

"Texas is in the south," I argue.

"I'm giving everyone the day off tomorrow. Make sure Leighton knows. Keep me updated on how next week goes."

I stand, knowing when I've been dismissed. I have no doubt he wants to get out of here quickly and get back to Anna and his son.

The breakroom is empty when I walk back through, but I settle in on the couch sure that someone will come wandering through, eventually. No one shows. Deacon walks through, telling me goodbye twenty minutes later.

Giving up, I head to the elevator. My BMW is waiting for me in the parking garage, and I have every intention of going home despite not wanting to be alone as I drive across town, but somehow I end up at Leighton's hotel. I park, and as I climb out of my car, I tell myself I'll just head into the bar for a drink. It's the best in town after all. I'd never pick up a woman here. There's just something dirty about hooking up with another woman after agreeing to sleeping with Leighton on a regular basis even though I've never done the regular sex thing with one person before.

I don't head left in the lobby but angle my body right in the direction of the front desk. Flirting with the front desk clerk comes easily to me. Telling her that I want to surprise my sister for her birthday makes my stomach turn, but I doubt she'll give me the information I want if I mention that she's anything other than family. I could easily call Wren for Leighton's room number, but he's already too far into my business as it is. I'm honestly shocked I haven't gotten texts about fucking this up with her already.

With her room number drilled in my head, I catch the elevator with an elderly couple who can't seem to get enough distance between the two of them. If they could've caught separate cars, I think they'd both be happier. I know this isn't how all marriages end up. My parents are happy. My grandfather died just as in love—if not more—with Lala than the day he married her. It saddens me to see it. They get off on the third floor, and I ride it up a couple of floors higher, slowly walking off on the fifth.

My feet are heavy as I inch toward room 526, wondering what I'm going to say to her. I could go with cheery and say that the weekend has started since Deacon has canceled the workday for everyone tomorrow. I could just kiss her the second she opens the door. I could tell her that I noticed her sad mood earlier and I'm here to make her forget it.

None of those seem right, but it doesn't stop me from lifting my hand and knocking, but it does stop me from putting much force behind announcing my arrival.

Those same insidious thoughts about her thinking I'm turning into the clingy one hit me in the chest because if this isn't proof of exactly that then I don't know what is. I press my head to her door, feeling like a damn fool and wondering when the tables turned so drastically. When did I turn into the man who isn't happy unless I am standing in front of her? When did things shift from wanting a different woman every night to needing only her skin brushing my fingertips?

I huff a laugh, my breath forming a wet spot on her hotel room door.

I look down at my watch, noting the time I realize I've turned into a stage-five clinger.

Chapter 26

Leighton

Gaige: Wear a sundress. I don't think I'll be able to keep my hands off of your skin all damn day.

I stare down at the text message on my phone. I've looked at the damn thing a hundred times. The first time I saw it when I woke up this morning, I wanted to throw the damn thing at the wall.

I hadn't heard from him since I got out of the hired car on Thursday afternoon.

Well, that's not true. I got an email late Thursday night from him, informing me that Deacon was giving everyone Friday off. It was business-like, impersonal.

Our weekend started a day early, and the asshole sends a fucking email.

Thursday morning after I got back from Sandra Halen's office, he was begging me to crawl into bed with him. Conversation on the plane was normal, and then something changed. By the time we got in the car to ride back to the hotel, he couldn't even meet my eyes. At the time, I was grateful for the quiet. I had a million things rolling through my head. It was one thing for Gaige to not care how I acted at Sandra's office, but Gaige doesn't run BBS. Deacon does. Plus, another week was drawing to a close without any success. I've had unsuccessful weeks before. It's nothing new for me, but I was never afraid I'd lose my job because of it. Dad would give me a pep talk and tell me that it happens.

"Can't win them all," he'd tell me.

Deacon isn't Dad, and he will fire me. When I got that email notification, I just knew that's what was happening, and of course it would be Gaige who did it.

I had the day off. Then I didn't hear from him all day. He didn't show up with his cock in his hand. He didn't text and tell me to meet him in the bar or at Paragon. I heard nothing. Then this damn text. He sent it early, a second one coming, notifying me that I needed to be ready at eleven. What kind of damn function starts so damn early in the day?

I've thought more than once about messaging and canceling. He didn't even mention the damn function when he stayed in the car when I got dropped off, but I made a deal, although I regretted it the second I stepped into that office and saw how Sandra treated her staff.

I'll hold up my end of the bargain, and I'll wear a damn sundress. I'll even let the man touch me if he wants because I'm not a fool. He has skilled fingers, a tongue that works me over like an expert, and I'm aching for him, but I won't be completely happy about it. Plus, it could be the last chance I get. Come Monday morning, I could have that email I expect to get, the one telling me BBS will no longer be needing my services.

I rush to get ready, already wasting too much time trying to decide if I'm going to cancel to spend much time on my hair. I leave it down and pull on sandals. If the dress code is casual enough for a sundress, then I want to be in comfortable shoes, anticipating a full day event since it's starting so early.

The knock comes sooner than I expect, considering I anticipated a text saying he was downstairs since I never gave him my room number. I'm sure I have Wren Nelson to thank for Gaige having this little piece of information.

I bite the inside of my cheek when I open the door and see him standing there in a pale blue polo, khaki shorts, and Sperry shoes. A chuckle escapes my mouth.

"You look like a frat douche."

His eyes roam my body from my sandals to the dark waves over my shoulders. "And you look like a fucking mid-morning snack."

I feel a little guilty for speaking my mind, but in the next second, we're both inside the room, and he's carrying me to the bed. I'm on my back with my dress shoved up around my waist and his hot mouth on my inner thigh.

"I came by Thursday night," he says against my skin, and I know he's keeping his mouth away from where my body needs him the most on purpose. "You didn't answer the door."

"Bath," I manage. "AirPods. Mmm."

He sounds a little jealous, like he's fishing for information, and I'll fucking tell him anything if he just moves that talented tongue three inches to the left. He rewards my confession by brushing the tip of his nose over my panties, nudging my clit.

"Oh God, you should've knocked harder." I start to pant. This man has the ability to make my body go from zero to a hundred in no time. "The tub is big enough for two."

He groans, the weight of him leaving me completely, and I glare up at him as he stands, adjusting a very eager erection in his shorts. His hand clasps mine as he pulls me from the bed. I glare at him the way any sane woman would.

He presses his mouth to mine, pulling back when I try to deepen the kiss.

What the hell is wrong with him?

He presses his thumb to my bottom lip but pulls it away when I try to bite it.

"Be good today, and we can try that tonight."

"You want me to bite your dick?"

"Not bite, but a little teeth sounds like fun."

My core clenches around nothing.

"Let's go. We don't want to be late," he says, urging me toward the door.

***

"Absolutely not," I hiss as he pulls his sleek car in front of a huge house.

"You're going to have a blast." His words are sincere, but this isn't happening.

"You said it wasn't a big family event."

"I said it wasn't a wedding."

"There are over thirty cars parked on the street."

He points to a pickup. "That belongs to the neighbor."

"And all the others?"

He shrugs.

"What kind of function is this?" I ask, looking up at the massive home.

I'm no stranger to big houses, that's not the issue. My family has money. I was raised in a home similar to this. I know how nice they are on the outside and how cold they are on the inside. I know how many secrets those pretty doors can lock away.

"It's Lala's birthday."

"What's a lala?"

"Lala is my grandmother on my father's side. She's turning ninety."

My eyes widen. "You brought your fuck buddy to your grandmother's party? Are you insane?"

He smiles that devious one he gave me right before he put his mouth on my pussy the very first time.

"Being here isn't the insane part, but you have to play along."

I'm shaking my head already.

"You grew up in a wealthy family, Leighton. You know how things can be. You know what expectations are like. I'm thirty-three, unmarried, unattached with no prospects on the horizon."

"Oh God," I mutter, already getting an idea of where this is going. "Please don't even say it."

"We've been dating for a couple of months. That's new enough that—"

"You want me to lie to a ninety-year-old woman? Gaige, no."

"Her birthday isn't until Tuesday."

I narrow my eyes at him as if the clarification makes any difference. "A couple of months isn't long enough for them to ask questions about marriage, so we'll be safe on that front."

"Them?"

"My entire family will be there."

"Your dad's side."

He shakes his head. "My entire family. Both sides are very close."

My palms start to sweat, and I wipe them down the front of my dress.

He clasps them both in my hands.

"You're a professional, Leighton. Make it through this, and I'll eat your pussy for hours."

"That entire thing makes me sound like a fucking hooker, Gaige."

"I don't—" He sighs. "I don't mean for it to. Please do this for me. You're good with people. You'll be fine. Come on."

He climbs out of the car, and I give in, waiting until he comes around to open my door because if anyone is watching from the house, it's what would be expected. He brushes his mouth on my cheek, a whispered thank you on his lips, and I wait as he pulls a professionally wrapped gift from the trunk of his car.

As he bends down, a smiling man approaches, his eyes appraising, his mouth held in a familiar cocky grin.

"Hi," he says as he walks closer.

Gaige straightens, frowning when he sees the man.

"Tyler," he mutters, smacking him on the back of the head before he can reach for me.

They do that bro clap hug thing guys do that shows affection while maintaining their masculinity.

"This is Leighton Redmond, my... friend."

Seems we're not lying to his brother.

"Hello, Gaige's friend."

It's like that's all the permission Gaige's younger brother needs to step closer and wrap me in a hug. He smells amazing, but the lift and twirl is a little over the top. I play along, knowing from the playful wink Tyler gave me right before he touched me that he's purposely trying to rile his brother up.

I squeeze him hard, pressing my face into his throat.

"Wow," I praise. "You're so strong."

"You smell amazing," Tyler says, his nose also in my neck.

I bite my lip to keep from laughing when I see Gaige's angry face.

Today may just be me satisfying my half of the deal we made, but the man definitely doesn't like seeing me in his brother's arms. I file that away for later as Tyler sets me back on my feet.

"Are you two done?" Gaige snaps, making his brother laugh.

Tyler runs his hand down my arm as if he's going to take my hand to walk us toward the front door of the house, and that must be Gaige's limit.

"Do you mind?" he hisses at his brother, finally taking a stand and slipping in between us.

He situates his palm on my back possessively and hands over the gift. I'm thankful to have something in my hands as we enter the home. It makes things less awkward for me.

"When I suggested bringing her to Lala's party, I never thought you'd do it," Tyler whispers. I'm not sure I was meant to hear it, so I ignore the conversation as Gaige ushers me through the massive front door.

"Drop it," Gaige says.

The house is lovely, just as I expected it to be, but it doesn't have that cold and impersonal feel that my childhood home did. The center table in the entryway is stacked with gifts, and I feel a pang of disappointment that I have to relinquish my shield so quickly. Gaige takes my hand shortly after, his grip light but reassuring as we make our way out to the patio.

"This is beautiful," I whisper as I take in the vast yard.

His parents take great pride in their space because flowers in every color line the yard.

"The gardener must stay incredibly busy."

"This is my mother's work," Gaige says. "She's never had a gardener."

This is another difference between our families.

"And the wolves descend," Tyler whispers as a group of people notice us. Tyler presses a kiss to my temple as if he's known me for years. "It was nice meeting you, Leighton."

He walks toward the group of women, intercepting them before they get to us.

"Don't be nervous," Gaige says, his hand giving mine a little squeeze.

"We never nailed down our story."

He turns to me, a hand cupping my cheek. I swallow with the intimacy of it as I look up at him.

"We don't need a story, Leighton. We met at work a couple of months ago. We hit it off. Things are amazing. It's that simple."

"Simple," I repeat.

He nods before leaning down and brushing a kiss to my cheek. It's a simple action, innocent, something no one would bat an eye at or witness and think anything of, but it feels personal, something meant only for the two of us.

My fingers tangle in his shirt, my need to drag him closer controlling my muscles.

"Leighton, are you purposely trying to get me hard in front of my family?" His voice is teasing, but I don't find the humor in it.

It's as if I've been drenched in ice-cold water. There was absolutely nothing sexual about my reaction, and that's eye-opening. My need in that moment was emotional. His was sexual. We're worlds apart right now, not even close as far as where our heads are at, and that's incredibly sobering.

I take a step back, forcing his hand to fall away from me.

I give him a weak smile.

"No, Mr. Ward. My apologies."

"So formal." He winks, still thinking I'm playing a game. "That doesn't help either."

"I'm sorry, sir. Do you have an invitation?"

I look around Gaige to see a beautiful older woman approach. Gaige shakes his head, mirth shining in his eyes as he turns to face her.

"I spoke with you last week, Mom." He wraps her in a hug so tight she squeaks but doesn't complain.

"Might as well be a year. I miss you boys when I don't get to hear your voices." Her eyes close, holding on to him until he's the one to step back. I know this woman would stay in his embrace as long as he would allow it. That's what a mother's love is supposed to look like. "Who is your friend?"

"Girlfriend," Gaige corrects. "Mom, this is Leighton Redmond. Sweetheart, Caroline Ward, my mother."

I hold my hand out as her jaw practically unhinges in shock, and even though her eyes sparkle, she doesn't immediately take my hand. It's awkward as my eyes dart to Gaige. He takes a deep breath, mouths *I'm sorry*, and then I have another pair of Ward arms around me. It's my turn to squeak from being squeezed too tightly.

She takes a step back, her hands still on my upper arms as she looks me up and down as if she doesn't want to let me go in fear that I'll disappear.

"She's real, Mom," Gaige mutters as if his mother is acting utterly ridiculous.

"He's never brought a girl home before."

And I feel like an asshole for playing a part in this deception.

"She's very pretty," she says over her shoulder.

"Absolutely gorgeous," he agrees, his eyes on me when the words leave his lips.

My cheeks heat. Attraction between us has never been an issue, but it's nice to hear.

"And who is this?" a stately gentleman asks as he walks up, and I don't even have to be introduced.

The man is an older version of Gaige, and lord have mercy. If this is what Gaige will look like in another thirty years, the woman he does finally settle down with is going to have to beat everyone off with a stick.

"Gaige's *girl*friend," Mrs. Ward says. "Leighton, this is Everett."

Mr. Ward shakes my hand when I offer it instead of a hug, but then he lifts the damn thing to his lips. Now I see where Gaige got his charm. He's probably been learning it since the day he was born.

"Nice to meet you, Leighton. Have you met Mother yet?"

"We just got here," Gaige reminds them.

Mrs. Ward slides her arm around my back, separating me from Gaige, and I give a look of desperation over my shoulder before I'm swept away.

"She's just going to love you, dear. This will make her year. I just know it."

We walk deeper into the yard, and I don't have time to appreciate the gorgeous foliage because we're approached by several people. Mrs. Ward gives several quick introductions before she moves us along. Each person I meet—whom I have no hope of keeping straight—seems equally surprised when they hear I'm Gaige's girlfriend. The lies keep stacking up even though it's the same one over and over.

"Lala," Mrs. Ward says as we approach a sitting woman who is looking out across the yard watching a small group of kids chase each other.

The birthday girl turns her head to look at us. Her smile never wavers.

"Caroline, did you notice how much little Pete has grown since Christmas? Will the clothes we bought for his birthday still fit?"

"I'll check with Megan. I saved the receipts. We can exchange them for a larger size if we need to."

"Oh, hi, dear," the senior Mrs. Ward says, noticing me for the first time. She looks up to Caroline for an introduction.

"Lala, this is Leighton Redmond." A pregnant pause hangs between us. "Gaige's girlfriend."

The woman doesn't react at first. It's as if her brain either can't handle the information or she is hard of hearing.

Then the smile that has been on her entire face transforms, growing wider. Her arms lift, forming a huge circle, making it clear I'm expected to step into it.

Of course, I do. I'd never deny this grinning woman that. But I'm also in a sundress. I press one hand to the back of my thighs and lean over to embrace her.

What I thought was going to be awkward is just the opposite. A woman I don't even know hugs me in the middle of a patio I've never stepped foot on before, and suddenly I feel like I'm at home, like the piece of my life I've been missing has just slid into place. Tears sting the backs of my eyes as she starts to rock back and forth the way you would when seeing someone after a very long absence, someone you love and have missed seeing for years.

When she finally eases back, her brittle fingers swipe at her own cheeks and then she shoves her hands into the pocket of her very sensible slacks and tugs free a tissue.

"I'm sorry, dear. Allergies, you know."

"Of course," I say, dabbing at my own eyes, grateful for the excuse.

"Have a seat, dear."

Lala points to a patio chair sitting right beside her and I drop into it.

"I'll let you two get better acquainted," Caroline says before walking away. "Leighton, would you like something to drink?"

"I'm fine but thank you."

For long moments, we just sit and watch the children play. Lala seems quite content to just observe her family enjoying being around each other, and that's exactly what they're doing. They laugh and joke, tease each other. Everyone is smiling and mingling. There are no side-eyes, and I remember that this is both sides of the family, both Gaige's mother's side and his father's, and it makes it all the more magical.

The questions start simple enough. Where did we meet? Is Gaige a gentleman? Does he open doors and treat me with respect? I tell her the truth. Well, I shift the timeline a little on the first question and tell her that we met at work.

But of course, Gaige was wrong about telling everyone that we've been dating a couple months meant we'd be able to avoid the serious questions.

"Caroline didn't have to tell me you two were dating," she says, her eyes still on the kids, that happy smile still on her wrinkled face.

"She didn't?"

"I saw the two of you walk out. I'd say even Tyler has a little crush on you. Everyone thinks I'm half blind, but I see just fine."

I chuckle. Elderly people are smart. This woman didn't make it to ninety without keeping a few cards close to the vest.

"I know love and devotion when I see it."

I give her a weak smile even though she isn't looking at me. I also don't tell her that her vision obviously isn't as good as she thinks it is if that's what she imagines she saw.

"I got married in the springtime," Lala says almost distantly, as if she's stuck in a memory rather than actually sharing. "But the guests sneezing was quite distracting. So I think a fall wedding would be better for the two of you."

"Fall weddings are beautiful," I say diplomatically.

"Evening time."

"Of course," I agree. "Soft candlelight. Lots of muted colors. Plum, maybe stone or bordeaux."

"That sounds lovely. An extensive wine list to match."

I chuckle. "Plan the entire reception around the wine list. That's a wedding I can get behind."

She laughs with me. "And children?"

"We'd have to start right away. I'm thirty. He's already thirty-three."

The conversation continues, the details and advice getting more and more personal as we talk and by the time Gaige approaches, I'm sure my face is as red as the wine Lala and I discussed serving with the steak at the wedding reception that will never happen.

"Hi," I say, begging him to rescue me.

He hands me a flute of champagne, and uncaring of what it looks like drinking midday in front of his entire family, I drain the entire thing in one go. He chuckles when I hand the empty glass back to him.

He hugs his grandmother before walking away, telling me that he'll get me another glass, and I realize I just shot myself in the foot with that one.

Conversation shifts as more people join the party, but it doesn't get better. Lala, transitioning from the incredibly lucid woman I carried a detailed conversation with, starts introducing me to family members as Gaige's fiancée. She does it with a glint in her eye that makes me realize this woman is completely lucid and possibly the biggest prankster in the group, but no one calls out a ninety-year-old woman at her birthday party, so I smile and nod when people respond with shock and a million questions. Lala tells them about our fall wedding, planned for next year of course because this year would be too soon and people would be looking at my stomach and counting off the months on their fingers wondering why the rush—nudge, nudge—insert old lady cackle here. The woman is hilarious, despite her comedy being at my expense.

It's another thirty minutes before I see Gaige again, and the look on my face must be enough because he walks up and holds his hand out to me.

"Lala, I need my girl for a minute."

"It was lovely to meet you," I tell her.

She gives me a sweet smile before we walk away. I wrap my arm around his waist, pinching his side as hard as I can. I know it hurts, but he doesn't hiss or pull away. Gaige grins down at me.

"Had I known you were just going to throw me off the boat in shark-infested waters, I never would've agreed to this."

"You were smiling the entire time. I thought you were having fun."

I actually was having fun, but that's not really the point. He deserted me.

"Did you know she's telling everyone we're getting married?"

He grins down at me. "I figured it out after the third congratulations."

"Next fall because apparently everyone will think I'm knocked up if we do it sooner."

"Fall weddings are nice. Not too hot, not too cold. Allergies are horrible in the spring for guests."

He must've heard about her wedding more than once for him to say something like that, and it hints at how close he is to her.

"She's worried my hips won't spread wide enough to birth your children."

Instead of his eyes growing wide at the thought of impregnating me, he takes a step back, eyes drifting to my lower half as he takes a sip of the champagne he never offered me. "That could be a problem."

"She wants to know if I plan to breastfeed." His eyes lift. "She doesn't seem to think I'm going to have any problems there."

He licks his lips, a smile in his eyes. "Probably not."

He places the glass in his hand on a table and slips his palm against mine. "What are you doing?"

"We're going to dance."

"No one else is dancing, Gaige. Are you purposely trying to embarrass me?"

"No." He tilts my chin as he pulls me close, and we start to sway. "It's just us."

What in the world is going on right now?

He spends time looking in my eyes, watching my mouth, his fingers sweeping slowly up and down my spine, and the rest of the world just fades away.

"She loves you," I whisper.

"And I love her."

"She says you're a kind and caring man." He gives a soft smile, as if those words coming from his grandmother mean the world to him. "She said you'll be gentle when you deflower me."

Gaige throws his head back and laughs, drawing the attention of every single person on the patio.

Chapter 27

Gaige

I knew my family would love Leighton. I just had no idea how much. The way my mother hugged her at first sight made my chest constrict. Tyler swinging her around in front of the house was a way to call my bluff when I mentioned her being just a friend, and it worked. I felt territorial the second he put his hands on her.

You smell amazing he told her.

I could've wrapped my hands around his neck.

The grin on Lala's face when Mom introduced them?

That gave me literal butterflies, a million wings flapping in my stomach.

I should've felt sick, should've wanted to grab her by the hand, told everyone it was a lie, and dragged her away from the house, but I just stood to the side talking with Dad while I watched them talk.

Mentioning marriage and kids, all the things I was certain no one in my family would bring up with a complete stranger should've terrified me.

It didn't.

I pictured what candlelight would look like reflecting off her dark hair. How long I'd have to innocently touch her while dancing before we could sneak away, and I could take her for the first time as my wife.

Babies?

That's something I never considered, but stepping back and looking at her hips, her breasts when she mentioned feeding my children made my balls ache. This is all so new to me, and the prospect thrills me, which should also be alarming.

It's not.

"No," I tell Tyler when he pulls out the chair on the opposite side of Leighton.

He grins, but he steps away and heads to the other side of the table.

"Not you either," I tell Jarrett, my older cousin.

Several of the men in my family laugh, but Jarrett walks away as well.

Assisted by my father, Lala shuffles closer, taking the seat on Leighton's other side. This is possibly even worse than two very flirtatious men, but I'm not going to say a word.

Leighton shifts in her seat, but she smiles as Lala settles beside her. If she's worried that Lala will say something to embarrass her in front of everyone, then that fear is warranted. My grandmother doesn't hold her tongue. If it enters her mind, it comes from her mouth, and we love her for it. No one is spared. She's equal opportunity that way. We've all been there.

Lunch begins, waiters carrying out platters of food and placing them in the center of the table. Large gatherings like this are the only time Mom doesn't cook. She'd rather spend her time visiting with family than in the kitchen. Dishes get passed around, Leighton earning more Lala points as she helps fill my grandmother's plate.

Then the chatter begins, and of course with the woman beside me being the newbie, all the focus is on us.

"Did he tell you about the time he split his pants trying to look cool at the homecoming dance?" Jarrett asks.

Leighton smiles as widely as she can with a mouthful of mashed potatoes, her head shaking.

"Or the time he tripped right in front of the head cheerleader in high school?" Tyler adds.

"He was an awkward child," Lala says.

"Very clumsy," Dad confirms.

"We had him tested for neurological problems," Mom says.

I find that it doesn't bother me at all. I want her to know all these things about me. Maybe it will help her to open up more about herself. I know the surface stuff. We chat about it often. I want to know the things she never tells anyone else.

"He'd come home and cry, but there was always one thing that made him feel better."

"Tyler," I warn.

My brother gives me a devious smile.

"What?"

Lala laughs, the sound that tells me if my brother doesn't say it, she will.

"Freckles," my brother says, the ultimate betrayal.

"What's Freckles?" Leighton asks as she reaches for her glass of water.

"It's this cute little stuffed rabbit," Lala explains, furthering the treachery.

Leighton looks over at me, grinning.

"It's still in his room upstairs. I'll show him to you after lunch," Mom says.

I snap my head in her direction, drawing a round of laughter from everyone at the table.

"I still have my stuffed teddy bear," Leighton says, throwing me a bone, and I squeeze her thigh under the tablecloth.

"Did you sleep with it until you were twelve?" Tyler asks.

She scoffs.

Another round of laughter.

"You couldn't pry that thing out of my arms until I left for college." She squeezes my leg right back.

The conversation shifts when my family realizes that Leighton is on my side. They ask her a million questions, ones I've never been brave enough to ask, things I really want to know. It's like a game, rapid fire, things that would be asked if we were on a dating game, but I discover so many things about her.

Favorite color—coral. I have no idea exactly what that is, but it sounds pretty.

Favorite food—the wings from Mario's in New York.

Favorite alcoholic beverage—mint julep. She only drinks white wine more often because she can't stop with just one of her favorites.

Favorite television show—she rarely watches television, and she doesn't understand the fascination with *Schitt's Creek*. She couldn't get past the first episode.

Tyler frowns at her because of this. Moira Rose is his spirit animal, apparently.

Once the meal is over, and we're waiting for dessert to be brought in, I inch closer to her, pressing myself to her side while Uncle Eddie shares a story about a recent trip to the Alps.

"You should take her," Eddie says once he's done. "Have you traveled a lot, Leighton?"

"Yes," she answers. "I've been very lucky in life."

"I'm the lucky one," I say, pressing my lips to her temple.

Everything shifts. What was pretend, now becomes real. What were lies, what were half-truths now feel like commandments in my chest, and it takes all my strength not to pull back and look her in the eyes to see if she feels it too.

This has gone beyond clingy, and she must sense it because she pulls away, a smile on her face that I can tell she doesn't feel. I've watched her enough over the last two weeks, seen her give prospective new hires this fake smile one too many times, been the recipient of her real one for it to work on me.

"You okay?" I whisper when someone else starts talking.

"Where's the restroom?"

I push myself back from the table, pulling her chair back once I stand and escort her from the room.

"Hey." I hold her hand, stopping her before she can enter the powder room. "What's wrong?"

She doesn't hesitate to step around me and close herself inside. The lock clicking into place doesn't have the same effect it did the other day when she left me in bed with an erection. That left disappointment in my nuts. Right now, my heart is what's hurting. The physical pain I could deal with easily. This new awareness is so foreign I stupidly press my fingers to my chest to try to rub the ache away.

"That won't fix it," my dad whispers from the end of the hall.

I pull my head from the wall, wondering when I pressed it there to begin with.

"What?"

"Seeing her happy is the only thing that makes that misery subside."

"I don't know what you're talking about." It's only a partial lie. I know what he's referring to, but because I don't exactly understand, it's not a full deception.

"You will." He gives me a sad smile, as if he's known the entire day that Leighton isn't my girl. "We're getting ready for the game. See you out back."

I'm still standing in the hall when Leighton steps out of the restroom, and I hate that she seems disappointed to see me. It's clear that she was hoping she stayed in there long enough that I would've walked away.

"I have a headache," she says before I can ask. "Will you take me home?"

I clasp her hand, nodding, refusing to call her out on her lie. I'd hoped that bringing her here would get my family off my back, but maybe it was too much. Maybe I'm too much for her.

Lala is shuffling toward the patio on our way through the dining room.

"Oh, there you are, Leighton. Help me out back. I don't want to miss kick-off."

Lala reaches for her hand.

"Leighton isn't—"

She squeezes my hand once before releasing it, then she takes Lala's hand and walks slowly beside her out the back door. Maybe the family isn't the thing she wants to get rid of. Maybe it's only me, because as soon as I join the rest of the guys on the grass, Leighton is smiling and joking with the women in my family like she didn't walk out of the bathroom with a frown on her pretty face.

I can't concentrate on the game at all. What is supposed to be a flag football game still sees me on my back more than a half dozen times because my eyes stay on her rather than paying attention to what's going on. If I didn't know her as well as I do, I'd think she was having a great time, but the longer I watch her, the easier it is for me to see that the same enthusiasm she had earlier has drained away.

She's miserable, and I should've insisted on taking her home instead of being selfish and letting Lala drag her out here because I wanted to spend a little more time with her.

No matter what I do with this woman, I just can't seem to do it right.

Chapter 28

Leighton

As put together and confident as Gaige looked when he arrived at my hotel this morning, he doesn't look like that now as the football game comes to an end. He's covered in bits of earth, grass stains on his khaki shorts, and there's a smudge of dirt on his cheek.

I find that I like the disheveled look of him a little too much.

His family begins to filter out, saying goodbyes, many of them having quite a distance to drive to get back home to prepare for the week ahead. Gaige doesn't seem as eager to leave, helping his dad and brother clean off tables on the patio as I sit with Lala.

She hasn't continued the line of questioning, but there isn't much about my life the entire family didn't ask about at lunch. She seems content to just sit in the sun and soak up the rays.

After another half hour, Gaige finally approaches, squatting in front of his grandmother with a soft smile on his lips. It's clear how much he adores the woman, and that same loving look is in her eyes as well when she cups her wrinkled hand on his golden cheek.

"Thank you for sharing Leighton with us today," she whispers.

He kisses her palm. "You're welcome, but we're going to head out. I need some time alone with her."

"Treat her like the lady she is."

"Always," he promises before wrapping her in a hug.

Lala's eyes squeeze tight, and she grunts with the effort she uses to hold him tight. She's reluctant to let him go, winking at me when he steps back.

"Don't be a stranger," she says to me before we walk away.

"I won't," I tell her, knowing it's a lie, and hating myself a little for it.

My hand grows clammy in his, much the way my body began to feel when we were at the table earlier. It was too easy to let myself start believing in the lies we were telling just by smiling and pretending to be this happy couple that was falling in love.

I know love and devotion when I see it.

Not only were we fooling an entire family and a precious ninety-year-old woman, but I was also starting to fool myself, and that spoke of the dangerous situation I was in.

My heart never gets involved. I don't give it time. My life is dedicated to my work and goals.

We're stopped on the way out, saying goodbye to his mom, dad, and Tyler. A look passes between Gaige and his dad, one I don't have any hope of understanding, but it's not really my place to start analyzing what the Ward men have going on. I'll never see the oldest one again. This was a business transaction of sorts, both parts of it—today and the one back in Texas—leaving me feeling dirty and in need of a shower.

I want to pull away from him as we walk to his car, but I have a feeling Caroline Ward is watching us from the window, no doubt with a smile on her face, thinking her son is finally going to settle down, the consummate bachelor hanging up his playboy ways.

I don't pull away even though I know I should. I live in the moment, in the fantasy for just a few seconds longer and lean into his shoulder, my throat threatening to close with each step closer we take toward his car. He releases my hand, his arm going around my waist, and he holds me to him. Right there in the middle of his parents' yard, Gaige Ward pulls me against his chest and lets me live in his world, allows me to picture the loving family I've always wanted but never had. He lets me own the sweet jokes and endless teasing that only people who truly care about each other can get away with, and then he tilts my head up, pressing a sweet kiss to my lips, his thumbs tracing my jaw.

"Thank you for today," I tell him.

I have to turn around. Looking at him is going to draw the tears, and I can't explain them.

This isn't a relationship. He laid it out that night at Paragon. Hell, I made the rule about no sex while working. I've known him two weeks, and half of that time I thought he was married. Fantasies and well-placed lies have a way of getting inside of your head and altering reality. That's all that this is, and I'd do well to remember that.

He opens the car door when I stand at it, quickly making his way around to the driver's side, and although he cranks it, he doesn't put it in gear and drive away from the curb.

He turns in his seat to face me, and it takes a moment for me to school my face so when I look at him, he doesn't read every emotion I'm trying to hide. I give him a small smile when I meet his gaze.

"Are we going to talk about the weird mood you're in? And don't tell me it's because you're tired or because you have a headache."

But I do have a headache. My entire body aches right now—my chest and the muscle beating there. My fingers ache to touch him, my throat from the effort not to cry.

"I don't like lying to people," I tell him, and that's a truth I can manage.

He nods, his eyes focusing out the front glass before he shifts into drive and pulls away. The drive back into the city is quiet, and it seems to take hours longer than the ride out to his parents' house, even with the anticipation earlier of not knowing where I was going. The music playing softly over the radio doesn't serve as much of a distraction as it's too low to even tell when one song transitions into the next, but I don't dare reach for the controls to change the station or turn it up. It may make him speak, and conversation could be a bad thing right now. It could raise questions, and those require answers. I'm not sure if any of that will be beneficial to either of us.

Gaige doesn't pull up in front of my hotel when we arrive, and as he parks like he's a guest in the side lot, anxiety ratchets through me. Earlier, my delusions made the day feel like the beginning of something incredible. Right now feels like the end.

"Can I come up with you?" His words are soft and pleading.

I nod because it's impossible to turn him down.

We exit the car at the same time, meeting in front of the vehicle but not touching as we walk inside. The ride up in the elevator is spent the very same way the car ride was—silent and reflective.

As we step off and enter the hotel room, I'm not sure either one of us is sure of what's going to happen as we look at each other.

"Today," he begins, but I hold my hand up.

I don't want to talk about it. I can't talk about it.

Today destroyed me.

Pulling up to that house, I was terrified I was being used as a pawn, walking into a situation much like the one I was raised in with snide remarks and scathing looks, well-placed insults disguised as helpful suggestions.

It was much worse. Today showed me what real love was, that it honestly existed, and I've been missing it all this time.

"I don't want to talk," I tell him as I lift the hem of my sundress and pull it over my head, leaving me standing in my bra and panties.

I kick my sandals away, unsnapping my bra before shoving my panties to the floor.

"You're a goddess," he whispers, his eyes on mine rather than running the length of my naked form.

Somehow, it seems even more invasive.

I reach for him, my fingers pushing the buttons at his throat through their respective holes as he stands still. The only thing moving on him is his chest as he takes shallow breaths. I pull his shirt over his head, next working open his khakis, shoving them along with his boxer briefs down. There's no skill or seduction in it. Getting us both naked is the means to the end. He kicks his shoes off at the same time he kicks his clothing away, and then we're both standing there naked. Neither of us touching.

"On the bed," I tell him, taking over the commands when he's normally the one giving them.

His cock bounces as he moves, and I find myself a little hypnotized by it. Once he's flat on his back, I start to climb on top of him, but remember the condom. I have to crawl back off and grab one from his wallet before returning.

"Kiss me," he whispers, reaching for me, but I can't.

We didn't that first night, and maybe that's where we started going wrong. Maybe that intimacy is where things started to turn.

I press my lips to his abdomen, letting the groan that escapes from his lips wash over me before leaning back and rolling the latex over his cock. His hips flex, muscles all over his body taut and rigid.

I don't waste time straddling him. I'm ready, so ready to sink down on him, and we both moan in relief when I do. His hands find my hips, but before long, one is on my back, urging me forward, so I have to lock both of my arms, hands splayed on his chest so he can't pull me against him.

"Fuck, Leighton, please," he begs. "Need you closer."

If he could give me what I needed, I'd give everything of me in return, but I'm too raw already, too exposed to risk further damage. I may not recover as it is.

I lift and fall, over and over, letting the pleasure my body is feeling erase the pain I feel elsewhere. It's close to working when the world turns upside down, and Gaige flips me onto my back. The loss of stability makes me lose the upper hand, and he's right there, covering me completely, his lips on mine, tongue gaining access to my mouth when I gasp in surprise.

He swallows my moans, drinks my pain and my pleasure, begging for more with each slow roll of his hips.

"Every time," he pants. "Better than the last."

He urges one leg higher on his back until my knee is practically in his arm pit, and I'm so open for him. His pelvic bone rubs my clit every single time he finds the end of me, and I cling to him.

I fight the orgasm, knowing exactly what it means, but the skillful way he moves his hips makes holding it off for forever impossible.

"No," he whispers when my eyes close. "Look at me, Leighton."

I open my eyes, but only manage partway. It seems to be enough.

His muscles flex, and mine do too. His mouth hangs open, and I can't help but mirror the action. When he starts to tremble, his hips moving so slow, but so perfectly deep, my body does the exact same thing.

"We're going to come," he whispers as if his finger is over the detonation button for both of us.

I guess it is because it happens the second he whispers, "Right now, Leighton."

Silence. Calm. Stillness. We don't move. We don't breathe as our bodies speak to each other. He pulses, I clench. They communicate, thanking each other.

Saying goodbye.

Chapter 29

Gaige

"That," I say as I finally regain my breath and roll to the side.

"Can't happen again," she whispers.

Emotion clogs my throat. "Yeah. We have to stop before—"

"Yeah," she agrees before I can finish.

I guess even putting any of that emotional shit into the air wouldn't be right. It's proof that we're not on the same page.

"We had fun," I say with false cheer in my voice.

"Loads of fun," she agrees quickly, rolling over and grabbing a half-empty bottle of water from the bedside table and taking a drink.

She doesn't turn back to face me when she's done, and I can't resist the sight of her bare back. I lean into her, pressing my lips to her skin, my fingers tracing her side.

"Thank you for coming with me today." I rest my chin on her arm, but I can't see her face.

"Just holding up my end of the deal. I had a good time. You have a lovely family." She clears her throat. "See you Monday at work."

A dismissal. This is the end. And not just the end of the sex. I doubt there will be any more laughter or small talk. No more dinner conversations or chitchat. We won't strategize or joke about anything any longer. All of it is over because I fucked up. I let emotions get involved. I broke the rules, and it's not what she wanted.

In for a penny, in for a pound, right?

I tug on her arm, urging her to her back and press my mouth to hers one last time. I don't dip my tongue into her mouth. This kiss is a goodbye, not a way to sexually entice her. When I pull away, tears are rolling from each eye toward her temples. I wipe them away and kiss her again before crawling out of the bed and getting dressed. She never opens her eyes. All she would have to do is ask me to stay or reach for me, and I'd be hers, but she doesn't.

It says she doesn't want me here, can't wait for me to be gone. I linger a little longer by the door but know I can't keep invading her space any longer. I blame the sobs I hear as I near the elevator on a television in another person's room because Leighton Redmond is not a woman who really cries. She's too strong for that. She's not going to get overly emotional over something ending, especially when she's the one who wanted it over. She's the one who said it couldn't happen again.

I was going to say it was the best I've ever had. I was prepared to ask the woman to move to St. Louis, to move in with me. Hell, I was feeling so good, I would've agreed to hand calligraphy on the wedding invitations.

She said it couldn't happen again. She was done. I'm far from it.

But it reminded me of the change in her mood, the distance when we crawled into bed, the way she didn't want to kiss me.

Stupidly, I thought if I could show her with my body what I was feeling inside, it would win her over. I was wrong. I was so fucking wrong. It just blew up in my face. Instead of sticking with the status quo, I just lost everything.

I try to convince myself that I'm not upset. It was great sex. It was a good ride.

But I'm miserable by the time I get to my car. Upon walking into BBS, I'm either homicidal or suicidal and honestly, I haven't decided which. I consider myself a very sane person, always have, but I'm starting to understand a little why people lose their shit when they lose a significant other or get their heart broken.

I press my fingers to my chest as I walk into the breakroom. Is this what heartbreak feels like? Shit. No wonder people swear off love.

"What the fuck are you doing here?" I snap at Wren when I see him heading into his office.

"Whitney is in California visiting her friend Sarah," he says with a shrug, ignoring my attitude as if he expected me to have one. "I'm bored. Figured I'd get caught up on some work."

"You look like shite," Finn says from the couch.

I flip him the bird. It's the usual fuckers in the breakroom. Besides Wren, all of us men without significant others are here. I go ahead and give Brooks and Kit a middle finger just because, before sitting down on the couch.

"Why does it look like you lost a fight with a college douche?" Brooks asks.

"Family flag football," I say, looking down at myself. I probably should've gone home and changed.

I know I still have the scent of Leighton's body on my skin. Forgetting about her will be easier the sooner I can get that done.

For all his talk about getting some work done, Wren takes a seat on one of the sofas.

"How was Lala's party?" the computer nerd asks.

I look over at him, wondering how long it's going to take him to ask about Leighton.

"It was good."

"Will it be just a fall wedding, or a fall-themed wedding?"

I glare at Wren, but his eyes are on his phone.

The other guys look between us, confused, and this is how it goes. Wren doesn't spill the tea until the tea has elsewhere been spilled.

The huge television screen on the far wall changes from the news that's always on to an image taken from the party, and as much as I want to snap at Wren to take it down before the other guys can see it, I can't seem to manage to open my mouth. No wonder my family is already in love with the woman. They're only feeding off of what they were getting from us. As I look at the picture, I notice that it's not just me, but her as well. She was feeling some sort of way about me in that moment. It's in the angle of her face, the look in her eyes as she gazed back up at me, the soft smile on her lips. She's even up on the tips of her toes as if she needed her face just a little closer to mine as we swayed to the soft instrumental music playing on the speakers.

My left hand is on the curve of her ass, and I can almost feel the softness of that sundress even now, hours later. My other hand rests softly on her jawline, my thumb tracing her chin. We look like soulmates with the sun high above us and my mother's flowers creating the perfect backdrop for two people in love.

"Fuck, man," Brooks says as he turns and looks at the television. "Not you, too."

The woman talked about getting married, having my babies. I didn't freak out then, and even after what happened earlier in the hotel room, I'm not freaking out now. I don't want to run away and disappear. I don't want to laugh it off and pretend the conversation didn't happen. If she hadn't told me that Lala said some shit about deflowering her when I've spent so much time inside of her already—throwing that conversation in a different direction—maybe I could've mentioned it then, and things would be different right now.

Coming home to Leighton every night isn't close to the worst thing that could happen to me. If anything, I think I'd enjoy it. She's easy to talk to. She's fun as hell in bed. She's got a quick smile. She's smart, caring. Lala likes her. I wanted to punch Tyler in the throat just for looking at her. Hell, I wanted to kick Dad's feet out from under him when he kissed the back of her hand, and I know that man is dedicated to my mother.

I felt all of that. I felt it when we were just swaying to the music in that picture, and what did I do? I walked away from her. I knew it was ending. I knew she didn't want another thing from me, and instead of laying it all out in her hotel room, I just walked away.

To what, save face? I feel like a complete fool. I shake my head, my throat threatening to close and not for the first time today.

"Yep," Kit says, responding to Brooks. "And he's just now realizing it too."

"And from that sour look on his face," Finn adds. "He's already fucked it up."

Chapter 30

Leighton

I learned long ago that crying will get me nowhere. Even as a child I knew tears rarely amounted to anything. Mother didn't care if my face was streaked with wetness so long as it was dry by the time I was in public. They never bothered her. Eventually, I didn't even bother with them.

I have cried more in the last couple of weeks than I have in the last fifteen years, starting with the night I caught my father with Margaret. I've cried nearly nonstop since Saturday afternoon, since Gaige walked out of this hotel room. My throat is raw from it. My eyes itchy and swollen.

But I made myself a deal before bed last night. I had to get them all out and today I was a new person. I was done crying over men who disappoint me. I was done resting my happiness in their hands, giving them the ability to hurt me.

I set the alarm, and at eleven fifty last night, I washed my face and put an end to it. Technically, the last tear fell a minute after midnight, but I'm calling it a win.

I've alternated between hot and cool cloths this morning to try and get the swelling down in my face, and I'll use makeup to cover up the rest. I doubt he'll be paying much attention to me as it is. Getting dressed is easy, another blouse, another pencil skirt, another pair of sensible heels. I have a forty-minute ride to the airport to prepare myself to see him, and that gives me plenty of time to get a better handle on my emotions, one last chance to lock everything up tight.

Before leaving the hotel room, I check my email one last time, shocked when I see the itinerary for the week rather than a termination letter. The car is waiting by the curb as always, but when the driver pulls the door open, Gaige is waiting inside instead of the back being empty.

"Mr. Ward," I say as I settle in the seat. I immediately pop my AirPods in my ears.

He pulls the left one out, holding it in his palm as he smiles at me.

From the look in his eyes, I can see that he'd be perfectly fine with continuing the sexual relationship we started, but that's impossible for me. I don't know that it has ever been just sex after I knew he wasn't married. It's going to be hard enough working with him. Sleeping with him would be torture on my heart.

"No," I tell him before he can speak. He's too smooth, too convincing. I can't risk it. "We're both professionals. Unless it has to do with work, it doesn't come out of your mouth."

His face falls. "You're sure?"

"One hundred percent."

He drops the AirPod into my hand and doesn't say another word.

The ride to the airport is silent as well as the flight to Georgia. He doesn't say a word other than introductions during our first meeting. He doesn't interject or offer information, and we leave that appointment much the way we've left all the others. I'm not southern, but I know *bless your heart* when we explained what we were looking for wasn't a good thing.

The ride to the hotel is quiet and miserable. I know he's doing exactly what I asked of him, but he's doing it so thoroughly it feels almost insulting, like a childlike silent treatment.

He waits for me on the curb when we arrive, but his attention is on his phone. We walk side by side, but we might as well be strangers.

As usual, I stand to the side while he speaks with the desk clerk, grabbing our room keys. When he returns, he hands me the small cards with two keys in it, making me realize he's been keeping the extra one of mine each time we've traveled. He no longer has an interest in it now. I should feel safety in that, but I don't. It's just more evidence of his disinterest.

"Dinner?" he asks, his eyes still down on the electronic device he was focused on during the car ride back from our appointment.

"No, thank you," I say, praying he'll remind me that it's in the contract and required.

He simply gives me a little nod and walks in the direction of the restaurant alone. Pain nearly cripples me right there in the lobby, seeing how easy it is for him to switch gears. Two days ago, he made his family think he loved me and tonight, he'll probably fuck another woman in the room beside mine.

I head to the elevator, reminding myself that my tears are done. Only four more days of this, and I'll have some time to myself. I can handle this. I head up to my room. Maybe there's a spa nearby. A full body massage sounds perfect right about now, and I've been so busy the last couple of years, that I haven't had time to schedule one.

Once I get to my room, nothing could convince me to leave. Maybe the thoughts of going back out and not holing myself inside were just false bravado to get me moving so some poor employee didn't need to spend time scraping me off the floor. Maybe it was the motivation to keep me from heading into the restaurant and asking Gaige to share a little of his assholishness so I could have some of that black heart I swore to him I had when I slapped him.

I change into my pajamas and order pasta. I eat more than I should, and when my tears drip into my pillow, I don't count them because my face is buried in the fabric. If they never meet the air then they don't exist, right?

Chapter 31

Gaige

I'm not surprised she turned down dinner.

She's not said a word to me all day since she declared it work only.

I didn't want to upset her more, so I kept my damn mouth shut. Yet, as the day progressed, it seemed like giving her exactly what she wanted only pissed her off more. Women are so fucking complicated.

I opt for the bar instead of dinner. I dine alone often, but doing it with Leighton upstairs just seems stupid. A liquid diet seems like the best idea ever after a shitty day, but I still keep it to a two-drink maximum. Three may have me knocking on her door because I stupidly gave her both of her damn door keys.

When the women start swarming, I itch to pull the gold band out of my pocket, but I remember I lost it somewhere in Texas.

I settle my tab and walk out of the hotel, waving off the guy out front when he asks if I need a cab. I stand on the sidewalk, wondering just what in the hell I'm doing with my life. I need help. I need answers. I know the solution to my problems, and she's upstairs, but there are roadblocks leading to her, ones she's putting up, and I don't know how to knock them down. Hell, I don't know if she's even receptive. I don't know if she's interested.

I didn't think she was, but I saw the picture Tyler took and posted to his Instagram account. She wasn't pretending in that picture. She was as lost in me as I was in her. No one existed in that moment but us. She wasn't playing a role. That wasn't her part of the deal. She may not be in love with me but she's fucking close. I did something or said something to fuck it up, to make her pull back, and until I figure out what it is and fix it, I'm stuck.

I pull out my phone, scrolling through my options.

I could call Wren, but I already know what his advice would be. He'd tell me to tie her up, duct tape her mouth, and only take it off to choke her with my cock until she agrees to hear me out. I get the feeling that Leighton wouldn't agree to those terms, but my dick seems to think trying it would be worth it.

I shake my head and take a few more steps further away from the hotel.

I hit call on Tyler's contact. He seems out of breath when he answers. "Hey, bro. What's up?"

"I fucked up with Leighton."

"Already?"

He pants again, then groans.

"What the fuck are you doing?"

"Don't ask." The phone seems like it's further away when I hear, "Aw fuck, do that again."

"Jesus, Tyler. Did you answer the phone while getting head?"

I hear a long drawn-out moan. "Feel how deep that one is, Bree? Can you work it out? Harder. Yeah. That's it. What did you say, Gaige?"

"Are you getting head?"

"Fuck, I wish. Deep tissue massage. I'm helping one of the students learn some new techniques."

"Roll over," I hear a woman say, her voice far from professional. "I'll do your quads. Let me grab some more oil."

"Hey, turn the camera toward us so we can evaluate your technique later," my brother says.

"That girl's going to end up on your dick," I mutter.

"From your mouth to God's ears," he whispers. "What do you need?"

"Help with Leighton."

"Look what I found, Dr. Ward."

"Orgasms," he hisses into the phone. "Oh, this is a naked massage?"

The call drops.

So fucking helpful. I grip my phone in my hand, barely holding on to the thing instead of throwing it across the damn street.

I hang my head as I place the next call. It may be opening up too many doors, ones I may have trouble closing later, but I couldn't not try to win this girl over or back. Hell, I have no idea where I stand right now.

"Gaige?"

"Hi," I say into the phone.

"Is something wrong?"

"Everything is fine."

"You're sure?"

"No."

"Is it work?"

"No."

"Is it family?"

"No."

"Then it's Leighton."

"Yes, ma'am."

"Already?"

"Lala." I groan.

She chuckles, her laughter a tinkle in my ear that would normally make me smile.

"Help me."

"How mad is she?"

"She won't even talk to me."

"Will she stay in the same room with you?"

"Only because we have to work together."

"And when the workday is over?"

"She's gone. Wouldn't have dinner with me."

"Have you tried talking with her?"

"She said work only."

"Did she tell you she hates you?"

"No."

"What did she say when you told her you loved her today?"

I'm silent.

"You did tell her that today, right? Women need to hear it every day."

"I haven't—we haven't gotten that far."

"You love that woman, Gaige," she snaps. "You need to tell her."

"I don't know that it's going to work right now. What else do you suggest?"

She gives me a different laugh, one that would make me think she's going to suggest the same thing Tyler did if she didn't mention deflowering to Leighton at her birthday party.

"I always enjoyed flowers when PopPop gave them to me."

"You always had flowers, Lala."

"PopPop was always in trouble." She takes a reflective moment, a gentle sigh leaving her lips. "He was a pissy Italian who let his mouth get away from him without thinking, so he had lots to make up for."

"I don't think flowers are going to fix this," I tell her, but I'd buy every one on this side of the Mason Dixon if I thought it would.

"Grand gestures are nice as well, but the apologies that always stood out the most to me were the ones when PopPop actually opened his mouth and told me what he was sorry for and why. When he used his words. Sounds simple, but apologies are anything but if you think about it."

"I'm not good with those types of words," I mutter, knowing I'm shit with emotions even less.

"And that's what makes the gesture so grand, my dear, but you make up with her. I'm expecting more great grandbabies. Leighton sure is beautiful. I'll never forgive you if you mess this up, Gaige. Promise me, Gaige. Promise me you'll marry that girl someday."

There's a long pause as I stare up at the hotel, knowing there's very little chance that she's up there looking down at me.

"I promise, Lala."

After I get off the phone with my grandmother, I spend an hour walking the block around the hotel, unsure of what kind of gesture would be grand enough to prove to Leighton that I'm no longer the man she met in the bar, that I'm worth taking a risk on. I can't guarantee she'll listen. She doesn't want me to talk to her, so that narrows down my options, so then it hits me.

If I can't tell her, I have to show her.

I make a half a dozen calls, regretfully getting Wren on board who seems to have been waiting for my call since Saturday afternoon.

Chapter 32

Leighton

Hope is so easy to build and so easy to crush. My phone ringing at nine in the evening shouldn't light me up, but it does. That hope vanishes just as fast when I see my mother's name on my screen instead of Gaige's.

"Hello," I answer, holding the phone to my ear and sitting up in bed.

"Leighton?" she snaps. "Were you already in bed? Are you ill?"

"I'm not ill. I've been traveling. It's jet lag."

It's probably more like depression, but I'd never admit that to my mother. She'd tell me to pop a pill and get over myself.

"I've been expecting your call."

"I've been working," I tell her.

"Redmond Enterprises no longer exists."

I don't respond. She knows I know this. Chelsea and I are close. There's not much going on with the family that I don't know. She's trying to bait me, and I'm sick of feeding into it. She's no longer my puppeteer. If I'm not working for her company, she no longer controls my strings.

"The company fell apart in your absence."

"You closed the doors and fired everyone. That has nothing to do with me, Mother."

"Do not take that tone with me, Leighton."

I hit the button to put her on speaker and drop the phone to the bed. It takes too much energy to hold the damn thing while being berated.

"I need you to come home."

"I'm under a contract."

"Break it."

"They could sue, Mother."

"And we could pay it, Leighton. I need you to clean this mess up."

"Excuse me?"

"I need Redmond Enterprises back up and running."

I blink down at the phone. That company is what I thought I always wanted and hearing her say this to me should make me want to do back flips, but the thought of leaving St. Louis makes my skin crawl despite knowing there's nothing between Gaige and me, at least on his end of things.

Is it what I still want?

"It's now or never, Leighton. What's it going to be?"

"How much time do I have?"

"I need you in the office tomorrow. If you're not back, the company is done. I already have a prospective buyer. You've been wasting your time, doing God knows what while everything is just burning to the ground up here. Your lack of dedication to this family is speaking very loudly right now."

"I'll—"

Three beeps indicate the dropped call.

My blood boils as I crawl off the bed and pace the room. My mother infuriates me. I swipe my phone from the bed and call Chelsea.

"Hello?" she says upon answering.

"Mom just called."

"Who is this? It's a little late for telemarketers."

I huff. "Okay, not in the mood I see."

"Sorry it's been so long since I called."

I haven't spoken to her since Thursday. It may not be long for some siblings, but we usually talk every day.

"What did she say?"

"She wants me to pack up, break the contract with Blackbridge, come back to New York, and clean up the mess she made with the company."

"I thought you were getting fired."

This was the last conversation I had with her after leaving Sandra Halen's office and telling her office clerk to tell her to go fuck herself. I was certain Deacon Black would get wind of it and let me go. I haven't heard from him.

"I haven't been fired. I told her I'd be in breach of contract. She said if he sued that she'd pay the penalty."

"Do you think he'll sue?"

"Probably not. More than likely, he'll be happy to see me gone. I haven't benefited his company at all."

Gaige will probably be happy he'll no longer have to work with me as well. It's a win-win for everyone except my poor, battered heart.

"Then come home. I miss you."

It's almost enough to have me rushing around the room to pack my things.

"I don't know," I tell her instead.

"Because there's something else keeping you there."

There is subjective because I'm not even in St. Louis. There is Gaige Ward.

She's too on the nose, and I haven't mentioned much more than him getting on my nerves, but as my sister and best friend, she's all too aware of my tells.

"You're falling for him."

"Who?" I ask, playing stupid.

"That jerk."

I'm silent.

I plop down on the bed, rubbing at my forehead just to spite my mother because she'd warned me of early wrinkles.

"He took me to a family function on Saturday."

"Are they horrible? I'd never force Gabe to go to any of ours. Ever. I love him too much."

"It was amazing," I mutter. "They actually love each other. Did you know people like that exist?"

"Kind of a culture shock, huh? I felt so weird after I went to a baby shower for Gabe's sister before we got married. I felt sick halfway through and wanted to leave."

I pull the phone away from my face, glaring down at the thing as if it personally offended me before putting it back to my ear.

"I felt that exact same way. Why did you never tell me?"

"I didn't want to sound like I was bragging. We didn't have that. You didn't have that. I felt guilty that I was going to get to have that while you weren't."

"I never would've been mad that you were going to be a part of that," I say, tears once again threatening. I hate that she hid part of her joy to protect me, and it's just one more thing our mother managed to mess up for us.

"Did they hug you?"

"Like they'd known me for years?"

"Did you cry?"

"Right on his grandmother's shoulder, and it's like she knew I needed it without even knowing my story. Do we look that broken?"

"Old people somehow just know. Gabe's mom just patted my hand and sat quietly with me. She let me cry in her bedroom and offered me her makeup when I was done. I looked horrible when I walked out. You know how tan they are and we're pasty white, but they were all so kind. No one said a thing."

"I was wrong," I confess.

"About what?"

"There are more than a few good men left in the world."

"I knew you were wrong when you said it, but you wouldn't have believed me if I had argued with you at the time. Is the guy you're working with, the one you're falling for, a good man?"

"I don't know," I answer truthfully.

Maybe. Possibly.

But he still walked away from me. He didn't fight for me. He didn't hold me and tell me that he wanted more.

So there's a chance he isn't.

Or maybe I'm not his one, when I so desperately want to be.

It happens like that sometimes.

Unrequited feelings are a real thing.

People suffer with it daily.

I just know I can't do it any longer.

I can't face him. I'm not strong enough.

"Have you told him how you feel about him?"

"No."

"You should."

Weren't the tears on my cheeks Saturday afternoon enough? They should've been. Had I seen them on his face, I wouldn't have been able to walk away. I would've had a conversation at least. Unless the sight of them were enough of a conversation for him. Unless the sight of them were the only answer to unspoken questions he needed.

"I'm coming home," I tell her. "I'll see you soon."

We end the call, and I pack. For the last two weeks I thought I had nothing to go home to, but I can throw myself right back into work. I didn't need a man or love or all of the things that go with it before, and I sure as hell don't need it now. This hurts too much. It's not worth it as far as I'm concerned.

I make flight arrangements on my phone, grateful to find a late flight leaving in two hours. I leave the room, stepping out of the way for a delivery guy with a paper-wrapped package before climbing on the elevator. While in the cab, I shoot an email to Deacon, apologizing for the short notice, explaining that I completely understand if he feels the need to seek legal action for breaking the contract, but my family needs me back in the city. I keep it professional and short.

As the wheels of the plane touch the tarmac at La Guardia, I imagine it's only going to take about twenty years for me to forget that Gaige Ward ever existed at all. Thank God, I have a lot of other things to focus on.

Chapter 33

Gaige

My fingers are sore from drumming them on my thigh for countless hours. The arrangements were made. The package is marked as delivered, but she hasn't come to me. She hasn't knocked on my door. I made sure to include in the note that I was across the hall this time because the hotel couldn't accommodate adjoining rooms.

She hasn't stepped foot out of her room either and I'm sure I have a circle around my eye from constantly pressing it to the peephole in the door. She doesn't answer the door when I give up on waiting and step across the hall and knock. I don't hear a peep when I bang louder. She doesn't even tell me to fuck off when I beg her to open the door.

She doesn't show the next morning when the car arrives to take us to our appointment for the day, and I don't get in the car either. I ask the driver to wait and head back inside, determined to kick her door in.

"Mr. Ward!" The front desk clerk waves at me as I stride toward the small bank of elevators.

"Yes," I say as I approach, agitated at being stopped on my mission up to her.

At this point, I'm worried sick that something has happened. She's fallen in the shower, or she has some debilitating illness that makes it impossible to answer her phone or the door.

"You've been listed as a secondary on Ms. Redmond's room. A delivery man left this for her, but she checked out last night."

"I'm sorry. What?"

"Ms. Redmond. Room 914? She checked out last night, and he was unable to deliver a package." I follow the point of her finger.

It sits behind the desk, unopened.

Is that her answer?

Part of me says yes, but if she didn't open it, then maybe no. If she saw it, she would understand.

"Are you able to make arrangements for me to have that shipped back?"

"To the company?"

"To my home," I clarify.

"Of course, Mr. Ward."

I spend the next twenty minutes making those arrangements, growing increasingly frustrated because this isn't something they normally do and it takes more time than it should. Eventually, I step away with confirmation numbers and a guarantee that it will be at my condo within three business days.

My phone rings on my way back into my own room.

Deacon.

"Hello," I snap.

"Ms. Redmond is breaking her contract with BBS."

"Okay. You just found this out?"

"She sent an email last night."

"And I'm just now hearing about this?"

"I'm fucking drowning right now, man. Little Deke has reflux. Do you know how irritable a newborn with reflux is? I haven't slept in what feels like months."

"I'm sorry," I tell him with sincerity.

I get the feeling I won't be sleeping well any time soon either.

"I can work the rest of the contacts," I assure him, but I know without a doubt, none of them will be fruitful. Leighton was right, these women have no interest in what we're offering.

Deacon sighs. "My focus shifted when you guys were in Texas. The reality of having a female team shifted last week."

"You told me last week to work hard in Georgia," I growl, remembering that I begged him to let me in on the damn game plan. I had a feeling this wasn't about building a damn female team. "What exactly is the plan now?"

"I was vetting Leighton Redmond for BBS."

My stomach turns. If he tells me to go get her, I may cry. Not only have I lost her for myself, but I've lost her again for Blackbridge.

"I want her to be our liaison. We need help organizing you guys. Pam wants to cut hours, and I need someone knowledgeable, someone really good with handling difficult people, someone good with the media and calling people out on their bullshit. I need someone with integrity, and I knew she was the one when she walked out on Sandra Halen. Did you know she found that poor assistant of Halen's a job with one of the other people you spoke with? He started work with them today."

"I didn't know that."

"See, she's humble, too. We need some of that around here."

"If you had told me—"

"Then you wouldn't have fucked it up?"

"Maybe," I mutter

"This isn't on you," Deacon says. "She went back to take over Redmond Enterprises. We lost her, Gaige."

I lost so much more.

"I'll have Wren make arrangements for you to get back home. We have shit piling up here. I know you don't like to travel much."

"Thanks, man," I tell him, and the call ends.

Was she already gone before I came back upstairs last night? Did I not try hard enough? Did I push too hard?

Jesus, this love shit is stupid. So fucking stupid. I should call Wren and tell him to get me a flight out of Atlanta to New York, but that won't work. She had a chance to at least say goodbye. I've texted her this morning. Of course, I didn't know she was gone, but she hasn't responded. She didn't CC me on the email last night. She purposely left me in the dark so she could make her escape. She wanted to put distance between us before I found out.

It speaks volumes. I pack, growing angrier and angrier at myself, at her, at everything, and everyone.

Things were perfect before her. My life was just damn fine before she came in and wrenched open the protective barriers around my heart. I didn't want or need these emotions. I just wanted fun and powerful orgasms, and somehow, she managed to just slip right in with her pretty smiles and that amazing laugh. She's like carbon monoxide, silent and deadly.

I get a text alert from Wren, letting me know I have an hour and a half to get to the airport. It's like he's punishing me for Leighton going back to New York. Atlanta traffic is horrific on a good day.

I took his advice last night when I asked about certain companies to use locally for what I needed. I took Lala's advice with the grand gesture bullshit. Hell, I was going to take Tyler's advice on the orgasms if she came to me.

I had open ears, and all of it backfired in my damn face.

Chapter 34

Leighton

The familiar thick air of New York doesn't bring any form of relief. If anything, it suffocates me even further. I send Mom a text, letting her know I'm back in town, meeting the ridiculous deadline she set. I go home only long enough to shower and change. If I crawl into bed to sleep, I may never leave again.

I head to the Redmond Enterprises offices through muscle memory alone because exhaustion drags me down. I'm spent, both emotionally and physically, but I'm determined. If my mother thinks I can handle rebuilding the company, then I'm going to give it my best shot.

At least that's the pep talk I've been giving myself for the last eight hours since I got off the phone with Chelsea.

It's not unusual to step off the elevator onto the Redmond Enterprises floor to complete silence. I would get to work fairly early most days. I pride myself in creating a happy environment for our employees and sometimes it's the little things that bring people the greatest comforts. One of those was always having coffee waiting when they arrived.

Today is different. I'm not walking into a freshly cleaned office smelling like lemons from the overnight crew. The offices are a mess, the bullpen in complete disarray from the rush of people leaving. Chairs are several feet from their respective desks, paperwork litters the floor—client confidentiality be damned—one computer keyboard hangs abandoned from its cord. This, I imagine, is what the place would look like during the apocalypse. My stomach turns into a knot.

The people who worked here were loyal. They worked hard, and we treated them fairly. My dad prided himself on taking care of his employees, citing that it helped with retention. Looking back, maybe it was guilt over what he was doing to destroy his own family that made him be so nice to others.

I avoid an overturned trash can, ignore the open door to my former office and walk into my father's. I don't bother turning on the light. The sun coming up over the horizon is enough for me right now. I don't know that I could stomach the sight of the place in full color right now. I crash in his office chair and take a moment for myself. With elbows on his—my—desk, I rest my forehead on my hands. I haven't even gotten started, and already I'm overwhelmed.

I know the people I worked with liked me, but there's no way I could convince them to come back, not when Estelle Redmond controls the company. They'd never take the chance that she'll have another mood swing and pull the rug out from under them again. Some of the employees have been working here for decades. Melinda in HR was Dad's first hire and has been around as long as the company has been around.

My heart breaks for each of them.

It breaks for the position I've been put in because it seems so impossible, and as I sit here, the more I realize I want no part of it. It's not the work. I'm a hard worker. My work ethic is strong, determined. It's the fact that a woman who has always been short on praise and long on criticism, a woman who prides herself on being an astute businesswoman, made a brash decision, creating a mess and now she expects me to clean it up. She's dangling the only thing I thought I ever wanted in front of me like I'm a starving horse and she's the abusive trainer holding the golden carrot. She expects me to bite, exactly like I've always done. Of course, I'm going to bite. It's what I've been trained to do, groomed to do.

Maybe it was the jab about dedication to the family that angers me so much. Her contribution has always been money. She makes a lot of it, and to her that should be enough. The time together and love shouldn't matter. It never has.

This is my legacy, my birthright. Maybe Chelsea was smart in wanting nothing to do with it even though she's always said nursing and not business was her calling. She hasn't severed ties completely with the family, but she's managed to create enough distance to find her own little slice of happiness, including Gabe's family who loves her, treats her like one of their own.

Refusing to let my mind wander back to the birthday party, I take a shuddering breath. I can't think of his touch, or his lips, or the last kiss we shared. It hurts too much. I'm too weak right now, too tired. My defenses aren't strong enough to fight those memories off. That kiss to my temple was final. I have to remember that.

Did he know that last time was the end? Was that why it was so sweet, so all-consuming?

I fought it as long as I could. I didn't want sweet and considerate. Those are things that hit you in the chest. Things would be different if he had pulled my hair, smacked my ass and walked out of there and said it was a great lay like he had the first time. Why did he have to wipe my tears and kiss me softly? It made me feel even more used. It broke me, ruined me, left me battered.

"Fuck him," I mutter, refusing to cry again.

I heave a sigh as I lift my head, scooting the chair closer to the desk so I can reach the computer keyboard. I have work, something I know I can get lost in. I move the mouse, and nothing happens. After pressing a key on the keyboard, the screen flashes once, and that's it. Everything is powered up, and the damn thing is dead.

I know in my heart, without having to look, that my dad knew Mom was going to do something with the company. He killed the entire system. He knew she was going to be vindictive, so he decided to do it first.

It's the final straw, and I'm done. Picking up where everything left off two weeks ago is one thing. Starting from the absolute bottom isn't going to happen. I did that on my own in St. Louis, and although I did it with Blackbridge with absolutely no success, I can keep doing it without the shadows and stains of Redmond Enterprises weighing me down.

I stand calmly, looking down at my father's neat desk. Everything in here is orderly, just as it has been my entire life.

I scream my frustrations as I sweep everything to the floor. I hate him. I hate my mother. I hate Gaige. I hate that I still love each of them even though loving them does nothing but cost me.

I wipe away the tears on my cheeks, drop the office keys on the desk and walk out of the office for the final time. I don't look back even knowing that I'll never step inside again.

I'd rather beg for money on the filthy streets of New York than clean up another person's mess.

Choke on that carrot, Mom, because I'd rather starve.

I didn't pay much attention when I came home earlier, but my apartment is in much better condition than the office. I prepared to leave when I went to St. Louis. The trip was originally planned through Redmond Enterprises, and I knew several weeks in advance that I was going to be traveling. The single houseplant I had was dead long before I left, so I don't feel guilty at seeing the wilted ivy in the corner of the living room. I'll dispose of it after I get some sleep.

My fridge is empty, but that doesn't stop me from opening the thing just in case.

I stripped my bed and laundered the linens, placing them in vacuum-sealed bags with a dryer sheet, something I'd somehow retained from small talk in the employee breakroom.

As I roll my suitcase toward my bedroom, I realize my apartment is just as sterile as Gaige's office is. I've stayed in hotel rooms that have more life to them than my home does, and it makes me feel even more depressed.

I know he works a lot. It's one of the things we discussed.

Does he also use the free time he did manage to find to get lost in someone else to take the edge off his loneliness like I do? Did he do that last night after I declined dinner?

Not my business. Not my concern.

And none of it matters.

I've already sent the email to Mr. Black. I no longer work for BBS, despite the reason for coming back to New York no longer existing. I won't go crawling back to either. I won't be in this apartment much longer. I may not be in the city much longer. It won't take long before I have to start dipping into savings, but if I'm smart, I can make that money stretch for a while. I'm not a big spender. I haven't had time to spend money because of how much I work—worked. I hate that I have to start thinking about things in the past tense, but I guess it's good to get used to it.

My stomach grumbles, but I ignore it. The only things I need are a shower and sleep.

Chapter 35

Gaige

I'm back at the BBS offices because where else would I be? Licking my wounds in private would probably make more sense, but silence for some reason hurts more than the chatter in the breakroom.

All day the guys spoke around me, but mostly left me out of their ribbing. When they did bring me into their conversation, it had nothing to do with Leighton or the job we were working on. Either they're great at reading my mood, or they were briefed to leave me the fuck alone about it. As the day drew on and turned into evening, the majority of the guys drifted out, the ones in relationships heading home to their significant others.

Before, I would cringe at the thought of having to go home to the same damn person day in and day out, but picturing Leighton as the woman I got to leave the office and run home to each day? Hell, I wouldn't even want to come to work. I knew I'd try to find a way to convince Deacon to let me work from home. He wanted her to come to work for BBS, and that sounds like the perfect plan to me. She could ride my cock while talking on the phone to organize shit. I could type up court briefs for clients while she sucked my cock. It would be the perfect work situation for both of us.

Then I remember that she's gone. She's in New York and I'm here. She's got no interest in me or my cock. What we had no longer exists. It has run its course. She had enough and dipped out.

The elevator dings, and a thrill of excitement runs through me. It's late, like two in the morning late, and I've been the only one here for two hours. Jude got his happily ever after this way not long ago. Parker showed up and kissed him not ten feet away from where I'm sitting, but it isn't Leighton walking in here in the middle of the night to confess her undying love.

It's just fucking Wren, and he looks pissed.

"Hey," I say when he approaches. "What are you doing here?"

"Deacon is a vindictive dick," Wren mutters.

I cock an eyebrow. Deacon is a levelheaded guy, always has been.

"What did you do?"

Wren narrows his eyes at me. "Nothing."

"Something," I argue.

"I helped him."

"You helped him, helped him, or you Wren helped him?"

"Is there a difference?" I slow-blink at him. "He couldn't get Deke to stop crying. I offered to hold him."

"And?"

"I held the baby."

"And?"

"The baby stopped crying."

"Okay."

"And now I'm here in the middle of the night because he needs something."

Maybe Deacon is a vindictive dick if he's forcing Wren out of bed in the middle of the night because he was able to get the baby to stop crying when he couldn't.

Wren heads to the coffee pot.

"It's like the man knows just when I'm about to have fun with my girl," he mutters.

"Aren't you always about to have fun with your girl?"

He and Whitney have a very active home life.

"Yeah." He chuckles. "But tonight, man, you should've seen her. We ordered this thing online that she—"

"Enough, Wren. I don't want to know."

He chuckles. "Still having girl trouble?"

"I'm here alone, aren't I?"

"Don't give up. I saw that picture. The proof is there."

"She didn't even see it. She left before the delivery was made. She hasn't returned my calls. Long distance won't work. She went back to take over Redmond Enterprises. She's going to be busy. I'm busy. Taking over Redmond Enterprises is her dream. I'm not going to stand in the way of that. My family is here. I'm not moving to New York. It's good that this happened now instead of later. Later would've been harder."

"Are you trying to convince me or yourself?" Wren asks.

"I'm—"

My phone chirps a text in my pocket, and I pull the thing out.

Nothing good comes from middle of the night communications.

Wren is calling after me because I'm running from the office a second later. My heart is racing, my palms sweating.

I don't remember the drive, or parking, or rushing through the front. When I get to the information desk, I have to be asked more than once before I can remember why I'm even here.

"Imogene Rose Ward," I tell the tired-looking woman.

She directs me to the floor, and then she has to do it a second time when I stare at her blankly because I couldn't hear her voice over the pounding in my ears the first time around.

Time slows, the elevator taking a thousand years. The waiting room is already full. Mom is crying. Dad is visibly upset, but I can tell he's trying to be strong. Tyler looks as destroyed as I feel. Uncle Eddie and his family are here, huddled together and weeping, and I know I'm too late. I stumble up to my mother, pulling her to my chest. Her tears dampen my shirt, and it surprises me that it's the first sensation I notice, the second the warmth of my dad's palm on my back.

"She's gone," I whisper, wondering where my own tears are.

I'm devastated, and I feel the pain of it, so where are the tears?

"No," Mom says, pulling her head back, and hope blooms like a garden in my chest.

Then I see her stricken face.

"Not yet."

"There's nothing they can do," Dad says, his voice husky and riddled with pain. "The damage from the heart attack was too extensive. She wouldn't survive surgery."

"You need to go and say goodbye."

"I can't," I argue. "I won't."

If I don't, then she'll live. I know it in my soul. I don't care how childlike it seems.

Mom cups my cheek. "Gaige, go."

I nod, and she guides me to the desk lined with kind-looking nurses. No words are spoken as they lead me to one of the small rooms. This isn't the first time I've seen Lala in a hospital bed. She had a hip replacement several years ago, but she was lucid and smiling by the time we were able to see her. Now, she's frail and tiny in the too-big bed, wires and cords attached to her body, machines beeping all around her. At first, they give me a tiny jolt of hope. Why have them if they aren't going to help?

But my mother and father wouldn't lie to me. If there was hope to be had, they would be the first to try and build that in Tyler and me. They've always been like that with us growing up. Sometimes it worked in our favor, sometimes it didn't. It was healthy either way.

If they say there is none, it's because there isn't.

The tears I couldn't find in the waiting room find me as I sit in the single chair beside the bed. Her hand is cooler than it should be, and I clasp it between mine to warm it. She doesn't move, doesn't smile the way she always does when I'm near her, and the tears fall harder. It isn't lost on me that it's technically the day after her ninetieth birthday. This time of year is always going to be so bittersweet for the family going forward.

I'm grateful for speaking with her so recently, and it's the recollection of that last conversation that makes the sob bubble from my throat. I made promises to her, ones I wanted to keep then, ones I know I have to keep now.

And yet, I gave up on Leighton so easily.

Hell, just before getting the text from Tyler, I gave Wren a long list of reasons why we could never work out. I'll be damned if all of those reasons will stop me. I hate the big city, but if living in New York is what she wants, I'll gladly go there for her. I can deal with smog and noise so long as I can breathe in her scent and listen to her say my name.

"I think I can convince her to marry in St. Louis," I whisper, my lips closer to her weathered hand. "Early fall when the leaves are just starting to turn so we have the best of both worlds, the greens and reds, you know? Leighton is going to be absolutely stunning. I'll cry when I first see her. I just know I will. I'm going to hate the slow beat of the wedding march. I'll want to speed it up. I'll want her to be mine quicker, but you already know how impatient I am."

I keep my eyes lowered, wanting to remember Lala as the smiling woman I've known all my life, not the fragile one lying in the bed. I curl her fingers around mine when she doesn't do it on her own.

"I won't relinquish her for a single dance. I won't allow her to leave my sight for a second that night. I don't think I'd be able to breathe without my arms around her. I'll watch her closely, every smile, every glance, keeping a close eye on her face, the way her cheeks will pink as she enjoys the wine, and I'll know Lala. I'll know when it's time to leave. Our babies are going to be beautiful, and she's going to be gorgeous carrying them. I'll pamper her, treat her like a queen every second I'm allowed to love her. I'll cherish Leighton, Lala. I'll do my best not to be like PopPop. I'll try my hardest not to have to spend much time apologizing to her."

I take a moment to wipe tears from my eyes on my shoulder because I can't imagine pulling my hands from hers even for a second.

"If we have a girl, we'll name her Rose. I won't make her suffer with Imogene. I know you hate that name. I know I'm making a lot of promises, but I plan to keep every single one of them. You've always had faith in me, Lala, and it's not misplaced. I love you."

I press my forehead to our combined hands as the beeping from the machines change. I know what it means, and it kills me that there's nothing that I can do about it.

Hospital staff come in and the beeping stops.

I know what that means too.

Chapter 36

Leighton

I slept for seven hours, woke up, ordered food for delivery, ate, and then went right back to sleep.

I'm still a little out of it when a text from an unknown number wakes me up at two-thirty in the morning.

Lala had a heart attack. He needs you.

It didn't come from Gaige's phone. I blocked his number. It was the only step I could take to try to be strong. If he called or messaged propositioning me, I know I couldn't resist. The walls were nonexistent, and hope is a fickle dangerous thing.

My heart is pounding in my chest as I fly out of bed. I grab literally nothing. I change into clothes decent enough for public, grab my wallet, phone, and I leave.

I book a flight in the cab on the way to the airport. Going to him is instinctual. I don't ask questions.

A second text comes as I'm boarding my flight which includes the name of the hospital and Lala's full, legal name. I stare at it until my phone threatens to die, and then I have to darken my screen to conserve the battery. The ride to the hospital is spent with twitching fingers and a knee that won't stop shaking. The cabbie doesn't seem to mind. The man is lost in his own world, and I'm grateful for the lack of forced small talk.

By the time I get to the information desk at the hospital, it's been five hours since I received the text.

"Good morning," the woman says in greeting as I approach.

"Hi. I need the room number for Imogene Rose Ward."

Her fingers work over the keyboard in front of her, and then I see it. The flinch. I work with people. I'm an expert in tells. I know it's bad news. The worst news.

"No," I whisper, pain hitting me in the chest, knotting my stomach.

She raises her eyes to mine. "I'm so sorry."

I know she's going to tell me that she can't give me any information, but she already revealed the secret I was hoping wasn't going to be true. I back away slowly, the tears already pooling in my eyes. I manage to nod, but words right now are impossible. I hope my weak smile is enough.

Exiting the hospital, I stand to the side and cry for a woman I barely knew, a woman I met only once, remembering the way she clung to Gaige when we were leaving like she just couldn't get enough of his warmth. Her eyes fluttered closed as if he had the ability to breathe life back into her tired bones, as if he was the boy she loved most in the world.

Lala's death for Gaige won't be the same as my grandparents' deaths were for me. He was loved by her. He has lost something, someone that brought value to his life.

I pull my phone from my pocket and fire off a text.

Where is he?

Office.

I'm not nervous this time heading to BBS. My fingers aren't trembling. My knee isn't shaking. I'm determined. He needs me, and although I have no idea how I'm going to be received, I'll be what he needs. If he needs a shoulder, I have two. If he tells me to fuck off, I can do that as well, but I need him to know the options are his.

But as the cab draws closer and the bravado fades away, nervousness settles in. It could go either way. He could push me away because his pain is just too big or he could pull me close, cling to me now only to push me away later when it subsides. Either way, I have to go to him. I want to ease his burden.

Pam looks somber when I step off the elevator.

She has to be aware of the contract I've broken when she sees me because she holds up her hand to prevent me from walking further into the office. It seems I'm no longer welcome. My access is being denied.

"I'm here to see Mr. Ward," I tell her, having no idea why I'm acting so formal when I'm in jeans and a t-shirt.

"Gaige isn't receiving visitor's today, Ms. Redmond."

Pam's phone rings, and as she answers, her eyes stay on me as if she's afraid I'll dart through the office and defy her. Honestly, I'm considering it. She nods a few times, saying nothing.

"You remember where his office is?" she asks when she hangs up the receiver.

I nod, and she sweeps her arm in that direction.

I move before she can change her mind.

The breakroom is filled with Blackbridge men, and they grow silent as I walk through, several waving at me, but none try to engage me in conversation. Finnegan and Brooks seem relieved that I'm here.

I take a deep breath outside of his office, just a second to compose myself before I turn the knob. I don't bother with knocking because I don't want to be denied. He's at his desk, head hung between his hands, and I imagine I looked much the same way sitting at my father's desk yesterday morning when I first returned to New York. My own problems seem so small now.

"I just need a few minutes, man." His voice is harsh, filled with emotions he seems to be struggling with holding back.

"Gaige?" I whisper.

His head snaps up, and it pains me to see him so disheveled. I know I look no better. I didn't even brush my hair before leaving my apartment. His eyes are red and swollen, tired.

"Leighton?" he asks in a way that makes me think he doesn't really believe that I'm standing across the room.

"Are you okay?" I ask as I step in and close the door behind me.

He shakes his head, a tear rolling down the right side of his handsome face.

The sight of it has the power to break me. I cross the room, and he stands as I reach him. My arms wrap around him, and it seems like we battle on who can squeeze the tightest. He wins of course as he buries his face in my throat and sobs. I cry as well.

For him.

For me.

For Lala.

For *us*.

We don't rock back and forth. We don't move. We're static except for the shudder in our chests as we cry. It seems to last forever, but somehow it's not long enough when he pulls back, his arms opening, and I find that I don't like breathing as much when it means he's not touching me.

His hands cup my face.

"I missed you so much," he whispers, his thumb tracing my jaw.

"I missed you, too," I confess.

"What are you doing here?"

"I thought you might need me." I didn't know we were going to start so soon with the confessions. I may be a little too raw for it right now.

"I do. I need you so much."

He leans forward, pressing his salty lips to mine. The kiss is soft and needy, so slow and powerful it takes my breath away. It's truths and promises.

And it's over much too soon.

He pulls me to his chest again, this second hug somehow tighter than the first.

"I'm so sorry for your loss. I'm here for you."

"You being here is the best thing in the world," he says, his words rumbling against my ear. "Come home with me?"

I nod, knowing I'd deny him nothing right now. We haven't solved anything, but now isn't the time for those serious conversations we need to have.

"Give me a few minutes?"

"Of course," I tell him as he backs away, but then he's right back in front of me, his fingers in my hair, lips pressed to mine.

"Don't go anywhere," he says against my lips. "Promise me."

"I'll be right here."

"I just have to wash my face." His eyes search mine as if he's afraid I'm going to disappear.

He rushes into the bathroom inside his office, but then he takes his time. I know he's trying to get himself back together before he has to walk out in front of all of his friends, but I also know there isn't a single man out there that would give him hell for being upset over losing a loved one.

Gaige Ward is a different man when he exits the bathroom. He's the confident, professional man I met when I came in to sign the contract with BBS, and I wonder how much it's costing him to have that mask in place. I stand from the sofa, and he immediately pulls me back against his chest. I have to tilt my head back to look into his eyes, but he doesn't kiss me.

"We have so much to talk about. There are so many things I need to tell you," he says as he looks down at me.

Then he kisses me, both of his hands on my ass, the stirring of an erection against my stomach.

This may be part of his grieving process, and although it may hurt me in the long run, I know I'll do whatever it takes to help the man heal.

Chapter 37

Gaige

I don't know how fast things work in Heaven, but if anyone could get to God quickly, then I knew it would be Lala. She had to have had a hand in Leighton showing up, but then I walk out of my office with her and see Wren standing just outside of his office and realize it's another eye in the sky that had a hand in getting her here.

I give him a quick nod of thanks, pressing my hand to Leighton's back as we walk through the breakroom. I'm grateful to the guys for staying quiet as we walk through. My throat is killing me from crying for the last couple of hours, and I imagine I have several more hours I'm going to use my voice begging her to be mine, so I need to conserve energy where I can.

I'm so raw, everything so fresh, but just being near her helps ease the pain. I won't waste the opportunity. I won't squander the chance to tell her everything. I won't let her walk away wondering or guessing. If she leaves St. Louis again, it will be fully informed. Plus, I need to know what she feels and where her head is at.

I'm a man of action, and I don't know when I stopped being that person. I know a good deal when I see it, and Leighton Redmond is one hell of a deal, a lifetime sort of deal. I'd be a fool to let her slip away.

She keeps her eyes on me the entire drive back to my condo, and I do my best to pay attention to the road. I love this woman, but I also ache for her physically. The last thing we need is to get tangled up in the sexual side of things before I can tell her what my heart needs me to say.

The elevator ride is another exercise in restraint. I feel I deserve a medal because I manage to keep standing when I really want to lay her out on the floor and push myself into her until she vows to be mine for eternity.

"This is nice," she says when we step inside.

I look around, seeing it for what it is. My apartment is bland, a combination of brick, steel, and white. Sterile is the word my mother used. Lala hated this place. She said it was cold and unwelcoming. Maybe it's why I'm always in the breakroom at the office.

"It looks a lot like mine," she says, and there's a hint of sadness in her voice. "I had wondered if yours also looked like it was unlived in because you work as much as me. Oh. Maybe you're making an effort."

She points to the wrapped picture leaning against the far wall of the living room. My housekeeper must've brought it in and carried it there. I haven't been here. I went straight to the office after Georgia. My suitcase is still in my office.

"That's for you actually," I tell her softly. "I had it delivered in Georgia, but you had already left."

I'm taking a chance since she doesn't seem to recognize it.

"Open it."

She looks at me for a long moment before reaching for the corner of the paper and peeling it away. Both hands cover her mouth as she stares down at it.

"We look so in love," she whispers behind her hands.

Another round of emotions threatens to clog my throat. "We do."

"Who took this picture?"

"Tyler. I'm going to have it reprinted. Want to see the original?"

She nods, her eyes staying locked on the framed one leaning against the wall. I pull out my phone.

"I didn't know the significance of it when I had it cropped." I open the screenshot and turn the phone toward her. The image is the same but under it, the Instagram post read *liked by @LalaWard*.

"Oh, Gaige." Her hand presses to her heart.

It feels like now or never, and the phone shakes a little in my fist before I can put it back in my pocket.

"Before she died, I promised her I was going to marry you. I guaranteed her the fall wedding you talked about, and those babies she didn't think you had the hips for."

Leighton takes a step back, looking a little freaked out.

"I'm not asking you to marry me right now, Leighton. I mean, I would, because fuck, I love the hell out of you, but I don't think you're ready. I can ease into this, but I want you to know if you take off back to New York, I'm going with you. If you sneak out of here, I'm following."

"You're grieving."

"I am," I confirm. "But I knew I loved you before she had the heart attack. I promised her before. I called her before you left Georgia. Or before I knew you left because I'm not certain of the exact timeline. I felt like I lost you. I regret walking away from you on Saturday, but I'm not good at reading women emotionally. I don't have much experience with it. Actually, I have no experience with it. You said it couldn't happen again after we made love that Saturday, and I had to agree. I thought you didn't want me. Then I saw the picture." Both of our eyes drift to it, and I point. "That's love. Can't you see it."

"I see it," she whispers.

"Lala said grand gestures worked when PopPop fucked up. Words were important. I'm not good with words."

"You seem to be doing fine right now."

I chuckle. "That picture was my grand gesture, but you took off before you could see it. Before I could prove how I felt. Before you could see how you felt."

"I've known how I felt for a while," she says softly, her eyes returning to mine.

"You're looking at me like you love me in that picture," I say. "Do you see it?"

"Yes."

"Do you?" I swallow. "Do you love me?"

She swallows. "So much."

"Yeah?"

The emotions I managed to get a hold of in the bathroom back at BBS swarm me once again, a sob escaping my throat. I wrap my arms around her, burying my nose in her throat. I hold on to her, feeling the weight of the world lift from my shoulders. That ache I've felt for weeks and that weirdness in my chest I could never rid myself of or explain are suddenly gone, and it's like I can finally breathe normally again.

"Leighton," I sigh into her hair. "Thank you. Thank you for loving me."

"It's one of the easiest things I've ever done."

She holds me tighter, seeming as reluctant to let me go as I am her.

"I'm not taking over my family's business."

I pull back from her. "I was serious about going with you. If that's your dream, I fully support you. I'd never ask you to give something like that up for me."

She shakes her head. "I don't know what my dreams are now, but that isn't it. I'm done with it."

"You're sure?"

She nods. "Mind if I crash on your couch until I figure things out?"

"No way," I tell her. "My couch sucks, but there's a spot in my bed that's empty."

She squeals, the happiest sound my condo has ever heard as I scoop her up and carry her through the place to my bedroom.

As anxious as I was to get her here, everything seems to slow down now that our confessions are all out in the open. We're in no rush. We aren't working against a clock. There are no timelines or rules. There's not a clock ticking away or the threat of changed minds. We haven't made plans, but we do know we love each other and that seems like enough.

We undress each other slowly, our hands wandering, enticing, making promises with fingertips as much as with our lips. We shower together slowly, and I don't risk breaking the moment by challenging her no shower sex rule. There will be time for that later. I dry her with a towel, and she returns the favor.

Our lips seem glued to each other as we make our way slowly to the bed, hands roaming, mouths making promises of pleasure and of our future together, some naughty, some about the wedding and babies we've only teased about before. Each thrill me with equal measure.

Taking an even greater risk, I lean closer to her ear as I cover my body with hers. "I want you bare."

"I'm yours to take," she pants, her legs spreading to accommodate the width of my hips.

"Leighton," I groan with her approval.

This woman is just too much. I don't know how I lucked out to be the first one to approach her that night at the bar, but I'll thank my lucky stars every damn day that I was.

"Feel me," I beg when I slide into her.

"Always," she whispers, her neck arching back, giving my mouth the perfect spot to suck and nip.

Her fingernails, those perfect talons, dig into my back, and as much as I want to enjoy this woman and slowly make love to her, I need a little of the dirty and fast too. She must realize it because she's giving me exactly what it takes to put me in that head space.

"Fuck," I grunt, coming up from my elbows to my palms so I can slam into her harder. "Open wider."

She moans her pleasure, hands cupping her perfect tits.

"Love you," she whimpers. "Love your cock."

I chuckle. "Love you. Cock loves you, too."

"Gaige, I'm going to come."

"Can you wait for me?"

Her head shakes, a violent back and forth, and I know it's already too late.

"What do you need?" I ask, but the answer is her clamping down on my cock, her core convulsing.

"Gonna come inside of you, Leighton."

She moans again, her eyes closed. It's not really asking, and I'd do my best to stop if she wanted me to.

"Leighton," I say, giving her one last chance, but her legs close, knees clamping at my sides, and I'm done. My cock kicks inside of her. I'm buried deep, and the only thought I have before lowering my mouth back down to hers is that we may end up needing to have that fall wedding this year instead of next.

I fall asleep with her in my arms and a smile on my deliriously happy face.

Chapter 38

Leighton

"Are you okay?"

I press a hand to Gaige's cheek. "Shouldn't I be the one asking you that question?"

"You had to take medicine this morning."

Bless this sweet man. I don't know if I deserve him. "I have cramps. We buried your grandmother. The two don't compare."

"I don't like seeing you in pain."

"Same goes, my love." I press my lips to the palm of his hand.

"Do you need a drink?"

"I'm fine."

"You sure?"

"Now you're worried about my hydration?"

He leans in close, his lips very close to my ear. "I'm worried about your throat."

I pinch his side, knowing exactly what he's talking about. He doesn't flinch away, and maybe some would think his behavior is inappropriate at his grandmother's wake, but Lala made sure to set the mood for the occasion. She found out about her heart condition six months ago and knew she was on borrowed time. There was nothing the doctors could've done then, and she wanted to live the rest of her days with her family and not worrying about a single thing. The hug I witnessed means so much more to me now.

She insisted a video be played at her funeral. It was upbeat, the matriarch of the family insisting that people dry their eyes and have a good time. She's already causing problems in Heaven and reunited with the love of her life. She didn't want people to be sad and grieve, and somehow people listened. There was a long line of people who stood up and shared stories about Imogene Rose's wild days, many of her friends also elderly and reminiscent.

Now we're at Gaige's family home, and the house is filled with laughter and smiles much the same way it was for the birthday party although it carries a hint of sadness. Even Lala's demands can't completely take away all the anguish.

I still see some of it in the corners of Gaige's eyes when he thinks no one is looking.

The BBS guys are here, looking right at home in the middle of Gaige's family. Deacon and Anna mingle, showing off the baby, and it makes me think about the many times Gaige and I have talked about kids in the last week since I returned to St. Louis. When the man makes his mind up about something, he fully commits. I wouldn't be surprised if he doesn't start tracking my cycle this next month.

"Did you get to meet Whitney and Remington?" Gaige asks as he pulls me to his chest.

"I did, both are very sweet."

"Did they invite you out for drinks?"

"No, but Whitney did invite me over for a girls' night in."

His smile is wide. "That's a toy party."

I huff. "I'm a little old for toys."

"Not these kinds of toys, you aren't."

I raise an eyebrow.

"Oh really?"

"I'll give you my credit card."

"You don't see those things as competition?"

"I'm secure in my manhood, Leighton."

"We need more rules."

"We have plenty of rules," he grumbles.

"We have no rules," I remind him. "So rule number one, don't rub your erection on me at family gatherings."

"Rule number two, don't give me an erection at family gatherings, and rule number three, if you give me an erection, then you have to take care of it. Come on. Let me show you Freckles. He's up in my bedroom."

"I'm on my period," I remind him.

"Your throat is fine," he says with a wide grin. "I want to fuck it."

"What are you guys over here grinning about?" Caroline Ward asks as she walks up, and I nearly choke.

He's going to embarrass me; I just know it.

"Leighton is on her cycle and not feeling well."

Not exactly what I thought he was going to say, but embarrassing enough, even as a thirty-year-old woman.

I give her a weak smile.

"Oh, sweetie. Do you need some painkillers? A heating pad? You can go lie down in Gaige's room."

"I'll show her where it is," Gaige offers helpfully. "Come on, sweetheart."

"I'll be fine," I assure her, digging my heels into the plush carpet and staying locked in place. Gaige glares at me playfully, eyes wide like I've popped his balloon.

We chat with Caroline a little longer and the crowd begins to thin out. At some point, Gaige disappears as well, but I stick to Caroline and help her carry dishes to the kitchen.

"How is he doing?" she asks once we're alone.

"He seems to be doing okay," I tell her honestly. "Deacon has been kind enough to give him some time off from work."

"And you guys are doing okay?"

"We are. You've raised an amazing man."

She wraps her arms around me. "He's lucky to have you. Please remember that. We're lucky that you're a part of this family."

Ah! Cue the waterworks.

I'm crying on his mother's shoulder when Gaige walks into the room.

"I leave for ten minutes, and you make her cry? Way to go, Mom!" Gaige teases as he tugs me away from his mother. He hands me a tissue, and I swat at his chest before pressing it to my eyes.

I mouth *thank you* to her as he wraps his arms around me. Everett, Gaige's dad, hugs his wife to his own chest.

"We need to get going," Gaige tells his parents. "Are we still on for dinner Saturday?"

"Yes," his mother confirms. "Don't forget to bring the wine."

"We won't," Gaige says before turning us around.

We hold hands on the walk to the car and on the drive to the office. Gaige has a few things he needs to take care of since he's been out for the last week. He's not returning to work until Monday but there was something Deacon needed taken care of that required an attorney so Gaige told him earlier that he would swing by on the way back to the condo.

"Come up with me?" he asks when he parks.

I don't hesitate. He's kind of sexy when he works.

Most everyone is back at the office, still in suits from the funeral, and they greet us when we walk in.

"Leighton, do you have a moment?" Deacon asks when he notices me.

Gaige presses a kiss to my temple before walking toward his office.

"I do," I tell him, an apology on my lips for the way I ended things with Blackbridge. It was hasty and unprofessional. "I want to say I'm sorry for—"

"I want you to work for BBS."

"—the way I just emailed—Excuse me? What?"

"You and Gaige are together, right? He mentioned you not returning to New York. Please tell me if I'm mistaken, but if you're staying in St. Louis, I'd like you to consider working for Blackbridge."

"The team you're trying to build isn't going to work, Mr. Black."

"I don't want a team, Leighton. I just want you. I need someone who can herd cats." He tosses his thumb over his shoulder to indicate the men arguing animatedly over the news on the television mounted on the wall. "I need someone with a good memory and organizational skills."

"I have those." Is it too soon to be excited?

"I know."

"I'd love to."

"We haven't discussed salary."

"I'd love to."

He chuckles.

"Let me show you your office."

I'm light on my feet as I follow him down the hallway, stopping in front of Gaige's office.

"Not in there," he says. "That's Gaige's office. You can use the one you used before."

My eyes narrow as he walks deeper down the hallway and flips the light on in an empty office.

"You can personalize it however you'd like," he says. "Can you start on Monday?"

"I'd love to," I tell him.

"Perfect." He shakes my hand. "I'll have Gaige draw up the paperwork."

I stand in my office long enough to give Deacon the time to relay that message to Gaige, then go to look for him. He lied to me. It wasn't the first, and it wasn't the last if I wanted to count all the omissions as lies as well, but I'm glad he had me work in his office that day. I had an amazing time that night after I stalked his dinner plans which I didn't know at the time included me.

I don't bother knocking on his door, but my smile falls from my face when I enter. He's on the phone, face worried.

"What?" I ask when he hangs up the phone.

"We need to go see Wren."

He grabs my hand, pressing his lips to the back, but he doesn't immediately pull me from the room. He turns me, his other hand tilting my face up, so I have to look him in the eye.

"I love you."

"I love you, too, but you're scaring me right now."

"Promise me that no matter what happens, you won't leave me."

"Did you cheat on me?" Tears burn my eyes.

"No, baby. Never."

"Are you having a baby with another woman?"

"Fuck, Leighton, no."

He pulls me to his chest.

"Is my sister okay?"

"As far as I know. Shit, come on. I think I'm just making it worse."

We head down the hall. I'm crying and I don't know why. The breakroom is full and questions hit us the second we step inside, but Gaige doesn't answer any of them as we cross over and go into Wren's office.

Gaige has talked about the guy so much over the last week, I feel like I know him. I know he's the one who sent the texts about Lala's heart attack.

"Wren," Gaige says as he closes us in the freezing office.

My arms immediately go around me, a false sense of security. Several computer screens cover the desks, and there's too much information on them for me to understand a single thing. Wren's face is somber when he turns around.

"Don't look at me like that," Gaige snaps. "I won't keep secrets from her any longer. Just say it."

"Hey, pretty girl."

I snap my head to the side and see a bird prancing back and forth on the other side of the room.

"Not now, Puff," Wren mutters.

"Don't cockblock, man. Hey, baby."

"Wren!" Gaige snaps.

"Okay," Wren grumbles. "Shit."

"What's going on?" I ask.

"Your dad has been embezzling money from Redmond for years," Wren begins.

I gasp. "He wouldn't."

"I thought he was embezzling money," Wren says. "I've been digging, and it's taken weeks, but I followed a lead, and I just found some new shit."

"He's not?" I verify.

"Your mother is."

"No," I argue. "She doesn't need the money."

"She doesn't," Wren agrees. "But she does want revenge. It seems she found out about your dad's affair a very long time ago, possibly shortly after it started and has been making it look like he's been skimming, and that Margaret is involved."

I huff. Now this sounds like my mom. "Seriously?"

"Yeah."

"What are you going to do?"

"What do you want me to do?"

"Have her arrested," I say without hesitation. "If she's a criminal, she needs to go to prison."

"Yeah?" Wren asks, looking a little surprised. "And if your dad was the one stealing?"

I hesitate just a half second longer. "Same goes."

"Ruthless," Wren says in awe. "I love it. You're sure?"

I nod.

"I'll set things in motion."

Gaige turns me so I'm looking at him.

"You don't hate me because I knew about the embezzling?"

I blink up at him. "Just how much do you know?"

He swallows, having the nerve to look embarrassed. "Probably too much, but if it's any consolation, I really wanted to learn about all of it from you."

"I didn't know the company was being embezzled from, Gaige."

He scoffs, pressing his lips to my forehead. "I know that, Leighton."

I pinch his side, the same way I did at his parents' house earlier, and he takes it. I promised to love him forever, and I will, but that doesn't mean I can't torture him a little for it.

"We'll talk about it when we get home."

"You still love me?"

"Always," I tell him.

"Daddy needs love, too!" the bird screeches as Gaige walks us out of the office.

Gaige is whispering in my ear all the things he wants to do to me to make up for the secrets he's kept when silence fills the room. I want to bury my face and hide, thinking that they're looking at us, and maybe they overheard something he said but then I feel Gaige freeze.

I look up, and the day just gets worse.

There's an angry woman standing in the middle of the room. Her hand is clasping a round tub with a red switch on the top, a wire running from the bottom of it to the inside of a leather jacket.

"Finnegan Jenkins!" she screams.

The Irishman turns from the counter near the coffee machine, an unimpressed look on his face as he lifts his *KISS ME, I'M IRISH* coffee cup to his lips.

With her free hand, she rips open her jacket, revealing a series of boxes at her waist. I don't watch much television, but I've seen enough to know exactly what we just walked in on, seen enough to know it wouldn't matter if we were in this room or in Wren's office. We won't survive the blast.

The door at our backs opens, and the bird flies out.

"Take cover, we're going to fucking die!"

Someone on the sofa chuckles, and I'm too terrified to look over and see who it was, but apparently, they're as terrified as me if nervous laughter is their go-to in a situation like this.

My heart is racing, and I cling to Gaige, wanting to tell him I love him a million times more before I die.

"You crazy woman!" Finnegan bellows on the other side of the room. "Are you trying to get shot coming in here like this?

"I'll blow this whole place up!"

"You'll do no such thing! Get your pretty ass over here!"

She doesn't move, her finger hovering over that red switch. As if agitated more than scared, Finnegan smacks his coffee cup on the counter, strolls across the room, and scoops the woman up over his shoulder and carries her out of the room. Before he can get to the hall, I hear the sound of his palm echoing off of her ass.

She calls him an asshole, but there's no explosion.

"I told that man about sticking his dick in crazy," Kit mutters.

"Was that—" Gaige begins.

"Empty baking soda boxes? Yes," Kit answers.

"And in her hand?" Wren asks.

"Spray painted roll of Lifesavers."

The men around the room chuckle.

"I just let her through," Pam says with a grin. "Figured you boys needed a good laugh."

The office manager heads back to her desk.

"I'm going home," Deacon says with a shake of his head before walking out.

"We are too," Gaige says as he grabs my hand. "I have some apologizing to do."

"I do need a foot massage," I tell him with a grin as we head toward the elevator.

"I'm at your service, Ms. Redmond."

THE END

OTHER BOOKS FROM MARIE JAMES

Blackbridge Security
Hostile Territory
Shot in the Dark
Contingency Plan
Truth Be Told
Calculated Risk
Heroic Measures
Sleight of Hand
Controlled Burn
Cease Fire

Standalones
Crowd Pleaser
Macon
We Said Forever
More Than a Memory

Cole Brothers SERIES
Love Me Like That
Teach Me Like That

Cerberus MC

Kincaid: Cerberus MC Book 1

Kid: Cerberus MC Book 2

Shadow: Cerberus MC Book 3

Dominic: Cerberus MC Book 4

Snatch: Cerberus MC Book 5

Lawson: Cerberus MC Book 6

Hound: Cerberus MC Book 7

Griffin: Cerberus MC Book 8

Samson: Cerberus MC Book 9

Tug: Cerberus MC Book 10

Scooter: Cerberus MC Book 11

Cannon: Cerberus MC Book 12

Rocker: Cerberus MC Book 13

Colton: Cerberus MC Book 14

Drew: Cerberus MC Book 15

Jinx: Cerberus MC Book 16

Thumper: Cerberus MC Book 17

Apollo: Cerberus MC Book 18

Legend: Cerberus MC Book 19

Grinch: Cerberus MC Book 20

Harley: Cerberus MC Book 21

A Very Cerberus Christmas

Cerberus MC Box Set 1

Cerberus MC Box Set 2

Cerberus MC Box Set 3

Ravens Ruin MC
Prequel: Desperate Beginnings
Book 1: Sins of the Father
Book 2: Luck of the Devil
Book 3: Dancing with the Devil

MM Romance
Grinder
Taunting Tony

Westover Prep Series
(bully/enemies to lovers romance)
One-Eighty
Catch Twenty-Two

Made in United States
Orlando, FL
26 June 2025

62403426R00154